T0267434

THE UMBRELLA ACADEMY
YOUNG BLOOD

THE UMBRELLA ACADEMY
YOUNG BLOOD

BY ALYSSA SHEINMEL

AMULET BOOKS • NEW YORK

Cataloging-in-Publication Data has been applied for and may be obtained from the Library of Congress.

ISBN 978-1-4197-6627-5

Printed and bound in the United States
10 9 8 7 6 5 4 3 2 1

Amulet Books are available at special discounts when purchased in quantity for premiums and promotions as well as fundraising or educational use. Special editions can also be created to specification. For details, contact specialsales@abramsbooks.com or the address below.

Amulet Books® is a registered trademark of Harry N. Abrams, Inc.

ABRAMS The Art of Books
195 Broadway, New York, NY 10007
abramsbooks.com

A NOTE FROM THE PUBLISHER

We worked in close collaboration with Elliot Page and the creators of *The Umbrella Academy* as well as with friends in the trans community to portray Viktor's story in these pages in a manner true to his unique journey.

In Season 3, Episode 2, Diego asks, "Who's Viktor?" To which Viktor replies, "I am. It's who I've always been." Although our prequel story is set prior to Viktor's transition, we have chosen to use his name and pronouns throughout in order to accurately and respectfully represent this character's identity.

LUTHER

Another successful mission for the books. Even as he and his siblings walk into the academy, Luther can still feel what it was like when he lifted an entire wall off an earthquake victim—like, actually *feel* it, his arms flexing, and the Hargreeves in his head telling him to move faster, stopwatch in hand, timing just how long it took him to rescue each victim, keeping count of which of Luther's siblings rescued the most people.

Luther doesn't need to ask Hargreeves for the exact numbers; he *knows* he saved the most victims. He's Number One; the strongest, the leader.

"Hurry up, Boy Scout," Diego calls as he bounds ahead. He says it like it's supposed to be an insult, but Luther takes it as a compliment—Boy Scouts are always prepared, they always do the right thing, they believe in community and civic duty. Not that Luther's ever actually been a Boy Scout. But that's what he's heard about them.

People often don't realize how strong Luther is just by looking at him. He's fit but not super-ripped—it's not like his muscles burst his jacket every time he flexes. Then again, that could be because Mom custom-made his jacket and reworks it every time he grows so much as an inch.

Luther runs his fingers through his blond hair as he walks up the steps that lead to the front door. Some dust gets in his eyes, making them water. The academy doesn't exactly have the most welcoming exterior. The front door is flanked by square pillars, and the door itself is wide enough to drive a car through. Still, it's the only home Luther's ever known. Hargreeves adopted Luther and his six siblings when they were newborn babies, bringing them each here from seven disparate spots all across the world. Nothing feels better, as far as Luther is concerned, than arriving back home after a successful mission.

He grabs Allison's hand as they cross the threshold, and she grins at him. Luther can feel the blood pumping in his veins, the adrenaline winding down, the high that comes after all that action. He presses his feet into the hardwood floor, relishing the way the wood shifts under his weight, knowing he's strong enough to kick a hole through the floor. Mom's waiting in the foyer, a tray of milk and cookies balanced in her hands. Luther grabs a cookie and downs a glass of milk so fast that it dribbles down his chin. He's so pumped that he has to stop himself from throwing the cup down and watching it shatter into a thousand pieces on the floor.

Carefully, he forces himself to put the glass gently back on Mom's tray. Despite his best efforts, he cracks it after all, just from gripping it too tightly.

"Don't know my own strength."

He means to sound apologetic—Mom will have to repair it—but the words end up coming out proud. He *is* proud. He stands even taller, his broad shoulders flexing. He notices Viktor standing in the shadows behind Mom, his violin case clutched in his hand.

He doesn't know what he's missing, Luther thinks, *stuck at home*. For a split second, he considers saying it out loud: *You don't know what you're missing.* But then Allison pounds on his back to smack dust from his navy-and-red uniform jacket, and Luther can't focus on anything else. Allison's pushed her mask up over her forehead, holding her curly black hair away from her face.

As the dust releases into the air, he and his siblings start to cough uncontrollably. Mom, of course, doesn't so much as blink.

"Sorry about the mess, Mom," Diego says.

"Not to worry," Mom promises, with a smile centered on her perfectly symmetrical face. Her blond hair is pulled back into a French twist at the nape of her neck, and she's wearing a gingham apron tied tightly at the waist. "Your clothes will be good as new by tomorrow. Just leave them out before bed, and I'll wash them tonight." She smiles her perfect smile again, always so happy to clean up after them.

"*Bibbidi-Bobbidi-Boo,*" Klaus sings. "It's like we have our own fairy godmother. Can you turn my raggedy old uniform into a ballgown next, Fairy-Mom?"

Mom blinks in confusion. *Apparently,* Luther thinks, *when Dad built their mother, he didn't program her to understand Cinderella references.*

"Don't worry about it, Mom," Ben says quickly. "Klaus was just joking."

"Oh," their mother says, then smiles as though she understood the joke. "Very funny, Klaus."

Luther knows he should be sorry about the dust—Mom will have so much to clean—but he's too psyched to really be sorry about anything right now. He can still feel the arms around him from all the people who hugged him and thanked him for rescuing them. A *waste of time*, Hargreeves would say (the Hargreeves in his head *did* say), so Luther had to cut the hugs short even though he wanted to linger. Not like Klaus, who took in the adulation with glee.

"Let's go over it again," Hargreeves begins, leading the way through the marble-paved foyer. As always, he's wearing a perfectly tailored suit, his gray mustache curled at the ends, his goatee ending in a neat point at his chin. They walk past the wide wooden staircase and through the arched pillars into the dining room. Hargreeves slips off his leather gloves and slaps them against his bare hands.

Luther presses his eye mask up over his head, tossing it on the floor. *I'll pick it up later*, he thinks, but he knows it's not true. Mom or Pogo will take care of it before he has a chance.

"We drove upstate and kicked ass," Diego says. "What more is there to go over?"

Diego's words are exactly what Luther's feeling, though he'd never say so. Allison lets out a little *whoop*, and Luther winks at her as they take their seats around the dining room table. Allison sits directly across from him. Her eyes are red and watering from the dust, her hair so covered it almost looks gray, but somehow she's still so beautiful. Dad's at the head of the table in between them.

"From the beginning, Number One," his father corrects, and Luther winces. He hates when Hargreeves's temper is turned on him, even though it happens so rarely.

He takes a deep breath and gives his answer like a student giving a presentation in a classroom. Not that Luther has ever been in a real classroom. Hargreeves and Mom led Luther's and his siblings' education, focused as much on training to use their powers as learning their letters and numbers. Luther can't remember exactly how old he was when he realized that other children were raised differently. Of course, other children—as Hargreeves liked to point out—had been *born* differently. Unlike Luther and his siblings, most children weren't born to mothers who spontaneously gave birth after not having been pregnant for the previous nine months. And unlike Luther and his siblings (except Viktor), other children didn't have superpowers, so they didn't require the sort of training the Umbrella Academy did.

Allison could make anyone do anything she wanted, just by whispering *I heard a rumor* in their ear; Klaus could commune with the dead; Diego could wield knives with extraordinary precision; Ben had hidden tentacles between his shoulder blades; Five could jump through space and time—or anyway, he *could*, until he got lost doing so. Luther isn't sure—no one is—whether Five still has his powers, wherever and whenever he is.

Luther's power isn't nearly as flashy or strange, but it's every bit as useful: He's exceptionally strong.

"There were reports of an earthquake about two hours north of the city," Luther begins. He notices that Allison has the tiniest milk moustache on her upper lip, but stops himself from reaching across the table to brush it away.

"Which is unusual," a small voice adds. Luther turns to see Viktor sitting in the seat beside him. He knows he shouldn't be surprised to see him there—he's his sibling just like the others. But not at all like the others really.

Luther stomps his feet beneath the table, releasing a small cloud of dust from his pants. Viktor coughs.

"Sorry," he offers.

"It's okay." Now Viktor's eyes are watering, too.

Luther rests his hands flat on the dark mahogany table. Dad always debriefs in here. *The dining room is perfect*, Luther thinks, not just for family meals but for reviewing their missions. But tonight, Luther has to concentrate to keep his hands still. He wants to get back out there, save another life, solve another mystery. At the very least, he wants to head to the gym and pump some iron. He needs something to do with this energy.

Luther tugs at his collar. Usually his uniform fits like a second skin, but right now he can feel that his skin is coated with dust, sticky because of his sweat. They've been wearing the same uniforms since they were kids. Well, obviously, not the *same* uniforms—Mom altered and resewed the outfits as they grew. Luther's still not done growing, still not done putting on muscle, not done getting stronger. He hopes that his jacket will soon get tight beneath his arms, the collar of his shirt pinching beneath his Adam's apple, and Mom will have to tailor his uniform all over again. He wonders just how big and strong he'll end up.

Luther gazes at Allison across the table. Mom hasn't had to remake Allison's uniform since their last birthday. It fits perfectly, but everything looks perfect on Allison. Luther watches as she fingers the necklace he gave her, the one she never, ever takes off. Allison catches him looking and smiles.

"Indeed, it is unusual, Number Seven," Hargreeves continues, bringing Luther's attention back to the review. "So although we were ostensibly driving upstate to assist in rescue operations, what was the true purpose of our mission? Number Two!" Hargreeves snaps, and Diego looks up from his plate, which Mom has piled high with roast beef, green beans, and new potatoes. Dust has settled on his cheeks so that it looks like he has a gray beard.

Luther knows better than to get distracted by food before Dad's finished his debrief. But that's why he's Number One, sitting at Dad's side, and Diego is down at the foot of the table. Maybe Dad will demote Diego and put Allison in his place. She'd make a better Number Two.

Hargreeves scoffs, "What was the true purpose of our mission?"

"To discover the source of the seismic activity," Diego answers, his mouth full. Luther shakes his head in disgust.

"And what was the true source?" Hargreeves asks, shifting his focus to Allison. "Number Three?"

"An illegal fracking site just miles away from a small town. Their work caused tectonic shifts in the earth and polluted the groundwater."

The best part of the mission, Luther thinks, *was pulling people from the rubble*. Breaking into the fracking company's offices to expose them was fine and all—but nothing like the high of saving people's lives in the moment. He wonders what those people are doing now. What they might say to the Umbrella Academy if given the chance.

Hargreeves sits back in his seat, resting his hands across his chest. "And how can you be certain this illegal drilling was the source of the earthquake?"

"What else could it have been?" Fortunately, this time Diego swallowed before opening his mouth.

"You should never assume you know the goal of a mission at the start. After all, what began as a rescue mission turned into an opportunity to expose dirty business practices, did it not?"

"It was still a rescue mission," Luther interjects. He can feel dusty, desperate fingers intertwined with his own as he pulled survivors from the rubble. He can still hear people saying "Thank you!" and "You saved me!" and "How could this happen here?"

Hargreeves holds up his hand to silence Luther. He supposes that he shouldn't have cut in. He looks at the chandelier above the table, the light twinkling among the crystals in a way that seems almost festive. Which was appropriate. They should feel festive; they should be *celebrating*.

But then Hargreeves says, "Tell me, Number Two, exactly what went wrong?"

DIEGO

Diego has to stop himself from rolling his eyes. Nothing would've gone wrong if *he'd* been in charge. Every single mission, every single time, Hargreeves drags them back to this dining room and lists every single misstep and miscalculation. But not once has he mentioned the common denominator of each mission: Luther being the one in charge.

If Luther had his way, they probably would've politely knocked on the oil company's door. Diego was the one who jimmied the locks with his knives, who tiptoed down the halls and held a knife to some exec's throat until he admitted their wrongdoing. Pulling victims from the rubble was great and all, but nothing can compare to the way it feels to actually exact *justice*.

Of course, Hargreeves didn't see any of *that*. Hargreeves never sees Diego at his best, because he's always outside the action, watching from a safe distance, more interested in his stupid stopwatch than what's actually going on. Maybe if he'd just look a little bit closer, he'd see that Diego is actually every bit as much a hero as Luther. More, even. Luther doesn't like to do the dirty work, but Diego doesn't let anything stop him from finishing a job.

Diego pulls up his knee socks, itchy where they squeeze his calves. He's sick and tired of dressing like a child. Someday, he's going to burn his argyle sweater-vest. But if he did that now, Mom would have a fresh one folded at the foot of his bed first thing the next morning.

"What does it matter what went wrong?" Diego grumbles as he shoves a forkful of food into his mouth. Missions make him hungry, and Mom knows it. She always has his favorite foods waiting when they return from a mission. He'd like to think it's something she does just for him, but she does it for every member of the academy. At least she cares, unlike Dad.

"We won," Diego continues, his mouth full. "We saved the citizens, exposed the evil oil company. We won." Diego can feel his knives tucked safely in place in the compartments Mom sewed into his uniform. One thing he actually likes about his uniform: It has secrets the others' don't. Mom modified Ben's uniform to accommodate his tentacles, but that's not the same thing. It's not nearly as cool as secret compartments for weapons meant for him alone to wield.

Not even Luther can do what we does. Diego imagines taking out his brother with one flick of his wrist. He'd never actually hurt him. But still—it's nice to know he *can*.

"Maybe Dad has a point," Allison cuts in. "Maybe winning isn't enough."

"What's that supposed to mean?" Diego tugs at his collar. If he had his way, they'd dress in all black for missions. Mom would have to modify those clothes, too, to accommodate his knives. But black would be so much more practical; perfect for sneaking around. They could keep the eye masks—vigilantes in disguise. But Dad likes the uniforms; he wants everyone to know who's saving the day.

"I mean, maybe the *way* we win is just as important as winning," Allison says.

"You're just mad because they haven't featured you on the cover of *Teen Dream* magazine since last year."

"Don't talk to her like that," Luther jumps in from across the table.

"Don't tell me how to talk," Diego snaps. "Besides, Allison can take care of herself." Sometimes Luther acts like their sister is some damsel in distress, but Diego knows she's anything but. She's as capable of kicking ass as the rest of them. Today, she beat the crap out of an oil executive twice her size.

Out of the corner of his eye, Diego can see Ben and Klaus side by side at the other end of the table, squabbling as Ben's trying to keep Klaus from stealing food off his plate.

"Your food tastes better than mine," Klaus whines.

"Maybe if there was something on your plate other than melting ice cream, it would taste better." Ben lifts his fork in threat.

Diego tunes out the sound of their bickering. Honestly, he doesn't know how Ben puts up with it.

"I'm not upset that I haven't been on a silly magazine cover recently," Allison insists. "It's just—maybe the reason they stopped putting us on covers is because—"

"They're idiots who don't know a good story when it literally falls from the sky," Diego interjects.

"Or because we're not doing good enough work," Allison says. "Think about it. There used to be crowds waiting at the door when we got back from a mission. Today, there were, like, five people, and they didn't even seem excited when we got out of the car."

"So, what—it's not worth helping people if you're not surrounded by adoring fans?" Diego snaps.

"I never said that," Allison argues.

"It's because of Five," Ben says quietly. Everyone turns to face him. Even Klaus stops picking food off his plate. "They stopped writing about us after Five went missing. After that, we weren't such a cute story anymore."

"We were never *cute*," Diego argues. "We were going around the world foiling criminals, saving lives. That's hardcore—not *cute*."

Ben shakes his head and points to the wall of framed magazine covers behind him. On every one, a member of the Umbrella Academy is smiling, arms folded across their chest or planted on their hips. The boys wear navy shorts with black knee socks, and Allison's in a plaid skirt. They all don the blazers, argyle sweater-vests, and eye masks. The masks are the only part of the uniform that make sense, as far as Diego is concerned. They're too old for the rest of it.

He has to admit that back in the day, the press probably did think they were cute. People don't make pocket-size action figures of you if they don't think you're at least kind of cute. But that wasn't the point. The *point* was to help people.

And they did that today, no matter what Hargreeves has to say about it.

"Children!" Hargreeves snaps. "Number Three is correct. You act like you've saved the day, but who knows what other threats the people in that small town could face in the days to come?"

"We exposed the oil company, Dad," Diego reminds him. "They'll stop fracking. There won't be any more earthquakes."

"How can you be sure?"

Again, Diego has to keep himself from rolling his eyes. No matter how well they did on a mission, Hargreeves has a way of making it feel like they'd failed.

At least tonight, Diego knows that when Mom lays out his freshly cleaned uniform for tomorrow morning, she'll tell him how proud she is of what they did today.

CHAPTER 3

ALLISON

Allison picks at her hot dog. She doesn't have the heart to tell Mom that it's not her favorite meal anymore. It hasn't been in years. Somehow, Mom notices the second any of them grows an inch and tailors their uniforms to accommodate it, but she's never noticed the way that Allison barely eats her supposed favorite meal anymore. Allison guesses it makes sense—it's not like Mom has to eat anything. Then again, Mom doesn't grow either.

Allison knows that the attention they get from the press doesn't really have anything to do with how good of a job they did. The public prefers when things go a little bit awry. Makes the whole thing more suspenseful, more exciting—a real show.

The truth is, right after Five disappeared, the press followed them more doggedly than ever. They were riveted because Hargreeves refused to offer any explanation. When the press asked questions about the Umbrella Academy, all they received was "No comment," which had never happened before. Dad had always welcomed reporters, inviting them into their home for photos shoots and interviews, so his change in attitude piqued the public's interest. Sometimes Allison wonders whether Dad did that on purpose, inviting the intrigue, welcoming the attention.

But they're older now. It's harder to sell the whole "adorable kids, family of superheroes" package now that they're not preteens.

Allison tilts her head to study the chandelier above the table. All the furniture in here is so dark—dark wooden table, dark wooden chairs. The floor is black-and-white marble, but somehow the white squares look gray, the same way the light from the chandelier is always dim. And of course, Hargreeves keeps the curtains closed tight—can't risk fans and reporters peeking inside. Not that anyone's really trying to nowadays.

Diego wasn't entirely wrong. Allison does kind of miss the adulation. Not because she loved seeing her face on magazine covers—though she did love that—but because being adored made her feel like she *belonged* to something, something other than the Umbrella Academy. Giving autographs, answering interview questions, posing for pictures—it all felt so good.

She recalls how she fought that oil exec this afternoon. It should've felt exciting, but honestly it felt like . . . nothing. She barely even had a thought before she threw out her leg, landed a punch. She felt like a robot who'd been programmed to move without thinking. She glances at Mom, standing patiently in the corner, waiting to clear the table when dinner is through. She wonders if Mom ever feels that way—aware of her programming. Then again, Mom doesn't *feel* anything, so probably not.

At least when they were surrounded by fans, Allison felt special. People wanted to be close to her because she was unlike anyone they'd seen before. Allison stares across the table at Luther, trying to gauge whether he ever feels this kind of unease, too, but Luther only grins at her in return. He loves when Dad and Diego fight, loves the reminder that Diego will never be Number One.

"Dad's right," Luther says firmly after a moment. "We have to do better next time. We should review the mission step-by-step to identify any errors."

"Well said, Number One," Hargreeves crows.

Ben sighs. "Can't we just have a *normal* meal instead of rehashing our missions?"

"Here, here!" Klaus says, raising his tumbler of milk like it's a glass of wine. "To normal mealtime." Klaus stands and circles the table like he's giving a grand toast at a formal dinner party.

If they were a different sort of family, Allison thinks, *they would have parties in this room. It's the sort of room that was built for hosting glamorous soirées.*

"Now let me think." Klaus cocks his head to the side. "What is it that *normal* families do at mealtimes?" He closes his eyes like he's trying to imagine it, then shakes his head. He continues circling the table, patting his siblings on the head.

"*Duck, duck, duck* . . ." he says with each pat. Then stops and turns abruptly. "Do normal families play Duck, Duck, Goose at mealtimes?" When no one answers, Klaus shakes his head and falls back into his seat. "Guess we'll never know!" he says, then laughs.

Allison can't help it; she finds herself laughing, too. It is absurd for any of them to imagine what an ordinary family would talk about at dinner—how could they possibly know?

But Ben stays stone-faced. "It's not funny, Klaus."

"Maybe it would be, if you didn't take everything so seriously." Klaus presses his lips into a straight line and folds his arms across his chest, trying to look somber. But even when Klaus frowns, there's still a twinkle in his eye like he might burst out laughing at any moment.

"This *is* serious," Ben insists. "Playing hero is our *job*, and dear old Dad is really our *boss*. This isn't a dinner table—it's a boardroom. That's not normal! Don't you see that, Klaus?"

But Klaus isn't paying attention anymore. Allison doesn't know if he's distracted by a ghost or if it's just his usual spaciness. She can never be sure with Klaus. No one can, except maybe Ben.

Hargreeves shakes his head. "You're not *normal* children."

Allison cups her mouth with her hands, trying to secretly ask Luther, "Can you tell what's up with Klaus?"

"Does that make you feel normal?" Hargreeves snaps. "Whispering rudely across the table?"

Allison drops her hands to her lap.

"What's next?" Hargreeves continues. He removes his monocle and wipes it idly with a handkerchief, as though Allison has bored him. "You'll pierce your nose? Dye your hair pink? Throw a slumber party? Sneak out and break curfew like *normal* teenagers?"

Allison feels a spark of longing at the notion of a slumber party. At the other end of the table, Klaus is paying attention again.

"Piercing my nose and dyeing my hair sounds good to me, old man."

"Ah, Number Four, so quick to weigh in with useful information as always. What other *normal* teen activities would you like to participate in?"

"Let's see—getting drunk and high behind my parents' backs? Wait! I already do that!" Klaus laughs uproariously.

Hargreeves looks disgusted. "Indeed, Number Four. So many precious coming-of-age rituals you've missed out on."

Allison can't help it; she flinches at the sarcasm in her father's voice. She imagines the rites of passage she hasn't participated in: her first date, her first kiss, getting her driver's license, buying a prom dress, applying to college, picking out clothes with her friends, even getting her heart broken. Allison knows that if she let it slip that she actually did long for those sorts of experiences, Hargreeves would speak to her as coldly as he had to Klaus just now, so she keeps her thoughts to herself.

Suddenly, Hargreeves stands and throws his cloth napkin onto the table, though there never was any actual food on his plate. There never is. Mom piles everyone else's plates with their favorites: peanut butter and jelly with a side of potato chips for Ben, bubble-gum flavored ice cream for Klaus, roast beef for Diego, a hamburger and fries for Luther, and a hot dog for Allison. Allison glances down the table, trying to remember what Viktor prefers, but he's hunched over his plate. His long brown hair is in his face, and even though Allison knows Mom tailors Viktor's uniform just as she does the rest of theirs, somehow Viktor's clothes always look slightly too big. Allison can't see what Viktor is eating. She feels a pang of guilt that she's never bothered noticing before now. Even worse, she can't remember what Five liked either.

"You children will never be normal," Hargreeves announces, his voice booming. "I haven't worked with you for the past seventeen years to end up with a house full of *normal* children."

"*Worked* with us," Ben says, raising his eyebrows. "Exactly my point."

"Just look at Viktor." Hargreeves continues as though Ben hadn't spoken, his voice rising to a shout. Hargreeves points to the table where Viktor is slouching.

He's already so small, Allison thinks. *He should sit up straight.*

Hargreeves spits, "Ask him how it feels to be *normal.*"

Viktor blinks, clearly surprised to be the center of attention. Allison can't remember the last time Viktor was the center of attention. She feels a sensation in her gut she can't quite identify, almost like guilt. Which is, obviously, ridiculous. It's not Allison's fault that Viktor doesn't have powers like the rest of them. That Viktor's *normal*, the word Hargreeves keeps spitting like a curse.

Allison wonders if Hargreeves ever considered returning Viktor to his birth mother after he realized he didn't have any powers, like a pair of pants you'd bought in the wrong size. Allison pictures Viktor packed into a box, the words RETURN TO SENDER scribbled on the side.

No, that's not right. None of their birth mothers *sent* them away. Hargreeves sought them out and brought them home.

Brought them *here*, to this enormous building where he spent more effort training them to become a *team* than raising them as a *family*.

CHAPTER 4

VIKTOR

Viktor doesn't understand what his siblings are complaining about. Being ordinary is the worst thing that ever happened to him.

This afternoon, the rest of them left to rush upstate to save the day, and Viktor was left at home to practice his violin. Mom sat listening and applauded between songs, but the praise felt hollow. Mom's the only person who ever complimented Viktor's music—and she's not actually a person, but a robot Hargreeves programmed to behave like a mother. Hargreeves has never been impressed when Viktor mastered a new song, and the most his siblings have ever done was to ask him to keep it down when he was practicing.

As far as the rest of the family was concerned, Viktor's musical talent mattered just as much as his crime-fighting talent. That is, not at all.

After dad leaves the room, Diego leans back in his chair and puts his feet on the table, boots and all, leaving a mess for Mom and Pogo later. Klaus slides from his chair to the floor, lying flat on his back beneath the table, sighing as though the rug is the world's softest mattress. "One way to get him to stop eating off my plate," Ben mumbles. Luther drags his chair to the other side of the table to be next to Allison, and the two continue eating, heads tucked close together.

"This is bullshit," Diego says. "I'm sick of Dad's nitpicking after every mission. We did good work tonight."

"Dad just wants us to do the best possible job," Luther insists.

"No," Diego says. "He wants to control every aspect of how we do a job."

"Does anyone else think it's strange that we're talking about having a *job* at all?" Ben breaks in. "I mean, it's weird, right? Most teenagers haven't been working their whole lives."

Ben's the only one—other than Viktor—who hasn't moved since Dad left the room. He's still sitting in his chair, eating his dinner.

"Dad talks about being normal like it's a tragedy—no offense," he adds, glancing at Viktor briefly, and Viktor feels his cheeks grow hot. "But I wonder what it would be like to have a meal where we talk about something besides our latest mission." Ben runs his fingers through his smooth black hair. Some dust falls from the ends, but otherwise, it looks perfect as always.

"What if we could use our powers differently?" Allison asks leaning forward in her chair.

"Differently how?" Luther asks. "You think we have un-tapped resources that could get the job done even more quickly? Maybe that's what Dad was getting at—like, he knows that if we push harder, we'll become even more pow-erful?" Luther flexes his muscles like he's imagining himself even bigger, even stronger.

When they were younger, their father used to bring Vik-tor along on missions to keep time while his siblings saved the day. They all seemed so powerful that it's hard to imagine they have any resources they haven't discovered yet.

"I meant what if we used our powers to do something else," Allison explains.

Luther looks incredulous, like he can't imagine there's a point to having powers beyond being vigilantes. If anyone asked Viktor, he could tell them dozens of other things their powers might be used for. Ben could use his tentacles to help farmers who can't afford the latest machinery. Klaus could help mourning families say their final goodbyes. Allison could broker peace between warring nations. Diego could be a world-class chef. Luther could help people move in and out of their homes. There are countless ways to help people that don't involve fighting crime.

But Viktor keeps his thoughts to himself. No one ever asks him anything. Hargreeves doesn't even ask him to keep time anymore. As he practiced Bach this afternoon, Viktor imagined his siblings upstate. In his mind's eye, Alli-son rumored evil villains to put their weapons down, while Luther restrained the ones out of earshot. Diego used his knives to pick every lock, while Ben bashed his tentacles through walls, and Klaus got intel from the villains' victims on the other side. Viktor's siblings won't even ask him how it feels to be normal. Not even when their father suggests it.

"Do you ever wonder how we might have used our powers if we'd gone to a regular school?" Allison asks now.

Diego throws knives against the wall like he's playing darts. "The other kids would be jealous," he says, adding a practiced spin to a few of his tosses so those knives return to him like boomerangs. "Think about it—you could rumor every teacher into giving you straight As."

"But I could rumor them to give my friends straight As, too."

"What friends?" Diego waves his hands at the room around them. No friends, just siblings.

When he moves, dust rises from his uniform, making Viktor cough. Diego retrieves his remaining knives from the wall and starts throwing them all over again.

Viktor wonders whether he would have friends if he'd gone to a regular school. Here, he's a freak because he doesn't have powers. But maybe he could've fit in at regular school.

Or maybe he'd be an outcast there, too.

"I would've made friends!" Allison replies hotly.

"Not being normal is a privilege," Luther says.

Viktor silently agrees with his big brother. Technically, they're exactly the same age, but it's impossible not to think of Luther as his big brother. Not just because he's literally *bigger*, but because he's Number One, and Viktor's Number Seven.

"Normal teenagers don't stop crimes," Luther presses. "They don't save lives. Think about what we did out there today!"

"That oil company's just going to find somewhere else to drill," Ben says, throwing his napkin on the table.

"Fat chance," Diego counters, twirling a knife between his fingers. "We destroyed their headquarters!"

"We destroyed a *building*," Ben says. "Which is pretty ironic, when you think about it."

"Why?" Diego asks.

"We went up there to save people who'd been buried in rubble because of an earthquake—"

"Which we did," Luther interjects.

"Only to destroy another building."

"Yeah, but that building belonged to the *bad guys*." Luther makes it sound so simple.

Ben sighs. "The point is, the oil company can set up shop someplace else. Which means everything that happened today could just happen somewhere else some other day."

"Well, then we'll go rescue those people, too!" Luther throws his hand in the air like he's expecting someone to offer him a high-five, but no one does.

"We could've been normal," Ben says. "If Dad hadn't adopted us, if we'd gone to regular school—"

"We never would've been *like the other kids*," Diego counters. "I hate to admit when Dad's right, but he has a point about that."

"We're special," Allison agrees. She makes the word *special* sound so important.

"Maybe we could've found a way to be special and still fit in," Ben suggests, sounding wistful.

Viktor looks at his brother, feeling a hopeful tug. If his siblings could just be a little bit more normal, maybe they'd include Viktor on their adventures once in a while.

"Let's do it!" Klaus shouts, popping his head out from under the table. The back of his uniform is covered in dust bunnies that Mom's vacuum cleaner must have missed. Or maybe it's still detritus from the mission.

"Do what, Klaus?" Allison asks impatiently.

"Pierce our noses, dye our hair, sneak out to a party after curfew—just like dear old Dad suggested." Viktor and his siblings look at Klaus blankly. He continues, "Come on, sibs, a *party*, just like normals. No offense," he adds, echoing Ben and sneaking a glance at Viktor.

Viktor isn't offended. At least Ben and Klaus acknowledged him.

Diego rolls his eyes. "We are not trudging through the sewage system, Klaus."

Viktor knows that Klaus sneaks out from time to time, though he's never figured out how. But apparently *that's* how?

Luther looks as disgusted as Viktor feels. "You've been sneaking out through the sewage tunnels?"

"Nothing ventured, nothing gained." Klaus answers like the idea of sneaking through literal shit is no big deal.

Viktor shudders, and Ben rolls his eyes.

"We'll get out another way," Klaus promises. "The point is to *get out*, right?"

Viktor sees Allison nodding along, but Ben says, "That's not the kind of thing I had in mind."

"Dad would want us to get to bed early. We have training in the morning," Luther adds.

Rain or shine, the Umbrella Academy gets up at dawn seven days a week to train. Even Viktor rises with the sun, though he's never asked to train. Most days, he sits with Mom in the kitchen, lingering over breakfast, and then practices his violin. Mom applauds between every song. Viktor has no idea if he's actually any good, or if that's just Mom's programming.

"Come on, Luther, *please*." Allison's face breaks into a smile. "Let's break the rules just this once."

"You're wasting your breath, Allison," Diego fumes. "Mr. Goody Two-Shoes is too scared to break even one little rule."

Now Luther stands. He's so strong that when he knocks his chair over, it cracks even though Viktor's sure he doesn't mean for it to, just like the glass he broke earlier.

"I'm not scared of anything," Luther growls.

"Prove it." Diego puffs out his chest. He's shorter than Luther, but Viktor can tell Diego's trying not to let it show, like height is nothing more than an optical illusion.

Luther huffs. "Fine, I'm in."

"Me, too," says Allison, bouncing to her feet with a grin.

"Me, three," trills Klaus, as if the whole thing wasn't his idea to begin with.

Ben shrugs. "Anything's better than staying here."

"Viktor?" Allison asks, turning to Viktor.

Viktor's eyes widen. He tries to remember the last time Allison said anything at all to him. It certainly never occurred to him that she might ask him to come, too.

CHAPTER
5

BEN

"Viktor can help," Allison explains with a shrug.

She has a point, Ben thinks. *Viktor's the only one of them with real experience in normal.*

Unlike Ben, Viktor didn't spend the afternoon with tentacles coming out of his back, being lifting high off the ground by them so he could offer a hand to an earthquake victim trapped on the tenth floor of an unstable apartment building. And he didn't use those same tentacles to beat an oil exec bloody, knowing that if he hesitated, he'd never hear the end of it—not just from Hargreeves, who'd criticize him for wasting time, but from the rest of the Umbrella Academy, too. They'd say Ben had gone soft—and soft endangers missions.

Ben doesn't think it's soft to consider whether an oil exec might be willing to discuss matters before beating him to a pulp. But he knows better than to voice that opinion to his siblings.

"One rule," Ben says now, trying to make his voice as firm and authoritative as Luther's. Despite his best efforts though, his words come out like a question. "No powers tonight."

"What do you mean?" Diego asks, his eyes narrowing.

"If the point is to have a normal night out, then we have to actually *be* normal. If we use our powers, we're not exactly going to blend in among everyone else."

Diego and Luther grumble, but Allison nods.

"Ben's right. A normal night means we can't stand out. Or at least, not because of our powers." She winks, like she thinks she'll find some other way to be special.

"A surprisingly wise response from the sibling who uses her powers to get literally everything she wants," Klaus quips.

Allison looks taken aback. "I do not!"

Klaus throws up his hands like he already doesn't remember what he said to upset Allison in the first place.

Sometimes Ben thinks he's the only one who doesn't actually *enjoy* using his powers. Klaus isn't wild about his powers either, but he isn't asked to use them in quite the same way. No one sends Klaus into a bank vault full of criminals expecting him to take out every last one. No one forces Klaus to be a killer.

Diego called him that today as they forced their way into the oil company's offices. *"Get in there, killer."* He winked when he said it, like it was all in good fun.

Ben didn't hesitate—he knows that isn't allowed—but he didn't think it was *fun* either.

Ben tries to remember their first few missions. Did he enjoy it then? Was he having fun like the rest of them? What would his life be like if he'd never had to use his powers to save the day—if they were just a part of him, the way other people have perfect vision, or are left-handed, or pick up new dance moves easily?

Ben looks at Viktor. For a second, he imagines what it would be like if *he* was the one without any powers: Number Seven, the one left behind for every mission. The thought should make him feel sad, but instead he feels a strange sort of tug around his belly, not entirely dissimilar from the feeling of his tentacles moving around beneath his skin, neatly folded up between his bones, wrapped around his organs. They give a pull every so often, reminding him that they're there, eager to move and stretch. That's what this feels like—a tug of *longing*.

"Okay then, normal Number Seven," Diego says, turning to Viktor. "How do you propose we get out of here?"

Klaus opens his mouth, but Diego holds up a fist before Klaus can say anything. "Viktor?" he prompts.

Viktor stumbles over a non-response. Ben doesn't blame him. Diego's gaze is intense.

Diego turns to Allison. "I don't think Viktor's going to be much help." He says, making it sound like the punchline to a joke.

"Viktor's as well equipped for this mission as the rest of us," Ben breaks in, shooting Viktor a reassuring look, though he hates himself for calling it a mission. This isn't one of

Dad's *missions*. That's the whole point. "None of the six of us"—Ben has to concentrate to keep himself from saying *seven of us*—"has any experience out there in the real world."

"Au contraire, mon frère," Klaus says, brushing dust bunnies off the sleeves of his jacket. "You forget that I've been sneaking out of this house for years."

Ben rolls his eyes. "Klaus, for the last time, I am not swimming through sewage."

"Like I'd share my secret passageways with you," Klaus scoffs, but Ben knows Klaus would like nothing more than to share his expertise. He's invited Ben to come along on his nights out countless times before, but Ben's never said yes.

"Okay, then what's your big idea?" Ben asks.

"Follow me," Klaus says, crooking a finger and cocking an eyebrow. Klaus always has to put on a show.

Ben and his siblings follow Klaus, tiptoeing toward the wide staircase in the foyer.

"We're going to have to split up," Klaus whispers ominously. "Half up top and half down below."

"What are you talking about?"

"Half of us will climb out the attic window and shimmy down the drainpipe, and the other half will go out the service entrance."

Ben sighs. Had he really been expecting a more elaborate plan from Klaus? "That's it? That's your brilliant plan? If it's that easy, then why do you bother with the sewage system?"

"The sewage system is the only way I can get out without triggering the alarm."

"Well, how are we going to get around triggering the alarm tonight?"

"I hadn't gotten to that part of the plan yet. C'mon, Ben, you're the brains of this operation." Klaus's eyes widen with anticipation, as though there's not a doubt in his mind that Ben will know what to do.

He doesn't.

KLAUS

Does he have to think of *everything*? It's not Klaus's fault his siblings aren't willing to go the tried-and-true route of the sewers. Sometimes Klaus forgot just how queasy everyone else could be. Takes a lot more to gross a person out when they're used to regularly hearing from the dead.

Sometimes ghosts want to tell him every gruesome detail about how they died. Like earlier today, when the ghosts of people who didn't survive the earthquake shared exactly how it felt to be crushed beneath the weight of half a building. Hargreeves and his siblings expected Klaus to be able to concentrate on their mission—saving the people who hadn't died yet, exacting justice on those oil execs—when they had no idea that people were shouting in his head about gray matter and seeing their own intestines on the ground beside them. Just once, Klaus would like Hargreeves to have to focus on fighting off a mob of bad guys while hearing details about punctured lungs and gunshot wounds and suffocation.

Maybe then Dad would actually understand instead of shouting at him to toughen up.

Over the years, Klaus has heard descriptions of what it felt like to drown, to suffocate, to wither away from disease. He's heard about how it feels to get hit by a bus and hear every single one of your bones cracking; he's heard how it feels to choke on your own blood. He's heard how it feels to suffer an allergic reaction so severe that your throat closes up until you're gasping for air, aware the whole time that you're about to die because someone didn't tell you that the chocolate cake had peanuts in it. He knows how it feels to die because an untreated broken toe turned septic, and the infection spreads up your leg and into your groin before the doctors could stop it.

Anyhow, compared to all that, a little sewage isn't so bad.

"Okay, scratch the drainpipe plan," Diego says. "Maybe we should focus on where we're going once we get out of here."

"Sounds like putting the cart before the horse, if you ask me," Klaus says. He makes *clip-clop* noises to emphasize his point.

"Well, no one did ask you," Diego snaps.

Klaus folds his arms across his chest and blows a tuft of his chestnut colored hair off his forehead. This would be so much easier if they'd get over their squeamishness about the sewers.

Klaus's blazer tugs across his shoulder blades. He's tall and lanky, and as far as he's concerned, the dull Umbrella

Academy uniform does nothing to show off his physique. The whole getup is so uncool: a navy blazer with red piping over a sweater-vest, a perfectly pressed black tie around his neck, and shorts that stop just above his knees. Left to his own devices, Klaus thinks he could imbue even this outfit with some flair, but he knows Hargreeves would never allow that.

"Where should we go, Klaus?" Allison asks.

"I thought no one was interested in my opinion," Klaus pouts, though he knows exactly where to go, and it doesn't take much for him to spill. "What's the one place in the city where there's guaranteed to be a party every night?"

"The docks," Diego suggests.

"A bar," Ben tries.

Klaus shakes his head. "You two really need to get out more."

"That's the idea," Ben reminds him.

"The *college*." Klaus says like it's obvious—because it is. "Across town."

"How are we going to get all the way across town?" Allison asks. "Anyway, we're too young for a college party."

"They won't exactly be checking IDs, sister-dear," Klaus promises. "And we'll just drive there."

A plan starts forming in Klaus's imagination, growing more intricate with every word he says.

"Drive?" Allison echoes.

"To the garage!" Klaus shouts triumphantly while Ben shushes him desperately. "To the garage," Klaus repeats more softly, leading the way to the back stairs and the entrance to the garage, where Hermes, Hargreeves's Rolls-Royce Silver Shadow, is parked.

"No! Absolutely not!" Ben hisses. "Sneaking out is one thing, but grand theft auto? Really, Klaus?"

"May as well be as in for a penny as for a pound," Klaus sing-songs.

"What the hell does that mean?" Diego asks.

It occurs to Klaus that it's not the sort of phrase most teenagers would know, let alone say. But most teenagers don't have centuries' worth of senior citizens with old-fashioned expressions taking up space in their brains.

It's okay, Klaus assures himself. Once they find a party to crash, the voices of the dead will be drowned out by the blaring music, shouted greetings, and fraternity brothers chanting *chug, chug, chug* while they hold someone upside down over a keg.

And if that's not enough to silence the voices, there are other, even more effective ways.

Klaus reaches for the doorknob that leads from the basement into the garage. Then he searches for the button that will open the enormous garage door over the driveway, but Allison grabs his wrist before he makes contact.

"You're going to set off the alarm," Allison whispers.

"Why are you whispering? There's no one else down here."

"Dad will flip if we trigger the alarm," Allison says.

"Yeah, that's why we have to move quickly."

"What?"

"We have to get in the car and peel the hell out before Dad has time to get down here."

"You're not even going to try to disable the alarm?" Ben sounds aghast.

Klaus shrugs. "I don't know how to." What are his siblings thinking? He's a telepath, not a mechanic.

"So your entire plan is run away so fast that Dad won't be able to catch us?" Diego asks.

"You got a better idea?"

Diego looks at him blankly, then turns to his siblings for help. Each one of them shrugs.

"All right, then—let 'er rip," Diego says, gesturing to the garage door.

Klaus smiles like he can't wait for things to go haywire. "You guys ready to run for it?"

"Do you even have Dad's keys?" Ben asks.

"I've been hot-wiring Hermes since I was twelve."

Klaus snuck down to the garage then, too. He sat in the driver's seat and grabbed the steering wheel, making *vroom* noises as he pretended to drive. Back then, he didn't open the garage door—he was just practicing for later. It took him one try after another, but finally he got the car started. He'd never been so excited. He can't remember now how long he sat there. It must've been a while, because the next thing he knew, Pogo was carrying him up to bed.

"All right, sibs," Klaus says now. "On the count of three, make a run for Hermes. I'll open the garage and hot-wire that baby, and then we'll be out of here. *One, two—*"

"Why wouldn't you get into the car and hot-wire it before opening the door?" Ben interrupts. "That way you have more time before the alarm goes off."

"Haven't you ever heard of carbon monoxide poisoning?" Luther asks. "We can't sit in the garage with the door closed and the car running."

Klaus shakes his head. "That's an old wives' tale." *Old wives' tale.* Another expression not many teenagers would use. "I sit in here all the time with Hermes's engine revved, and I'm just fine."

"Fine is relative," Ben teases, knocking Klaus on the head.

"Carbon monoxide poisoning isn't a myth," Allison points out, and Klaus does vaguely recall meeting a ghost who died that way. Hmm. Maybe he's immune. Anyway, that's not what he should be thinking about right now.

Right now, he should be thinking about getting his siblings out of this house before they lose their nerve. He thinks Luther will be the first to crack. Or maybe Viktor—even if he's the most ordinary one in the group, he's always the one with the least experience in the outside world. He doesn't even come along to watch the missions anymore.

"You know, I'm beginning to think that you guys don't really want to go out tonight," Klaus says, cocking his head to the side. He tries to make it sound like a dare. No one can resist a dare.

"Of course we want to go," Luther says, but he doesn't sound certain. Klaus suspects that some part of Luther is hoping Hargreeves will stop them before they get out the door.

But Klaus had to admit: Diego and Ben look determined. Even Allison's eyes are blazing, though that could just be left-over irritation from the earthquake dust. (Which reminds Klaus: They're going to have to get cleaned up. They can't show up at the party looking like *this*.) Meanwhile, Viktor hasn't said a word, but Klaus can't help noticing that there's more excitement in his eyes than he's ever seen before.

"All right then, let's get out of here. *One, two—*"

BEN

Ben wraps a hand around Klaus's wrist before he gets to *three*.

"What now?" Klaus whines, but Ben brings a finger up to his lips. When his siblings finally quiet down, they can hear the telltale padding of Pogo's footsteps against the hardwood floors. Even though Pogo walks upright—unlike every other chimpanzee on the planet—his gait is distinct. His glasses balance on his nose, and his striped tie is knotted perfectly. Ben tries to recall if he's ever seen Pogo wear anything but a three-piece suit.

"Good evening, young Hargreeveses," Pogo says, and Ben flinches at the formal greeting. "Fine work upstate this afternoon."

"Dad didn't seem to think so," Allison mumbles, crossing her arms. Ben notices a look of surprise on Luther's face. He's not used to Allison complaining about their dad.

"Your father is proud of your hard work, I assure you," Pogo offers, but only Luther nods in agreement.

"Heading up to bed?" Pogo asks, after a moment. Ben thinks there's a suggestive note in his tone, as though Pogo suspects they're up to something. Why else would they be hovering around the door that leads to the garage? Sometimes Ben thinks Pogo is listening at every doorway. How could he know everything that goes on in this house?

"Of course, Pogs," Klaus answers, an exaggerated innocence in his voice. "We were just stretching our legs before heading upstairs."

Pogo nods. "I only ask because I'll be updating the security system tonight."

Ben's ears perk up as Pogo continues: "The alarm will be offline from ten to ten fifteen. Be sure your windows are locked—anyone could sneak in during those fifteen minutes."

"I think we can handle it, Pogo," Luther answers, puffing out his chest.

"Roger that," Klaus answers, giving a salute as Pogo walks away.

Diego rolls his eyes. "Leave it to Dad to have an elaborate security system that requires us to sleep with our windows shut and locked."

"Yeah, Dad's a real monster for wanting to keep us safe," Luther says sarcastically.

Ben can hardly believe how clueless his siblings are. "Weren't you guys *listening*?"

"Listening to what?" Viktor asks. Unlike the rest of his siblings, Viktor's voice is calm and serious.

"Pogo told us when the alarm's going to be offline. We can sneak out without tripping the alarm then."

Klaus huffs. "I told you guys, the alarm was secondary—"

"The alarm will be back online by the time we get back," Allison says.

"We'll worry about getting back in later," Klaus insists. There's urgency in his voice. Ben knows Klaus is worried everyone else is going to lose their nerve.

Well, Ben thinks, *Klaus doesn't have to worry that I'm going to lose mine. Nothing's going to stop me from having a normal night out.*

Until Hargreeves mentioned it over dinner, Ben hadn't realized how badly he wanted it. He'll even let Klaus drag him through the pipes if he has to.

"Let's do it," Ben says firmly.

"Come on, then!" Klaus shouts, and everyone else shushes him. Ben grabs Klaus's hand before he can open the garage door.

"Not until ten p.m., remember?"

Klaus slumps his shoulders like he's never been so disappointed.

"Come on," Ben says, leading the way from the garage into the playroom. They sit at the narrow table where they eat breakfast and lunch—only dinner is upstairs in the dining room with Dad—across from the deli counter that passes for a kitchen. Here, the floors aren't wide planks of hardwood or thick slabs of marble, but linoleum. Instead of arched ceilings with pillars adorning the corners of the room, there's a flimsy-looking popcorn ceiling. The table is low, left over from when they were kids.

Ben grabs a paper towel and wipes the dust from his hair and face. He tosses towels to his siblings so they can do the same. Ben tugs at the cuffs of his sleeves. He can feel that beneath his sweater vest, his white shirt is wrinkled against his chest, still slightly moist from sweating during their mission earlier. Ben wonders what mealtimes are like in other families' houses. Maybe it's not actually unusual the way Dad reviews their performances; maybe in other houses, fathers discuss homework assignments and SAT scores with the same urgency. Maybe Dad's constant disappointment is one of the more normal things about him after all. Ben's seen it on TV shows (when they sneak into Dad's study to watch) and read about it in books (provided by Mom and Pogo; the only reading materials Dad provides are related to their missions): fathers lecturing their children about studying harder, getting better grades. Maybe Dad *should* be grading their performances like report cards. Maybe that would be one step closer to normal.

Then again, Ben's also seen shows and read stories about parents who are supportive and proud. Mom plays that part, but Mom isn't like anyone else's mother, no matter how carefully Dad designed her. Mom may be the one who gave them names and who nurses their cuts and prepares their food and even kisses them good night, but Ben's willing to bet she's the only mom in the world who plugs into the wall to recharge at night, the only mom who could be deactivated entirely.

Everyone else seems to think that the security system update is some kind of happy coincidence, but Ben isn't so sure. Pogo may be genetically engineered—or whatever it was Dad did to him—but sometimes Ben thinks he's the most normal one of them all. Certainly, he's the only adult in the house who could understand why Ben and his siblings might want to sneak out in the middle of the night. Although, he's so loyal to Dad that—

Suddenly, Klaus looks at his watch and announces, "9:55!"

They sit in silence until he says, "9:56," and then, "9:54!"

"What?" Ben asks.

Klaus winks. "Just kidding—9:57!"

Ben knows that Klaus was joking around, but his heart sank at the thought that time could be going backward, that they might not make it out the door tonight. He feels a flutter of butterflies across his stomach. He can't wait to get out of here.

At 9:59, Klaus begins a second-by-second countdown.

"Everybody ready?" Klaus announces. "*Three, two, one!*"

Klaus practically sprints to the garage door. Ben follows at his heels, almost as excited as his brother.

ALLISON

When did you get a driver's license?" Luther asks as Klaus expertly backs Hermes out of the garage and on to the street.

"Who said anything about a license?" Klaus laughs, pressing his foot on the gas so hard that Allison's thrown back in her seat.

She's squeezed between Luther and Diego in the back. Klaus is driving, and Viktor and Ben share the passenger seat. Allison knows this isn't legal, but she's not entirely sure it isn't safe. Anyway, it's not as though most of the Umbrella Academy's activities are *legal*. Hargreeves doesn't exactly check with law enforcement before sending them in to save the day.

It's not as though their missions are particularly safe either. That's kind of the point, isn't it? If it was *safe*, then anyone could do it. The thought makes Allison sit up a little straighter, her shoulders bumping into Luther and Diego on either side.

She has to admit though, license or no license, Klaus seems to know what he's doing.

"Who taught you how to drive?" she asks, feeling a prick of jealousy. Maybe there's some lesson Hargreeves offered Klaus that he kept from the rest of them.

"Last year a NASCAR driver took up residence here." Klaus taps his forehead. "Died in a spectacular crash on the track, but that doesn't mean he didn't know what he was doing."

Of course, Klaus has had countless lessons the rest of them haven't. Dad used to lock him in a crypt in an attempt to get him to "overcome his fears."

"Well," Allison says awkwardly, "You're really good."

"Thank you," Klaus turns around to face her and seems genuinely pleased with the praise.

"Eyes on the road!" Ben shouts.

"Huh?" Klaus asks.

Ben reaches across the front seat and physically turns Klaus's head to face the road in front of them.

"Lighten up, brother," Klaus says. He leans forward to open the glove compartment, pulling out a pair of leather gloves. "Betcha didn't know this is where Dad keeps his special driving gloves."

"Where else would he keep them?" Ben mutters.

Klaus takes both hands off the wheel to put the gloves on. Ben lurches across the car to plant his hands on the steering wheel, trying to keep them in the lane.

"Such a worrywart!" Klaus pouts as he puts his hands back on the wheel, straightening out the car like he doesn't have a care in the world.

Allison leans over Luther to roll down the window. She breathes in the fresh air like it's all new, like an inmate who's just been released from prison. She knows that's absurd. They've been outside a million times before. Earlier today they were scrambling over rubble upstate.

So why does she feel like she's just broken free?

"Now what?" Ben asks. Allison can see him clutching his seat belt so tightly that his knuckles are white, not as impressed with Klaus's driving kills as Allison is. Klaus leans over, trying to force Ben to release his grip, but Ben swats Klaus's hands away.

"Now we do whatever we want!" Diego whoops.

Luther gives Allison's shoulder a squeeze, and she can't tell if he's excited or nervous.

Klaus laughs. "Now we head to the other side of town."

"And then what?" Viktor asks.

Klaus leans across the car conspiratorially. "And then, the whole world." He straightens up. "Okay well maybe not the whole world, but the local university. Like I said, there's always a party on campus to join. Where do you think I always sneak out to?"

"I never gave it much thought," Ben answers, but Allison can hear the lie in his voice. She wonders how many nights he's spent waiting up to make sure Klaus comes home in one piece.

Allison gazes out the window, watching the city pass them by. It's dark out, but the streets are lit up by milky yellow streetlamps. In between their glow, the buildings all look gray, their windows darkened. As they keep driving, they pass through a residential neighborhood, the buildings are shorter and more windows are lit up, glowing behind curtains and blinds. Allison imagines the families inside: kids doing their homework, parents watching the news, dogs begging to be let outside. All those strangers doing whatever it is normal families do. And tonight, Allison's one step closer to them than she's ever been before.

"What do you want?" Allison asks Luther breathlessly.

"Huh?" he asks, a smile pulling at his lips.

"Where would you go, what would you do, if we could do anything?"

Luther shrugs.

"Come on, there must be something," Allison prods.

Luther furrows his brow like he's concentrating. Finally he answers, "I guess I'd just want to hang out with you."

She smiles. She wants that, too, but she also wants . . . *more*. Maybe tonight will help fill in the blanks.

"It is weird, right?" Allison asks, gazing out the window once more. "That this is the first time we've ever been outside without some kind of supervision?"

"I never thought about it," Luther says. "We've snuck around the academy so much." Luther waves in the general direction of the building they left behind. "I figured we discovered all kind of nooks and crannies Dad didn't know about. Never felt like I couldn't get away from his supervision if I really wanted to."

Allison nods, even though she doesn't agree. Every time they've snuck off, Dad always found them. Tonight is the first time she's ever felt truly out of his reach. Which makes fitting in out here that much more important—like it's her chance to prove she can make it without Hargreeves keeping watch.

Allison looks down at herself. No way can she fit in like *this*. None of them can. They're all still wearing their uniforms.

"We should've changed before we left," she says.

"There wasn't any time," Diego points out. "Besides, change into what? Our pajamas?"

Diego has a point. They don't really have any clothes besides their uniforms, their training sweats, and their pj's.

Allison closes her eyes, remembering a photo shoot she'd done for some teen magazine. They did her hair and makeup, and put her in a bright blue silky dress like she was going to a school dance. But before the camera could take a single photo, her father insisted she wear her uniform. The Umbrella Academy had an image to uphold. Allison hadn't understood why her wearing a dress would tarnish their image, but now she does: Dad never wanted anyone to notice her before they noticed her uniform. He didn't want readers to do a double take before they recognized her as a member of the Umbrella Academy.

Maybe she could've borrowed something from Mom's closet tonight. Her clothes aren't exactly current, but Allison's confident she could rock a retro look if given the chance.

"Well, we can't go to a party dressed like this," Allison says firmly. "Klaus!" she shouts. Getting his attention is almost impossible these days. Allison can't be sure if it's because of all the voices in his head, or the brandy she's seen him swiping from their father's liquor cabinet, or something worse.

"Yes, lovely Allison?" Klaus answers on the first try, turning in his seat again.

"Eyes on the road!" Ben says.

"Worrywart!" Klaus shouts back.

"What do you wear when you go to those parties?" Allison asks.

"Oh, if only you'd agreed to exit through the pipes. You should see the outfits I have stored in there."

Allison wrinkles her nose at the thought of it.

"But not to worry," Klaus adds with a wink. "I've got you covered."

Klaus takes a sharp left—he runs a red light, but at least he signals, which is more than Allison expected.

Allison's never felt jealous of Klaus before. She's never been jealous of any of her siblings, really; she doesn't mind being Number Three, and she likes her own power better than any of theirs. It's so much more useful out in the real world. But tonight, for the first time, she feels a tug of envy. Klaus never waited for Hargreeves to offer him the real world; he just took it.

Tonight, Allison will, too.

VIKTOR

Klaus parked in front of a thrift store. Well, technically, he parked in front of a hydrant in front of a thrift store, and even Viktor knows that's definitely not allowed, but he's too impressed by his brother's parallel parking skills to say anything about it. His siblings don't mention it either.

Once he's turned the car off, Klaus hops out of the driver's seat like he's on springs, Viktor and Ben unfold themselves from the passenger seat, and his siblings in the back step out one by one. Klaus leads the way toward the thrift store like he's been here a dozen times before.

"How'd you know this place would be open?" Viktor asks.

"Not my first rodeo," Klaus answers with a wink. "And, it's the perfect place to get our bearings. We're only a block away from campus."

"The college campus you've been sneaking to regularly?"

Klaus winks again. "You're welcome to join me any night," he whispers, like it's a secret he's offering only to

Viktor. Which Viktor knows isn't true. Klaus is very "love the one you're with"—if it had been Allison (or Ben or Luther or Diego) asking the question, he'd have offered to take them, too. Klaus isn't picky.

Still, Klaus's attention makes Viktor feel special somehow. Maybe it's because Viktor is so rarely given any attention at all, but Viktor thinks it's more than that. Klaus is one of those people who lights up every room he walks into. People notice him, and not in a *Who is that freak? Get him out of here!* kind of way. Unlike Viktor, who always seems to blend into the scenery. Actually, that's not true: At home, he tries to blend in, but he ends up standing out, because he's the only one without powers. Out in the real world, back when Hargreeves used to bring Viktor along on missions—to keep time, to watch his siblings carefully—no one ever noticed him.

Viktor imagines his siblings walking into a party with a bunch of ordinary people tonight. For once, Viktor will be the one who fits in. Not that his siblings have ever protested about standing out before. But tonight, everyone wants to fly under the radar. That's why they made their no-powers pact. But for Viktor, fitting in should come easy tonight.

"Follow me, siblings," Klaus calls as he opens the door to the thrift shop, a bell ringing over his head.

The store is huge, and the siblings quickly split up to explore. Row after row of clothes are piled high like walls, no rhyme or reason to where things are located in this labyrinth of a store—or at least, not one that Viktor can discern. He starts by following a few steps behind Allison—the store doesn't really appear to be split into sections, with menswear on one side and women's wear on the other; the clothes aren't organized by size or style either. Viktor eyes some ripped-up blue jeans hanging over a pair of shiny silver boots.

"It's like digging for treasure," Klaus yells from an aisle away, pulling out a mesh top from a pile of what looks like dirty laundry. Klaus begins undressing right there in the center of the store to try it on.

"Klaus!" Ben shouts. "You can't strip in public."

"Who's gonna stop me?"

"The dressing room is right there!" Ben shouts, pointing to a row of curtained-off rooms in the back of the store.

"Prude!" Klaus cries, but he heads in the direction of the dressing rooms, stopping to pick up a few more clothes along the way.

Viktor keeps browsing. Many of the clothes are vintage, he realizes. Seventies bell-bottoms are next to eighties tie-dye leggings are next to nineties-era hip-hugging, bootcut jeans. Like his siblings, Viktor's never had a chance to pick out his own clothes before. He looks down at his uniform: the blazer, the formal shoes. It never felt right, wearing the Umbrella Academy uniform when he's not really one of them. He's surprised Hargreeves doesn't insist that he wear something else. Then again, Hargreeves would've had to come up with whatever that something else was, and that's more effort than he's ever put into Viktor.

Allison piles Luther's arms high with one pastel-colored dress after another. Diego's picking up only black clothes—black shirts, black sweaters, black pants, black boots.

"You going to a funeral?" Klaus asks him.

"Technically, a funeral is a kind of party," Diego growls. "The guest of honor just doesn't know they're being celebrated."

"That doesn't make any sense," Luther shouts from the other side of the store, his voice muffled beneath piles of taffeta.

"It's a gathering of people who've come together to celebrate someone. It's practically the same thing as a birthday party," Diego counters.

"Deathday party," Viktor mumbles, and Klaus bursts out laughing.

"A deathday party sounds *so* much more fun than a funeral," he says. "Viktor, promise me that when I die, you'll throw me a deathday party, not a funeral."

Viktor feels himself blush, but he nods, which Klaus must take as a promise because he smiles in return. Klaus pulls what looks like a skirt off the rack in front of him and adds it to his growing pile of clothes. Klaus doesn't care that most boys don't wear skirts; *he* wants to try this one on. That thought sends a shiver of excitement down Viktor's spine.

Viktor catches a glimpse of his reflection in one of the store's mirrors, half obscured by a tall pile of clothes. He reaches into a pocket and takes out one of his pills, downs it dry. Since Viktor was twelve, Dad said to take a pill any time he felt agitated, anxious, uncomfortable. Which is a lot of the time. Does everyone feel so strange in their skin? Or is it just everyone who's powerless? Maybe he's not supposed to look this way because he's supposed to be special, like his siblings.

Allison lets out a squeal that echoes from one side of the store to the other, a sure sign that she's found another beautiful dress or a stylish pair of jeans that she can't wait to try on. Diego lets out a gruff *Yes!*—he must've found exactly what he was looking for, too. Viktor bets that whatever it is, it'll fit perfectly. His siblings all seem to know exactly what they want to wear.

Maybe that comes from years of comfort inside your own skin. Then again, Ben never seemed quite so at ease as the rest of them. It took Ben years to learn to control his tentacles. Mom always had to alter his uniform to accommodate them—she created secret slits in his shirts and blazers that the tentacles could release and retract from. Viktor wonders how Ben will manage in normal clothes, then remembers that his siblings all promised not to use their powers tonight, so Ben won't have to worry about ripping holes in his new clothes. Viktor watches Ben find a white T-shirt, blue jeans, black leather jacket. Ben walks confidently toward the curtained dressing rooms at the back of the store.

Viktor runs his hands over the rack in front of him, tracing the edges of old dresses and ripped-up shirts and threadbare jackets. He lands abruptly on a pair of black jeans that look small enough for his narrow frame. He keeps searching until he finds a worn-in graphic T-shirt—it has a faded picture of a surfer on it—with a neckline that's only slightly stretched out, but at least it looks clean. Last, he finds a beat-up brown bomber jacket, the kind he's seen pictures of World War II airmen wearing in the textbooks Mom gave him to read while his siblings were out on missions.

Viktor's hands are shaking as he rushes to the dressing room and pulls off his uniform. There's no mirror in here; the walls are made out of crushed velvet curtains that smell like incense. But Viktor doesn't have to look in a mirror. This outfit, these clothes that belonged to strangers years or maybe even decades ago, feel like they fit him better than the uniform his mother carefully sewed to fit his body, now crumpled into a pile at his feet.

Bespoke, that's what Mom called it. Custom-made clothes were bespoke. The word sounded rich and heavy, like it was meant for men in business suits, not children running around, fighting crime. His bespoke uniform never felt like it fit. He always thought it was because he wasn't a real member of the Umbrella Academy.

Viktor leaves the dressing room behind and heads toward the front of the store where there are bins of accessories. He digs around for a while, then looks up to find himself face-to-face with Klaus, who's wearing what appears to be a plaid kilt with a sheer black sweater on top. Somehow, he's also found dark black eyeliner to smear around his eyes, and his lips are shiny with gloss. For a split second, Viktor feels a pang of anger: Klaus's kilt isn't that different from the plaid skirt that's part of the Umbrella Academy uniform. Viktor can't understand why Klaus, who could have chosen to wear anything tonight, chose *that*.

Klaus looks Viktor up and down and nods approvingly. "Classic look," he says approvingly. Any trace of anger vanishes as Viktor feels himself blushing again. Klaus's praise feels strange, but also as good as the new clothes on his back.

Viktor isn't sure he's ever felt quite this good.

KLAUS

A woman is hollering at him that he's stretching out her sweater, and a man with a thick Scottish brogue keeps shouting that he needs a sporran to match his kilt.

Klaus wishes these people would shut up. Not his siblings—to be fair, his siblings won't shut up either, but Klaus is skilled at tuning out their chatter, and anyway, he kind of likes it. No, the people yelling at him are the previous owners of Klaus's new clothes. The downside of thrift shops is the endless commentary.

"What the hell is a sporran?" Klaus mumbles. He didn't pick the kilt because he was going for a traditional Scottish ensemble, but it's perfect for his grungy, field-hockey look. He finds a pair of combat boots forgotten under a pile of wrinkled clothes, black with threadbare laces. They're too big, but they complete his look so nicely! Then Klaus hunts until he finds a pair of thick socks that make the boots *almost* fit.

"Close enough," he says, trying and failing to ignore the voice telling him that he was wearing those boots the day he died.

"Shut up!" Klaus begs through gritted teeth.

He sticks his hand into the pockets of one women's coat after another until he finds some forgotten makeup. Allison would scream if she saw him using a stranger's lipstick and eyeliner. But of course it isn't a stranger's makeup; there's a voice in his head explaining exactly how to apply her old stick of kohl, longingly recalling the last time she wore it.

Klaus is sick of the voices and their stories. He's itching to drown it all out.

Just a little bit longer, he tells himself, *and we'll be on campus. Just a little bit longer, and they'll be at a crowded party.* If there's one thing he's learned over the past year or so, it's that at the right sort of party, someone is always holding. And that someone, whoever they are, is the key to the *quiet*, the key to *oblivion*, the key to putting on makeup without hearing someone's voice in his head telling him whether he's doing it right or not.

At least tonight's voice did actually help him, but it's a high price to pay for the perfect smoky eye. Although, catching a glimpse of his reflection in a nearby mirror, he knows he looks *good*.

Klaus musses his hair. He hasn't washed it in days, so it's greasy enough to hold whatever style he shapes it into. He adds volume to the front, a few strands falling artfully across his forehead, then smooths it down in the back. Some dust from their earlier mission falls out as Klaus combs his hair with his fingers, and he coughs. *Maybe we should've taken the time to shower before we went out into the world tonight,* he thinks. But no—if he'd given his siblings time to stop and shower, they might have lost their nerve. Better that Klaus kept the momentum of their night going.

"Don't get spittle all over my kilt!" the Scotsman commands.

Klaus rolls his eyes. *Just a little bit longer.*

Diego steps out of his dressing room, clad in black from head to toe: tight black cargo pants, fitted black T-shirt, black combat boots.

"Those pants are so tight I can see your *knives*, brother," Klaus says, not disapprovingly. He guesses that Diego had to improvise without the secret compartments that mom sewed into his uniform. Mom even built Diego shoes with secret compartments. Klaus likes the idea of fashion that is more than meets the eye. Not that the Umbrella Academy uniforms are anything resembling *fashion*.

"Jesus, how many do you have?" Klaus adds, trying to count the bumps and lumps beneath his brother's pants.

"Enough to kick anyone's ass," Diego answers with a grin.

Allison emerges next wearing—there's no other name for it—a prom dress. A ghost whispers in Klaus's ear that she wore it to the homecoming dance in 1989. Allison spins, layers of purple taffeta enveloping her. The dress cuts straight across her chest; the sleeves are powder puffs off her shoulders. The bodice is fitted to a drop-waist skirt, where the dress expands into a full layers of stiff tulle. She looks like she stepped straight out of an eighties movie.

From the next dressing room, Luther steps out wearing a tuxedo that's at least two sizes too small. Allison stands on her tiptoes to button his shirt, but the buttons holding the collar down literally burst off his neck.

"You break it, you buy it, Number One," Klaus explains.

Luther tugs at his collar, his Adam's apple bouncing up and down as he swallows.

"What kind of policy is that?" Luther growls, but Allison smooths his collar, assuring him that he looks perfect. Klaus has to hold back a snort. They'd look perfect if this was a costume party. The purple dress's previous owner scoffs and then goes quiet. If only everyone would shut up when he offended them, Klaus wouldn't have to go to such extreme lengths.

Ben grabs Klaus from behind and spins him around. "Any luck?" Ben asks. He's wearing an innocuous outfit: jeans, T-shirt, leather jacket. Ben looks, Klaus has to admit, pretty cool. He'll fit right in at the party. *Until he rips his new clothes into shreds when his tentacles come out*, Klaus thinks sadly. *What a waste of a good outfit.*

"Luck with what? Getting our siblings dressed for a party? I never would've guessed that you and Viktor would be the only ones who wouldn't embarrass me."

"You don't embarrass easy," Ben points out, and Klaus shrugs. He's right.

"Anyway," Ben leans in, his voice softer, "you know that's not the luck I'm talking about."

"Oh, right," Klaus checks an imaginary watch on his wrist. "It's time for Ben's daily check-in." *Can't he give it a break for just one day?*

"And?" Ben prompts.

"And what?" Klaus plays dumb, though he knows exactly what his brother wants to hear.

"And—have you heard from him?" Ben's voice is an octave higher than usual. It happens whenever he asks about Five.

"No, Ben." Klaus stomps down one of the store's labyrinthine aisles. "I haven't heard from our long-lost brother."

Ben exhales. Every day, he asks Klaus if he's heard from their brother, and every day when Klaus says no, he looks so relieved that Klaus has long since decided that even if he *did* hear from Five, he wouldn't tell. Because as long as Klaus doesn't hear from Five, Ben can go on holding out hope that their missing brother is still alive, that he could come back any day, any time, any place. Just *pop* out of thin air. (That is how he disappeared, after all.) Klaus knows that Ben harbors a fantasy that someday all seven of them will be together again.

Ben doesn't know that Klaus has been plotting his escape for months. One way or another, he's getting the hell out of Dodge.

Maybe tonight will make his siblings realize they need to get out, too. One night out in the real world, and they'll see what they've been missing. Not every outing has to be a mission, not every public appearance a photo shoot (though Klaus doesn't mind the attention). One perfect night and Klaus won't be the only one leaving the Umbrella Academy behind. It should be easy enough to show everyone that parties are way better than crime-fighting rescue missions.

LUTHER

What do you think Klaus meant, 'You break it, you buy it'? We don't have any money."

As Luther says it, he thinks for the first time that it might be strange: He's seventeen years old, and he's never actually handled cash, never had a credit card, never stepped up to a counter in a store to make a purchase. He remembers that when they were little, they had a toy cash register with plastic coins. He and Allison used to pretend they were running a grocery store, charging their siblings every time they sat down for breakfast and lunch. Come to think of it, that's the closest Luther's come to actually buying something.

Luther understands that things cost money. He's not some spoiled rich kid with no appreciation of his privilege. It's just that Dad always handled that side of their lives. The fridge in the basement is kept stocked, and a new uniform always appears neatly folded on his bed whenever he needs it.

"Allison," he hisses, tugging at the collar of his new (old) shirt urgently, "how are we going to pay for all this?"

"I guess Klaus will take care of it," Allison says with a shrug, though Luther can tell she's no more certain than he is. "He's been here before. He must have some kind of arrangement with the owner."

Luther tries to figure out what kind of arrangement that would be.

"Is everyone ready?" Klaus shouts from the other side of the store. Luther rolls his shoulders. The tuxedo jacket Allison picked for him is tight, and it rips down the back as he moves.

"You can wear your Academy blazer," Allison suggests, picking it up off the floor where Luther tossed it when he changed. "It almost matches."

Luther slips back on his familiar sport coat.

It doesn't match, and Allison knows it: It's navy blue, clashing with the tuxedo's sleek black pants, and the Umbrella Academy patch Mom sewed over Luther's heart is unmistakable. But it feels better than the stranger's jacket. Luther can't help noticing just how much more comfortable it is, and not just because Mom tailored it to fit his body perfectly.

Klaus heads to the front door, and Luther follows anxiously, grabbing his brother before he can go outside.

"Don't we have to pay?" Luther asks.

Klaus rolls his eyes. "In case you haven't noticed, this isn't the sort of establishment where the owner keeps a careful inventory of his stock."

Klaus gestures to the front desk where a teenager is chewing gum, headphones firmly planted over his ears, nose in a magazine. His eyes have a glazed look that Luther has seen in Klaus's from time to time; Luther suspects the clerk isn't entirely sober and certainly doesn't take his job very seriously. He probably doesn't care if Luther and his siblings walk out of here wearing stolen clothes. It's not like they've been subtle since they walked in.

"We can't just *steal*." Luther is horrified. The Umbrella Academy captures thieves; they don't *become* them.

"These clothes are one step above trash, Luther. It's not stealing, it's . . ." Klaus seems to search the right word. "It's *conservation*. If we don't take these clothes, they'll end up in some landfill. Do you really want to be responsible for the pollution of the planet?"

"Of course not," Luther says quickly, though he feels confused. Klaus has a way of twisting things so that it sounds like he's right, even when Luther's sure he isn't. Luther can't quite work out how he does it.

"It's all right, brother," Klaus says, putting a hand on his shoulder. "I know you care about the survival of Mother Earth." Klaus winks, then turns to the rest of the group. "Besides, we'll leave our uniforms behind, so it's like a give-a-penny, take-a-penny tray."

"A what?" Luther asks desperately. He hates this feeling—Klaus is the only one of them with experience out in the world, so he seems so much wiser than Luther. But Luther can't tell how much of Klaus's wisdom is real and how much is his usual gibberish.

Klaus has a way of making nonsense seem reasonable, of making the outrageous seem ordinary. Right now, for example, he's wearing a skirt and a see-through sweater, but somehow he looks so at ease.

Before Luther can gather his thoughts, Klaus shouts, "And we're off!" with a flourish, leading the way out the door.

Luther resolves that he'll come back here tomorrow. With money. Somehow. He'll pay for what they took. And retrieve their uniforms.

He picks his siblings' discarded clothes up off the floor and brings them to the front desk.

"I'll be back tomorrow," he promises. "Can you hang on to these for me?"

The clerk looks up from his magazine long enough to take the clothes from Luther. He seems mildly surprised that there's anyone else in the store at all. He picks up Klaus's jacket and laughs when he recognizes the embroidered crest.

"These'll sell big come Halloween."

"They're not for sale," Luther explains. "Like I said, I'm coming back for them tomorrow."

"What?" the clerk asks. He can't hear Luther over the sound of the music in his headphones.

"They're not for sale!" Luther shouts.

"That's a shame. Umbrella Academy costumes are big sellers."

"They're not costumes. They're uniforms." The clerk doesn't respond, so Luther repeats it louder.

"Whatever, man." The clerk reaches out for the clothes just as Luther sees a flash of light out of the corner of his eye.

Thanks to Hargreeves's training, Luther's first instinct is to suspect danger and protect the innocent. Before he has time to think, Luther is diving over the desk to tackle the clerk to the ground.

"What the hell?" the clerk screams, but his voice is overwhelmed by the rumble of thunder so loud, it's like it's coming from inside the planet instead of the sky above. The light flashes again. In an instant, Luther's on his feet.

"What's going on?" Allison asks.

"Man, that's assault!" the clerk shouts, his voice shaking. "I'm calling the police!" He reaches for an old-fashioned rotary phone on the countertop.

"I was trying to protect you—" Luther begins.

"From what?"

"Whatever *that* was," Luther gestures to the street outside.

"You tackled me!" the clerk protests.

"I was saving you!" Luther insists.

At once, there's another flash of light, and another rumble of thunder.

The clerk yelps, panic making his pale face turn bright pink.

Allison jumps over the counter and grabs the clerk's wrists. "I heard a rumor you were perfectly calm," she says, "and grateful that my brother saved you."

The boy recites, "I'm perfectly calm." He turns to Luther like he's seeing him for the first time. "And so grateful you saved me."

"No problem," Luther says. Even though Allison rumored the boy into thanking him, it still feels good. Although the truth is Luther isn't quite so sure he saved anyone. Not yet. Something strange is still going on outside.

"Hey!" Ben shouts. "What happened to no powers?"

"It was an emergency," Luther insists.

"It's a thunderstorm," Ben says. "You've just been so brainwashed into thinking every outing is a mission that you believe a little bit of thunder is a cause for alarm."

"A little bit of thunder?" Luther echoes incredulously. Whatever it is he's hearing, it's not a little bit of anything. Still, something in Ben's voice makes him waver for a single heartbeat—did Ben say they were *brainwashed*?

"There's someone out there," Allison says, gesturing to the huge windows at the front of the store. She doesn't sound alarmed, but Luther can't help it—he rushes toward the door.

And into a blinding burst of light.

The ground beneath his feet starts to rumble.

"What was that?" Allison shouts, coming up beside him on the sidewalk.

"An aftershock?" Luther suggests. "From the earthquakes this afternoon?" He looks around, frantic to find the person Allison saw through the window.

"No way," Ben says. "The earthquake upstate was hundreds of miles away."

"Who knows what kind of damage all that fracking did?" Allison points out. She's trying to sound reasonable, but her voice is wavering.

Another burst of light illuminates the street with a loud crack.

It's thunder and lightning, but the sky overhead is clear. It's not raining. Ben said it was a storm, but *this* isn't a storm. *This* doesn't make sense.

Before Luther can point any of this out to Ben, there's the sound of glass shattering.

"Duck!" Allison shouts as the floor-to-ceiling windows of the thrift shop shatter.

"Move, now!" Diego yells. Luther and his siblings move away from the windows as the glass shards shatter across the shaking floor.

"Wait!" Luther bursts through what's left of the broken windows to grab the clerk, still perfectly calm thanks to Allison's rumoring.

Luther and the clerk run out of the store just in time. Luther dives for the sidewalk, the clerk slung across his shoulder as a piece of the ceiling crashes down onto the piles of clothes below. A section of red bricks from the side of the building fall to the sidewalk. The destruction sends a wave of dust into the air. Luther's eyes begin to water. He hardly has a chance to catch his breath before he hears someone scream.

It must be the person Allison saw on the street earlier, the reason he rushed outside to begin with.

"Did you hear that?" Luther shouts as water fills the air. He assumes it's rain, but then realizes it's coming from the thrift shop. A pipe must've cracked when the ceiling caved in. "Did you see who screamed?" Luther asks.

Viktor answers. Or rather he points in response, his arm trembling in his new bomber jacket, his face and hair slick with water.

Luther lowers the clerk to the ground as gently as possible. "Man, my boss is going to kill me," he mumbles.

Luther rushes toward a person lying on the ground, surrounded by the bricks that fell from the side of the building. Luther goes straight into mission mode: He struggles to lift bricks off the person's body, just as he did hours ago upstate. He gets that same feeling—that *good* feeling, that *right* feeling—like he knows exactly what to do.

"It's a kid!" he shouts to his siblings as they gather around him. "Well, not a little kid, it looks like . . ."

"He's our age," Allison finishes, coming up behind him. "Maybe a little older." Her new high heels—purple to match her dress—click against the ground, nothing like the flat shoes with thick rubber soles that she wears on missions.

"Maybe he's a college student," Luther says. Not someone sneaking on campus like Luther and his siblings. Just someone on his way home who got caught up in the bad weather.

"Nice guess, genius," Diego says, pointing to the boy's sweatshirt, embroidered with the nearby university's name.

Luther bends over the kid; he's unconscious, but still breathing. Luther looks up at his siblings with a smile on his face.

"He's alive! We have to help him."

He watches disappointment spread across Allison's features, her shoulders slumping in her new dress. *Can you call it new when it came from a thrift store?* he wonders, then shakes his head. That's not the question he should be asking right now. Right now, he should be figuring out how to get their plans for the evening back on track so he won't have to see that look on Allison's face anymore. Of course, she's not disappointed that this kid—whoever he is, wrong place, wrong time—is alive. She's disappointed that an impromptu mission is messing with their plans for a normal night out.

"We should call 911," Ben says. "They're the medical professionals, not us."

"But we can't just leave him here," Luther insists. Luther sees Klaus's shoulders slump in disappointment. He knows that none of his siblings would abandon someone in need— but they're longing to go to the party, too. "You guys go ahead," he suggests finally. "I'll stay behind and take care of this. I'll meet you at the party."

"Always so quick to play hero," Diego sneers. "I saw the way you ran in to save that clerk."

"Was I supposed to leave him behind to get crushed by falling bricks?" Luther asks, his brow furrowed.

"Whatever. You've done enough for one night," Diego insists. "I'll stay behind. You go."

"None of us are supposed to play hero tonight," Ben reminds them.

"It's a little late for that," Klaus mumbles.

"Leave it to you to enforce the rules the one night we're out from under Dad's thumb," Diego complains.

"I'm not playing hero!" Luther coughs in the dust rising from the crumbling building. "But we can't just leave the guy."

"*We* won't," Diego says. "You go, and I'll stay."

"I'll stay with you," Allison offers, and Luther shakes his head. The whole point of offering to stay was so that it *wouldn't* mess up Allison's good time.

"Only one of us needs to stay—" Luther insists.

"Right—*me*," Diego interjects.

"Oh my god, can't you let it go for just one night?" Ben moans. "Let's flip a coin or something."

"Do you have a coin?" Luther asks, though he can't imagine that Diego should be the one to stay. This is so obviously a job for Number One.

Ben sighs, "Well, no, but—"

"So what are we going to do?" Allison moans.

"Rock Paper Scissors?" Viktor suggests. As always, his voice is softer than the rest of theirs, so that Luther feels like he's shouting even when he's not.

"Brilliant!" Allison says, giving Viktor a squeeze. Viktor

looks surprised by the affection. Allison gestures to Diego and Luther. "You two. Rock Paper Scissors. Go."

Luther turns to face Diego. "*Rock, paper, scissors, shoot!*" they chant in unison. First, two rocks. Then two scissors.

"We'll be here all night!" Klaus wails. "I'm *wasting* my killer outfit standing on the street with you."

"You could both stay, and the rest of us will head to the party," Ben suggests.

"No way," Klaus protests. "Bad enough if one of us misses out on the fun."

"Anyway, I'm not staying with *him*," Diego snorts.

Luther shakes his head. What did he ever do to make his brother hate him so much? Hargreeves assigned him Number One; he didn't choose it. It's simply what he was meant to be, like Diego was meant to be Number Two.

Finally, Diego puts out rock when Luther chooses paper.

"Paper covers rock," Viktor announces.

"You sure you don't want me to stay?" Allison offers.

"No way," Luther answers, just as Klaus says the same thing in unison. It's chilly, and in the light from the streetlamps above them, Luther can see Allison is shivering in her dress. "I'll be right behind you."

"Just follow the sound of mayhem," Klaus suggests with a grin. "It's the surest way to find the best party on campus."

Luther waves as his siblings walk away. "I'll catch up in no time," he promises, but the truth is, now that he's all alone with an unconscious person at his feet, he doesn't have the slightest idea what to do.

Rushing into a crumbling building is easy. Luther and his siblings have been training for that their whole lives. Dealing with the aftermath is something else entirely.

The Umbrella Academy has never stuck around after a mission to clean up the mess they left behind.

ALLISON

Klaus leads the way into the fraternity house. The college campus doesn't look like the ones Allison's seen in movies and TV shows; it's in the middle of a sprawling city rather than in the ivy-covered countryside.

This house is tall and narrow, a house lined up on a block of them, one right after the other. Klaus points out which ones he's attended parties at, which ones never have parties, and which basements he's passed out in, party or no party.

There are seven steep steps up to the entrance of the house from the sidewalk. People are spread across the stoop, smoking and drinking. The front windows are open, and the sounds of the party pour onto the street, just like Klaus promised—loud music, laughter, friendly shouts. Allison expects that the people on the stoop will question the Umbrella Academy before they can go inside. Surely they'll be asked who invited them, which of the nearby dorms they live in.

Maybe they'll need a ticket or some such to get inside. But no one so much as looks up as Allison ascends the stairs. Allison isn't sure whether she feels relieved or offended.

Directly across from the front door is a poky, narrow staircase. To the right, a tight hall opens into a large room where people are standing around holding plastic cups, swaying absently in time with the blasting music. The lighting is dim, but Allison can see that no one is dressed as she expected. She's the only person here wearing a dress—or at least the only one wearing a *fancy* dress. Mostly, people are wearing jeans, though she notices leggings, black pants, even a pair of plaid pajama bottoms. Allison's never felt so out of place. She wishes Luther were here, but then she remembers the outfit she dressed him in; he'd stick out just as badly as she does. The air is thick with the scent of beer and cigarette smoke. There's nothing remotely glamorous about this party: no bowties, no dance floor, no candlelight. They might as well be in someone's basement.

Allison feels people eyeing her dress and throws her shoulders back. She's used to standing out. Every room she's walked into, all her life, people have turned to stare at her. Then again, those rooms—outside of the academy—were usually crime scenes, briefing rooms, photo shoots. But for some reason, here, in this room, standing out doesn't feel as good as it usually does.

It hits Allison suddenly that she's never been to a real party before. Every year on their birthday—October first—Mom throws them a party, but it's only the six (or seven, before Five left) of them, plus Mom, Pogo, and sometimes Dad. But he only stays long enough to remind them to get to bed early for training in the morning. Allison's shoulders slump all over again. Whatever that is, it's not a party.

This is a party. Kids falling all over each other, drinking sticky concoctions out of plastic cups. Everyone in jeans and T-shirts, beat-up sneakers or heavy black combat boots.

There's music playing. Not the old-fashioned background music Mom listens to, but the sort of loud rhythm Allison's heard coming from Klaus's room more times than she can count. She's never told Klaus that she likes his music; over the years she's memorized the lyrics, forced Luther to dance across the floor of her room.

"Now what?" Diego asks, and Allison feels herself breathe a sigh of relief. She's glad Diego's the one who asked the question so she didn't have to. Diego looks almost as panicked as Allison feels: his jaw is hanging open, eyes darting from side to side like he's trying to take in everything at once. Allison can tell Diego's taking a mental account of the room—tracking where the exits are, where the crowds gather, how many people are inside—just like they were trained to do.

"Now we party!" Klaus throws his hands over his head and steps into the crowd. He says it like it's obvious, like they've trained to party just as diligently as they have for missions—like they know exactly what to do. "Follow me to the drinks."

Ben follows without hesitating, but Diego waits a beat before he does the same. Allison pauses, glancing at Viktor. His eyes are wide, but Allison thinks she detects the tiniest smile peeking out from the corners of his lips.

Does Allison actually expect *Viktor* to step farther inside before she does? When has Allison ever expected Viktor to be better at anything than she is, braver than she is? Why is walking into this party scarier than walking into a bank vault filled with armed robbers?

Allison knows the answer: because one is a scenario she trained for, and the other is something she knows absolutely nothing about.

She takes a deep breath and steps toward the makeshift bar. It's nothing like the mahogany-and-brass bar back at the academy. This bar is built from empty boxes and has cans of beer piled on top of it in a pyramid. Someone throws a football from one side of the room to the other, and a burly-looking guy crashes into the beer-can pyramid in an attempt to catch it. But no one yells at him for making a mess. Instead, the crowd cheers, like he just did something incredibly clever.

Do students actually live here, Allison wonders, *or does this building exist for parties alone?* She imagines that upstairs, someone is trying to sleep, trying to study, putting in every effort to ignore the sounds coming from below.

Allison turns to ask Klaus what he knows about this place—what fraternity is it, who lives here—but he's already on the other side of the bar, handing a beer to Diego and knocking back one of his own.

"Klaus!" she shouts, but he and Diego are locked in conversation.

She turns to Ben, tempted to repeat Diego's earlier question—*Now what?*—but she doesn't want to admit that she doesn't know what she's doing here.

"We won't blend in like this," Ben says finally. "Standing here together. And the whole point is to blend in."

Is it? Allison wonders. That's why they promised not to use their powers tonight, right? So they could fit in with the normals.

"Right," Diego agrees, appearing beside Ben. Allison looks for Klaus, but he's already vanished into the crowd. Diego hops up and down in place, and Allison can tell that nervous energy is coursing through him. He grabs a beer can from the makeshift bar and chugs it, almost as expertly as Klaus did. "Let's do this," he says, as though it's the start of a mission. Within seconds, Diego is merging into the crowd, too.

"You okay?" Ben asks.

"Of course," Allison says. She's not about to admit otherwise; she's been in scarier places than this—hasn't she? She smiles as Ben steps up to the bar, and she grabs a drink of her own.

Allison suddenly realizes that Viktor didn't follow her to the bar. She glances back toward the front door, but he is nowhere to be found. She wonders how much longer it will be until Luther gets here.

Despite herself, Allison scans the room just like Diego was doing before. She can practically hear Hargreeves's voice telling her to *discover an opening and force your way inside.*

Across the room, huddled on a couch, is a group of three girls. Like everyone else here, they're dressed casually, but something in the way they hold themselves lets Allison know they're the coolest girls at this party.

One is wearing an oversized white T-shirt tucked into ripped blue jeans. Her dirty blond hair is pulled into a messy bun on top of her head. Her eyes are ringed with thick black liner, and she's wearing a stack of plastic bracelets up one arm.

The next girl has straight dark hair parted in the middle, framing her narrow face. She appears to be makeup-free, but there's a smattering of freckles across her nose. Her jeans are black and tight, paired with sneakers and a dark gray T-shirt.

The third girl has a short Afro. She's wearing purple lipstick, and Allison can see that beneath the cuffs of her jeans, her socks are the exact same color as her lips—proving she put effort into her outfit. The purple is almost the same shade as Allison's outdated dress, but somehow it looks so much cooler on the other girl.

Allison makes her way across the room and sits at the end of the couch. The three girls don't acknowledge her at all.

Allison has never been ignored before, and she's not going to start now.

"Hi, I'm Allison Hargreeves." She says, holding her hand out for the nearest girl—the one with the straight hair framing her face—to shake.

"May Tan," the girl answers. She holds out her hand without making eye contact. "God, did you hear about Rebecca Abbott?" she asks, and it takes Allison a second to realize that May isn't talking to her but to the other girls.

Allison tries again. "I came here straight from a cocktail party," she lies, trying to explain away her dress.

Neither May or the other girls respond, so Allison says it again, louder this time.

Finally, the girl with the purple lipstick turns to her. "Sorry, do we know you?"

Allison smiles her biggest smile. "Not yet," she says, with the same voice she uses to answer interview questions for magazines. "Allison Hargreeves," she repeats, holding out her hand again.

"This is kind of a private conversation, Allison Hargreeves," Purple Lipstick says.

"I'm not sure this is the right place for a private conversation," Allison responds, still smiling. Her jaw is starting to hurt.

"Are you saying we should leave?" Purple Lipstick asks hotly.

"No!" Allison scrambles, "I just meant, maybe we could

all have a conversation, you know? It's a party, and I came here to—"

"Do you even go to this school?" Messy Bun asks. "I don't recognize you, and you don't actually look old enough to go to college."

Crap. They've found her out. If only she'd picked a more appropriate outfit at the thrift shop so that she'd blend in. She realizes suddenly that even Viktor had a better idea of what to wear than she did. Allison wishes more than anything that she could force May to trade her jeans and T-shirt for Allison's ridiculous dress.

Even as she thinks it, she remembers: *She* can.

Of course she can.

But she's not supposed to. They're not supposed to use their powers tonight.

Because they're supposed to be trying to fit in.

And Allison would only be doing it to fit in.

So maybe it would be okay.

"Anyway, what were you saying about Rebecca Abbott?" Messy Bun asks. May flips her hair, and Messy Bun squeals. "Hey, careful with that!"

May giggles. "Sorry."

Allison cringes. They're sharing some inside joke she's not a part of.

"Anyway, I heard a rumor that Rebecca Abbott hooked up with Ryan just to get an invite tonight," May says.

Allison's stomach flips. May said the words that Allison

has said more times than she can count. And nothing bad happened. The ceiling didn't cave in. Messy Bun and Purple Lipstick don't lose their self-control. Instead they giggle like they've never heard something more interesting than this juicy rumor about Rebecca Abbott.

It feels so good when people believe you. When they hang on your every word.

The words are out of Allison's mouth before she can stop herself. It's not like these girls have given her a choice, the way they've been practically ignoring her.

"I heard a rumor that you *love* my dress."

KLAUS

Klaus didn't mean to get here and immediately abandon his siblings. After all, the point was to spend the night together, right? One perfect evening of sibling togetherness, knowing it's only a matter of time before they go their separate ways. As the only one of the Academy members who's actually been to a party before, Klaus felt a responsibility for his siblings' well-being. Or at least for making sure they have a good time.

So he meant to show them the ropes. Like when they got to the bar, and Diego grabbed a beer and chugged it.

"Whoa there, brother," Klaus cautioned. "It's early. We've got a long night ahead of us."

"Who are you to lecture me about self-control?" Diego asked, wiping his mouth. Klaus had to admit his brother had a point.

Diego smashed the empty beer can under his heel, opening and closing his fists like he was already looking for his next drink. It hit Klaus suddenly that Diego was *nervous*. Klaus reached for his brother and patted him on the back.

"You fit right in," he offered. "Nothing says *party* like black on black on black."

Klaus felt his brother's shoulders tense beneath his hand. Not only has Klaus never been the responsible one, he's never been the knowledgeable one either.

Diego shrugged off Klaus's touch. And Klaus was honestly a little relieved—Diego didn't want or need his guidance.

And sure, maybe Klaus could've stuck with his siblings instead of spinning off into the crowd, his kilt billowing around his legs.

But the Scotsman was still screaming in his ears that he was wearing the kilt all wrong, and Klaus *had* to shut him up. Which meant venturing further into the party on his own to find exactly what he needed.

Now, Klaus reasons that he can't be expected to babysit his siblings all night. It's not like anyone held his hand when he crashed his first party. They'll probably actually have a better time if he leaves them to their own devices.

He tries to remember whether—before tonight—any of his siblings have ever asked him for advice. He doesn't think so: It's always Luther in charge, and then Diego insisting he knows better, and Allison taking Luther's side, and Ben trying to keep the peace, and Viktor being quiet in the background. But tonight, it was Klaus they turned to for a plan to get out of the house, Klaus who knew where they could find new clothes and a good party. They were even impressed with his driving. It's strange to be the sibling who knows best.

"Nice outfit!" someone calls out, and Klaus glows under the compliment.

"Cool makeup," someone else says.

Is this how Luther feels leading a mission? Like he's doing everything right? Partying is the only thing that's ever come naturally to Klaus. Maybe because he wants it more than he's ever wanted anything else. Which means what Luther wants most is to lead a mission. Klaus can't imagine wanting to be in charge that much.

Anyway, he didn't mean to leave his siblings all alone, but he's on a mission of his own tonight. Yes, he wanted to come here so his siblings could party, but that's not the *only* reason.

The truth is he can't stand one more minute of being sober.

He's allowed to have more than one reason. Multitasking isn't a *crime*.

Klaus has been to enough of these parties to know exactly how to navigate them. The good stuff is never on the first floor. The first floor is, like, general admission. To get upstairs, you need a ticket, a VIP pass, a wink and a nod from the right person. Klaus has never had trouble getting that though. Sometimes it's the outfit he's wearing or the person who's arm he's hanging on to, but Klaus has never had trouble getting people to like him. Well, that's not true. At home, it's much harder getting people to take his side than it is out in the world. Maybe that's the reason he started sneaking out.

Sometimes he gets what he wants by following his nose. Like, he can *smell* the good booze, the good drugs. To be fair, some of it does have a pretty distinct odor. But it's more like instinct. Or maybe it's the voices in his head pointing him in the right direction. At least they're good for *something*.

He leaps over a couple making out, their bodies stretched across the staircase. He knocks over some half-empty beer cans; the liquid nearly spills onto the couple, but they don't seem to notice.

"Oh, to be young and in love," Klaus coos.

"Bro!" someone shouts as he reaches the second-floor landing, putting his arm around Klaus's shoulders like they're old friends. "Sick outfit!"

Klaus regards the other boy's clothes: black jeans, ripped-up T-shirt, scuffed leather boots. His eyes lined with kohl and a ring through his nose. Klaus knows without asking that this is the sort of person who listens exclusively to sad music. And he might just be his VIP pass tonight.

"Thanks, man," Klaus says. He slides the beer bottle from his new friend's hand and takes a long swig. Already better than the swill coming out of the kegs downstairs. He wonders what his siblings are drinking, recalling the way Diego chugged that beer. Should he have told them that the good stuff is upstairs? No, more for him if they stay down with the riffraff.

"You looking for something a little bit stronger?" The boy raises an eyebrow.

"What gave me away?" Klaus asks with a smile. The boy grins in return.

"I'm Chris, by the way," he says.

"Klaus."

"What's your deal, Klaus?"

Klaus sighs heavily. "Honey, it would take all night to explain my deal."

Chris winks. "I got time."

Flirting with this cute boy feels so good, but it's not enough to drown out the voices in his head—they're pulling him away from Chris, away from the party, just like they pulled him away from his siblings in the thrift store. Klaus feels like he's constantly being pulled in a dozen different directions, from the present to the past, from the living to the dead.

"Tell me just one thing about your deal," Chris says. Klaus thinks that Chris has the most beautiful thick eyebrows he's ever seen. "The weirdest thing."

"The weirdest thing?" he asks. "You sure?"

"Positive."

Klaus cocks his head to the side as if he's considering, but he's already made up his mind: If Chris is interested in weird, Klaus can give him weird.

Smoothly, he says, "I can talk to ghosts."

Instead of laughing or recoiling—the two reactions Klaus was most expecting—Chris just grins even wider. "You gotta come upstairs. You're just what we've been looking for."

Never one to refuse such a flattering invitation—*just what they've been looking for?*—Klaus follows Chris up to a room on the third floor. *Chris and Klaus* has a nice ring to it. Inside, all the lights are off, but at least a dozen candles are flickering. In the firelight, Klaus can make out a group of six or seven people sitting cross-legged in a circle on the floor. They're dressed similarly to Chris: dark colors, heavy eye makeup.

"Guys!" Chris shouts. "Look who I found—Klaus!"

Klaus likes the way Chris introduces him, as though his arrival was always imminent.

Everyone turns to him and cheers. Klaus bows exaggeratedly, like he's here to put on a show.

"C'mon, man—have a seat," Chris offers. "We're holding a séance. Did you know that, like, twenty years ago, the fraternity brother who lived in this room *died?*"

Chris says the word *died* like it's something exotic and outrageous, instead of the one thing guaranteed to happen to everyone someday.

"Rumor has it there was a hazing ritual gone awry," Chris continues. "The university covered it up so the fraternity wouldn't lose its charter."

Klaus pretends to look shocked, but the truth is no one had to tell him that someone died here.

The minute he stepped into the room, a voice started shouting about alcohol poisoning and justice that went unserved.

Klaus is tempted to turn and run the other way. But then he sees Chris's stash peeking out of the top of his desk drawer, the *something stronger* he was promised. He circles the room, pocketing the drugs as he does so, subtly enough that no one seems to notice.

Then Klaus takes a seat beside a girl wearing denim cut-off shorts over fishnet stockings and enormous, lug-soled boots. Chris climbs across the circle to sit beside him, their knees touching. Everyone looks at Klaus eagerly, as though they're all pleased that he's joined them.

If these people want to commune with the dead, Klaus will put on a real show. Small price to pay in exchange for their drugs and alcohol.

Besides, he loves putting on a show. And he's long since forgotten that he and his siblings promised not to use their powers tonight.

CHAPTER
14

BEN

Ben winds his way through party, past the makeshift bar in the center of the room, across from the couch where Allison has settled next to the three most stylish-looking girls at the party—the sort of girls who seem stylish regardless of what they're actually wearing. It's all in the way they hold themselves, certain that everyone wants to be their friend. *No surprise*, Ben thinks. If they'd actually gone to an ordinary high school, Ben has no doubt Allison would have been the most popular girl in school: the head cheerleader, dating the captain of the football team.

Ben isn't quite so sure where he'd fit in a regular high school ecosystem. Actually, he's not sure what regular high school is actually like. Is it actually cool to be head cheerleader or captain of the football team, or is that just something he saw in an old movie? There's not much Ben can do about his lack of knowledge now.

Ben spots a pool table in the back of the room. Looks like a game is winding down—almost all of the balls are sunk. He takes note of a chalkboard on the wall. Someone named Alex is the reigning champion; all semester long, no one's beat him once.

"Can I take winners?" Ben asks.

A tall guy—Ben assumes Alex—is leaning over the table, lining up his next shot. Alex is wearing a baby-blue collared shirt with a tiny polo horse stitched over the chest, paired with khaki pants. His dark brown hair flops across his forehead, and he blows a few strands out of his eyes. From the look of things, Alex's opponent has only managed to get a couple of balls—stripes—into a pocket. There's only one solid left.

"You're welcome to try," Alex says as he sinks his last ball.

Ben smiles, shrugging off his black leather jacket. It feels good to be trying an actual game—not a new training exercise or mission prep—for a change.

Alex racks the balls and tosses Ben a cue.

"You wanna break?" Alex offers.

"Nah, man, you go ahead," Ben answers.

Ben has to admit that Alex is good. He sinks one ball, then another and another. Finally, on his fourth shot, he misses. He groans, then steps aside so Ben can line up his shot.

Ben studies the table, selecting his first shot. He leans over the table just like Alex did, holding the cue just like he did.

And then when he tries to take a shot, the cue slips right between his fingers and to the floor with a clatter.

Alex and his preppy friends start laughing as he crouches down to pick up his cue.

"Man, what is this, your first time holding a pool cue?"

"Actually, yes," Ben admits.

Alex stops laughing, but he doesn't look unfriendly. "All right, man—let me give you some pointers." He takes the cue from Ben's hand and lines up a shot, showing Ben exactly how to hold it, resting loosely between his knuckles.

"How about we give you a handicap?" Alex says. "I won't take another shot until you sink your first ball."

It's a nice offer, but Ben can tell he's not extending it to be generous; he wants to prove that he can win even when he's giving his opponent an advantage.

"Then what?"

"Well, then it'll be my turn again after you miss." It's clear from his tone that he thinks Ben won't be able to sink two balls in a row.

"Fair enough," Ben says.

Alex hands the cue back to Ben and folds his arms across his chels if to say *The table's all yours.*

Ben leans over the table, holding the cue in his hands just like Alex showed him. He takes another shot—he doesn't sink a ball, but he does manage to keep the cue on top of the table, which is progress.

He tries again. Another miss, but he does manage to at least hit something. The balls scatter across the table.

Ben is the sort of person who actually becomes calmer in situations where other people grow frustrated. It occurs to him that years of managing his . . . *extremities* have made him uniquely skilled. He lines up his next spot, this time treating the cue as if it's another extension of himself.

He sinks one striped ball. Alex claps but picks up his cue, clearly expecting Ben to miss his next shot.

Instead, Ben sinks another ball, then another. Alex looks surprised, but not angry. As Ben the fourth ball rolls into a corner pocket, Alex's friends are watching intently. Like Alex, they're dressed in some version of khaki pants and collared shirts. Ben counts the colors of their shirts: two pink, one navy, one white, and then Alex's light blue. Not every shirt has a little horse stitched on the chest; Ben notices one with a set of initials, another a tiny crocodile.

"Is someone actually going to blow your streak?" the boy with the crocodile shirt asks. Even though it's cold outside, he's wearing shorts, as though he just came from a tennis match.

"Looks like it." Alex grins. "What are you, some kind of hustler?"

Ben shrugs. "Just a fast learner."

Ben sinks another ball. It's loud in here, between the spectators and the music and the partygoers settled in the other corners of the room who don't have any idea about the pool match going on. But the crowd around the table erupts in cheers as Ben sinks his final ball.

"What's your name, man?" Alex asks over the din. He doesn't seem the least bit bummed about being beat.

"Ben Hargreeves."

"Where you been all semester, Ben Hargreeves? No one's put up a challenge in months. It's been dull as hell here!" Alex offers Ben his hand, which Ben shakes heartily. Then Alex smacks him on the back and Ben winces. His hand landed exactly where Ben's tentacles emerge. The skin there is thinner, and always tender from being ripped open. Ben's never told anyone that, not even Klaus. (There's no point sharing a secret with Klaus; he'd tell everyone.)

Ben wonders what might happen if he never released his tentacles again: Would the skin there heal, thickening until it was no different from the skin on the rest of his body? Would his tentacles settle beneath his skin and bones, sleeping around his organs until he could forget they were there at all?

Alex offers Ben a beer, which he accepts with a grin. Alex's friends keep smacking his shoulders with congratulations while Ben grits his teeth. He feels his tentacles twitching beneath his skin. He takes a deep breath, stilling the movement inside him. He can't remember the last time he was anywhere that he wasn't expected to use his powers. Where people didn't even know he had powers. Despite the motion beneath his skin, Ben doesn't think he's ever felt so relaxed.

Alex holds up his pool cue. "What do you say, man—ready for a rematch?"

Ben smiles wide. "Absolutely."

VIKTOR

Viktor doesn't think Klaus noticed when he followed him up the stairs. Viktor wasn't trying to be sneaky, but— the first floor was so *loud*. Viktor guesses that his siblings are used to that kind of noise, that kind of crowd, what with missions and adoring fans and press conferences and photo shoots. The loudest sound Viktor's used to is the sound of his own violin as he plays with his ears poised over the strings. He's certainly not used to such a *crowded* sort of noise. He's not used to the noise of so many other people.

He's used to being alone. Left behind while his siblings go on their missions. Sure, Mom and Pogo are usually in the house, too, but they all retreat to their own areas when Hargreeves and the rest of the Umbrella Academy are gone. Mom uses the quiet to recharge, Pogo to reorganize, and Viktor to rehearse.

Klaus is grabbed by someone and disappears behind a closed door on the third floor. Viktor shouldn't be surprised;

Klaus is the sort of person other people notice. Just like the rest of his siblings. Viktor saw the way Allison's face fell when they walked into the party. She wasn't wearing the right thing for maybe the first time in her life. As the only *normal* sibling, he should've known exactly what to wear. He should've warned Allison that her outfit was wrong. After all, that's why Allison invited him along tonight—she said so herself. But Viktor doesn't know any better than his siblings (except Klaus). Like them, he's worn a uniform most of his life.

Viktor reaches into his pocket for another pill. He thinks of Klaus, getting high for fun, drawing people closer, the life of the party, the center of attention. Viktor takes pills to be brought back down to earth.

The thing is, Viktor actually *is* wearing the right clothes. His outfit blends in more than Allison's. There are kids here wearing almost the exact same thing. He smooths his shirt over his flat stomach and takes a deep breath.

Time to see what else he can do right—time to take this outfit for a spin.

Viktor approaches three kids sitting side by side on the stairwell, blocking the way up to the fourth floor.

"Hey," he begins. He can still taste the chalky remnants of his pill.

"Hey," one of the stair-blockers responds.

Viktor hovers, unsure of what to say next.

"Are we in your way?" the stair-blocker asks, not unkindly—more like the person couldn't imagine another reason that Viktor might be approaching them.

Viktor tries to think of a more interesting answer than *yes* or *no*. He tries to think of something that might spark a connection, a conversation, and keep things going beyond a few words. But he's out of practice. In fact, he's not sure he's had *any* practice. He tries to remember the last time he had a conversation with anyone other than his siblings, Mom, Dad, or Pogo. He never expected to be good at playing the violin without practice; why should this be any different?

Finally, he says, "Yeah, trying to get through."

The stair-blocker who spoke moves so that Viktor can pass. When Viktor is a few steps above, the blocker calls out, "Hey, dude!"

Viktor turns. The blocker is shouting, probably drunk, but his words make Viktor feel pleasantly warm.

"Nice jacket," the blocker says, sitting back down.

"Thanks," Viktor manages. He ascends the stairs to the fourth floor, the top floor of the tall, narrow fraternity house, warmth trickling down from his face and settling in his belly.

With each step, the noise from the party grows a little bit softer. There are posters on the walls: music groups Viktor's never heard of, movies he's never seen. He wonders how long until his siblings are ready to go home. And when they do decide to leave, will Klaus be sober enough to drive by then, or will another of his siblings will have to learn to drive on the fly? He almost laughs when he imagines Diego and Luther arguing over which of them will take the driver's seat, even though neither of them would have the faintest idea of what they are doing.

If any of them asked, Viktor could tell them that actually, *he* knows how to drive. Pogo taught him last year. Viktor even has his license. It was Hargreeves's idea. Viktor guesses that Dad figured Viktor would need normal-person skills for his inevitably normal-person life. But his siblings never ask what Viktor does when they're not around, so Viktor's never had a chance to tell them. Now, on the fourth-floor landing, Viktor reaches for the nearest doorknob and turns.

"Hey!" someone shouts from inside as Viktor opens the door. Viktor can't tell if it's a greeting or a protest.

The room isn't dark and empty like Viktor expected— he'd been hoping to explore without being noticed. Instead, this room is dimly lit, the only light coming from a desk lamp on the floor in the corner. Quickly, Viktor closes the door behind him—too much brightness is pouring into the room from the hallway outside. There's a narrow bed against one wall beneath the window. The window is open, and the shade flutters in the breeze. The bed is unmade, a pile of clothes at the foot. There's a desk on the opposite wall, piled high with books and magazines. Viktor thinks he sees a laptop behind the papers, but he can't be sure. Whoever lives here is clearly more interested in books than technology. The bedroom reminds Viktor of the attic rooms he's read about in books like *A Little Princess* and *The Lion, the Witch and the Wardrobe*—at once forgotten and the very best room in the house.

There's a small lamp on the floor in front of the desk. And beside the lamp is a kid crouched beside an old-fashioned stereo, a pile of vinyl records on the floor beside him. There isn't any music playing, but the boy is reaching for a record like he's about to put it on the turntable. Viktor sees the name on the album sleeve and smiles.

"I love Bach," he says. He was practicing Bach just this afternoon. On the wall above, instead of a poster of a rock band, Viktor can make out an advertisement for the local symphony. The sort of thing he *does* recognize for a change.

"Me, too," the boy on the floor answers. He presses himself up to stand. "I'm Ryan."

Viktor opens his mouth to say his name, then pauses. *Dude*, the kid on the stairs had called him. Somehow that generic word felt better than being called *Viktor* ever had. It occurs to Viktor that *Viktor* is exactly like his Umbrella Academy uniform: Someone else gave it to him, and they never gave him a choice in the matter. And it *should* fit, just like his uniform *should* fit, sewn so carefully by Mom, the measurements clear and exact. And yet somehow, it doesn't. Somehow, the clothes from the thrift shop—the ones he picked out *himself* tonight—fit much better.

"What's your name?" Ryan prompts.

"Sorry," Viktor says. "Viktor." He stumbles over the second syllable, so that he has to repeat himself. He tightens the ponytail at the nape of his neck, tucking it into his shirt. He says it because he can't think of anything else to say. Because he knows this is just one night, and at the end of it, he'll have to change back into his uniform and go back at the academy. But the name feels like as much of a lie as the uniform. He's always felt like an imposter wearing it, since he's not *really* a member of the Umbrella Academy. He supposes that means he's not *really* Viktor either.

But he's not sure exactly who he is yet.

"Nice to meet you, Viktor." Ryan smiles, holding out his hand expectantly. He has light brown hair cropped closely to his scalp in a buzz cut. Like Viktor, Ryan's wearing jeans and a black T-shirt, though his shirt is emblazoned with the name of an old band across his chest. His hazel eyes narrow warmly when he smiles. "You probably think I'm a freak, hiding up here when the party's raging downstairs," Ryan adds sheepishly as Viktor shakes his hand. "Sometimes I just need a break though, you know?"

"I know exactly what you mean." Viktor nods. "Is this your room?"

As soon as he asks, Viktor realizes it's a stupid question. Why would Ryan be in here if it wasn't?

"Yeah," Ryan answers. It doesn't sound like he thinks Viktor is dumb for asking. "The fraternity offered me any room I wanted, and I picked this one. They thought I was making a terrible choice." Ryan laughs.

"Are you kidding?" Viktor asks incredulously. "This is the best room in the house!"

"I know, right?" Ryan says. "It's the smallest bedroom, but I don't need a lot of space. Plus, it's so much quieter than downstairs. Anywhere else, I'd never even be able to hear my music."

Viktor nods. With the door closed, he can't hear any of the din coming from the party down below.

"Have you lived here since September?" Viktor asks, guessing that Ryan moved in at the start of the school year.

Ryan shrugs. "I've lived here long enough that this place feels like home now."

Viktor likes the sound of that. He's never felt entirely at home at the Umbrella Academy. Maybe someday, he'll find a home where he fits in, a room so comfortable he can't remember what it felt like at the Umbrella Academy. Maybe someone will give him the chance to pick out his own room. Back at the academy, Hargreeves decided which room Viktor and his siblings would grow up in. The bedrooms are meant to be identical—the same size, same furniture, same layout—but over the years, Viktor and his siblings have found ways to personalize their spaces. Allison's room had posters on the walls and scattered jewelry on her desk. Diego painted his room black and hung targets on the walls so he could practice with his knives. Luther's room has weights piled in the corner so he can exercise even when it's not officially time to train.

Only Viktor's room stayed bare.

"I grew up in the city," Viktor offers. "But I don't think I want to live here forever."

"I love it here," Ryan says. "But I get it. I'm not sure any of us want to end up living in the towns we grew up in. Unless you had, like, a perfect childhood—but who had that?"

Viktor thinks of his siblings. Their childhoods may have been better than his, but they definitely weren't *perfect*.

"Where'd you grow up?" Viktor asks.

"A tiny town upstate called Dobbsville. Trust me, you've never heard of it."

Ryan grins, and Viktor returns the smile. Dobbsville actually sounds familiar, though he can't remember why. Geography lessons with Mom, probably.

"Anyway, ready for some Bach?" Ryan asks.

"Always," Viktor answers enthusiastically.

"It's his Concerto for Two Violins in D Minor," Ryan explains as he takes the record out of its sleeve. "Most people would think it's super nerdy that I hole up here playing classical music."

"Maybe the concerto is nerdy," Viktor says, "but I love it. I can play both parts." Viktor crosses the room and crouches on the floor beside Ryan.

"Sounds like you need someone to play with," Ryan answers with a grin.

LUTHER

Luther's been crouching beside the boy on the ground for so long that his legs ache, but he's not about to move. The boy has dark hair and a shadow of stubble across his cheeks like it's been a few days since he shaved. He's wearing jeans and a sweatshirt with the name of the college stitched to the front.

It seems like it takes hours for the ambulance to arrive. The boy hasn't regained consciousness yet, but Luther periodically checks to make sure he's still breathing, his heart still beating steadily.

Luther can't remember the last time he'd been alone. Technically, he isn't alone—there's the boy on the ground, and the kid from the thrift shop is hovering nearby, having called the ambulance. But still, except for sleeping at night and getting ready in the morning, this is the longest Luther has been without the endless soundtrack of his siblings' voices.

Which leaves Luther with way more time to think than he's used to. He notices that the palms of the boy's hands are black, as if they'd been burned. He leans down to sniff. There's no denying it—the boy's hands smell of smoke, like a candle that had just been blown out. Maybe it had something to do with the lightning earlier? Maybe the boy was struck by it?

But Luther doesn't have time to dwell on details, trying to piece together exactly what happened. He worries that he and his siblings wasted too much time arguing over who was going to stay behind and play the hero. If Diego had just shut the hell up, they could've called for an ambulance that much sooner. But Diego never shuts up. It's as though he thinks he ought to have a turn at being Number One every once in a while, which obviously isn't how these things work. Luther *is* Number One; Diego *is* Number Two. If Mom hadn't given them names, they'd never have been anything else.

Luther wonders if Mom had a name picked out for Five before he disappeared. Maybe she was waiting for the right time to give it to him, but then she never had the chance. Luther knows Ben doesn't believe Five is dead. He heard Ben interrogating Klaus earlier, asking if he's heard from their missing brother.

For what feels like the thousandth time, Luther tries to shake the boy on the ground awake. A wave of dust floats off the boy's shirt. Luther guesses that the dust came from the damaged building, just like the dust from the collapsed buildings upstate during their mission this afternoon.

Luther never knew that a building gave off so much debris when it came crashing down, but it makes sense when he thinks about it. Bricks and concrete and cinderblocks turning to rubble.

Now, finally—it feels like it's been *hours* since the rest of the Umbrella Academy left him here—the boy beneath Luther starts coughing, just as the sound of sirens fill the air.

Luther doesn't flinch as the ambulance screeches to a halt near where he's crouched. He helps the boy sit up.

"You okay, man?" The boy blinks but doesn't answer. "I think you got struck by lightning," Luther adds, gesturing to his burned hands.

"No," the boy begins. "I was just goofing around. Practicing, you know?" He tries to stand, but Luther stops him.

"The lightning hit this building." Luther gestures to the detritus behind him. "You were knocked unconscious."

Again the boy says, "I was practicing."

"You're in shock," Luther explains. "You don't remember what happened. That's totally normal."

The paramedics rush over, rolling the boy onto a flat board, then lifting him onto a stretcher. It takes two of them to do it.

They could've just asked me to do it, Luther thinks.

"This a friend of yours?" one of them asks.

Luther shakes his head.

"You called the ambulance and waited with him?" the other EMT asks.

"Yeah," Luther says.

"Good job," the paramedic says, patting him on the back. "Not everyone would do that for a stranger."

Luther glows under the praise, and he holds up a hand in a salute as the ambulance rides away. He hopes the boy will be okay. He kind of wishes he'd gotten his name, so he could check up on him tomorrow. But how could he check up on him once they're back home? If Luther tried to go to the hospital, Hargreeves would want to know why, and Luther could never explain. Unlike Luther, Klaus would be able to come up with a cover story on the spot, but Luther's a terrible liar.

Luther notices a small bundle on the ground. The boy's wallet must've fallen out of his pocket. Luther picks it up and pulls out a student ID. The kid's name is Mateo, and he goes to school on the nearby campus. (Luther guessed as much from his sweatshirt.) Surely he'll be able to find someone at the party who knows Mateo and can get his wallet back to him.

As he steps away, he can still smell that burnt scent from Mateo's hands.

How could one bolt of lightning have hit the building *and* Mateo's hands? Luther doesn't know much about thermodynamics, but it just seems unlikely. And what causes lightning when it's not actually raining?

Then again, it wasn't just lightning but also an earthquake that damaged the building—causing the windows to break, the ceiling to cave in.

Allison thought it might have been an aftershock, but

could the fracking upstate have done enough damage beneath the surface of the Earth to spread all the way down to the city?

Luther takes a deep breath, trying to think. But then he starts coughing. There's still dust in the air, the same dust that floated up off Mateo's sweatshirt when Luther was trying to wake him. The tickle in Luther's throat feels so familiar. Could that oil company from upstate be doing more illegal fracking closer to the city?

Luther stands upright and shakes himself like a puppy. Ben would say he's so used to saving the day that he's trying to turn a coincidence into a mission. He doesn't have time for silly distractions and invented conspiracies. Allison and the others are waiting. Plus he has to find someone to return Mateo's wallet to him.

Luther starts jogging toward campus, following the sound of loud music and mayhem just like Klaus told him to.

DIEGO

From the minute he stepped inside tonight, Diego has felt all wrong. Not that he usually feels right. In fact, there are only a handful of times in his life he can remember feeling *just right*. Alone with Mom in the kitchen, watching her sew compartments for his knives into his uniform. Once, on a mission, when he got to take the lead for a few minutes because Luther was busy fighting off a dozen would-be kidnappers. Cleaning his knives after a successful operation. Practicing hitting one bullseye after another while Mom cheered him on like it was hard, when—for Diego—hitting a target was the easiest thing in the world. As easy as breathing.

Not that breathing is always so easy. Not when for half your childhood, you could barely catch your breath to get out the words you wanted to say.

Diego can still remember the sensation: words getting stuck not in his throat but somewhere in the back of his mouth, twisted between his tongue and his teeth. He can remember the looks on his siblings' faces, the impatience and the way they'd fill in the unspoken syllables when they got tired of waiting. Only Mom never lost her patience.

Now, three drinks in and no calmer, Diego leans against a wall and watches a group of kids dancing. There's no real dance floor in the messy, crowded fraternity house, but the music is loud and has a good beat, so a crowd of dancers has made its way to the center of the room. *It looks*, Diego thinks, *more like a mosh pit than a dance floor.*

He can feel the edges of his knives tucked into his tight black pants. These pants don't really fit; certainly they're nothing like the ones Mom sews him. But even though these pants are at least one size too small, it's not as though he could've left his knives in the thrift shop. And he certainly wasn't going to leave them behind at home, despite his siblings' promise not to use their powers tonight. Leaving his knives behind would've been like going outside naked. As he changed clothes at the store, Diego took each knife from his uniform and carefully placed it somewhere in his new outfit. Luckily, these pants have plenty of pockets and compartments. If someone looked carefully, they could make out the edges of his knives tucked between the tight pants and the muscles of his legs, but he doesn't think anyone will look that closely, and he likes being able to feel his knives anyhow. When he ran out of pockets, Diego tucked knives into his waistband, and now he can feel the warmth of the metal against his skin. Someone else might feel threatened by the press of steel against flesh, but Diego feels comforted, like his knives are his security blanket—if he'd ever had that sort of thing, which of course he didn't.

Diego was two and a half the first time he reached for a knife from the dinner table and aimed it across the room. He can still remember the way it sounded when it shattered a glass on Hargreeves's desk. Mom applauded. Hargreeves seemed relieved that Diego's talent had presented himself.

Now Diego pulls out a knife and flicks it over his knuckles, concealing it between his fingers like a magician with a penny. This doesn't count as using his powers, he reasons. He's doing it just for himself.

"You gonna pull that thing from behind my ear next?"

Diego looks up to find a girl with round blue eyes and straight reddish hair grinning at him. She's wearing tight jeans and a black T-shirt, beat-up sneakers on her feet. She's clutching a nearly empty plastic cup, and her freckled white cheeks are flushed pink. For the first time, Diego notices how warm it is in the fraternity house.

"It's a knife, not a penny," Diego answers.

"A knife makes for a more interesting magic trick," the girl says.

"Or a more dangerous one," Diego replies with a smile. "How'd you get that?" He points to a tiny scar on the girl's chin.

She answers quickly, "Fell off my bike the first time I rode a two-wheeler. Hit a rock on the ground."

Diego thinks of the scars that line his body, places where the knives nicked him over the years. He wonders how he'd explain them away if this girl asked about them.

"Must've hurt," Diego says finally.

"What I really remember about it is the way my parents freaked out. My mom said she'd never seen so much blood. My dad drove us to the hospital as fast as he could, then screamed that he wouldn't let anyone but a plastic surgeon stitch me up. Like he was worried if a regular doctor did it, I'd be disfigured or something, and he couldn't bear the idea of having a hideous daughter." The girl rolls her eyes. "So sexist."

"Dads, right?" Diego says with a shrug. He tucks the knife he'd been toying with into a pocket.

He tries to think of a story about Hargreeves he could tell that would match this girl's story about her father. When Diego cut himself, Hargreeves never rushed him to the hospital, and he certainly never worried about how the cuts would look when they healed. Usually, Diego had to keep training even as he bled, and only afterward did Mom come to his room and nurse the cuts. Dad programmed her to be able to stitch Diego's wounds when necessary. Diego doesn't think Dad programmed her to have a plastic surgeon's skills.

"Don't get me started!" the girl answers, tucking her hair behind her ears. She downs the rest of her drink and drops her plastic cup on the sticky hardwood floor, crushing it beneath her heel. Diego sips the remains of his third beer. "So," the girl says, "are you gonna ask me to dance or what?"

"Dance?" Diego echoes. He's never danced. Not, like, with a person he's attracted to. Not like this.

The girl smiles again, and her cheeks are so pink.

Whatever, Diego thinks. *It'll be better than trying to keep still.*

He takes the girl's hand. He doesn't even know her name; he wonders if he should ask, but as they move to the center of the room the music gets so loud that he doesn't think he'd be able to hear her answer. So instead, he twirls her around. He thinks he hears her squeal over the din of the music. One thing Diego's always been able to do is move; he's not self-conscious about dancing. He closes his eyes and concentrates on the rhythm of the song, the heat of the girl's hands in his. He shifts his hips and turns in place.

"You're really good!" the red-haired girl shouts.

Diego grins in response, twirling her around and then moving around her. A small pocket of the dance floor opens up, giving them more space. He pulls the girl close, then spins her away again. He lifts her off her feet and glides in a circle. When he puts her back down, she kisses his cheek.

"Where'd you learn how to dance like that?" She catches her breath as the circle of dancers closes around them once more.

"Just born with skills, I guess," Diego shrugs, feigning modesty. He knows it's a lie. He may have been born with rhythm, but movement has been drilled into him for most of his life. Learning to fight involves as much choreography as learning to dance. Someone in the crowd wolf whistles, and Diego feels exactly as he does when people cheer for him during a mission. He spins the redheaded girl around, taking up more space on the dance floor.

"Hey!" someone shouts, hip-checking Diego. "Watch where you're going, fancy feet."

Fancy feet sounds like an insult. Diego spins around to see a boy towering over him, taller than Luther and more muscular. Like Diego, he's wearing black pants, though his aren't nearly so tight. His hair is dark brown and short, gelled into spikes. Diego scowls.

"You're not the only one dancing here," the tall boy snaps.

"I can't help it if my moves are bigger than yours." Diego doesn't care how tall this guy is. No way does he have strength or skills to match Diego's.

Diego feels like the entire crowd is holding their breath. No one's dancing anymore. *It's almost ironic*, Diego thinks, *that this guy who was complaining about wanting more space has cleared the floor.*

Diego drops the girl's hand, and she blinks like he's rejected her. She looks from Diego's face to the face of the guy who bumped into him, and takes one step back, then another. She seems to know what's coming almost as quickly as Diego does.

The big guy with the spiky hair isn't fast enough. Diego blocks his first punch with his right arm and grabs the guy's fist with his left, twisting his arm behind his back.

Finally, the nervous energy that's been coursing through his veins since he stepped inside this building dissipates. Or maybe it's that now the energy has somewhere to go, something to do. He thinks of how quickly his opponent picked this fight. Maybe he's not the only person here itching for some action.

The makeshift dance floor clears almost immediately, though the music keeps thumping. He lets the guy go long enough to get his footing—defeat him too fast, and the fight will be over in seconds, and that's the last thing Diego wants.

Diego jumps to the side when the guy tries to land another punch, and comes down hard on the back of the guy's neck just like he's been trained to do. The guy sprawls on the floor, and Diego backs up, giving him a chance to stand again. But the guy stays down.

Breathing heavily, Diego looks up at the faces around him. He catches the eye of the girl he was dancing with just minutes before. He expects her to look impressed at how quickly he won, maybe even to laugh at how little it took for Diego to get him on the ground, but she looks horrified. Her pretty features are twisted into a grimace. Beneath her freckles, her cheeks have lost all their color.

Diego is sweating. He realizes that to her—to all the kids here, judging from the looks on their faces—it's *weird* that he's this good at fighting, *weird* that things got so intense.

Diego backs away, squeezing through the crowd. In the far corner of the room, there's a door propped open leading to the fraternity house's backyard, though it's not really a yard so much as a pile of crushed beer cans and smashed bottles. Diego runs outside and breathes in the air, his heart rate slowing.

He hates to admit it, but the truth is fighting felt even better than dancing.

He turns back toward the party, knowing that the guy he just beat is probably back on his feet, waiting for round two. Maybe he's even got a few of his friends on his side now, ready to jump in when Diego knocks him down.

Diego flexes his fists. He'll take them all on.

ALLISON

It started innocently. She rumored May into liking her dress. No big deal. Sure, she wasn't supposed to use her powers tonight, but it's not as though she was using them to fight a mission or conquer the world. She merely wanted to fit in. No one could blame her for that.

But the thing is, it only let her part of the way in. It got May talking to her, but not the other girls—Messy Bun and Purple Lipstick.

So Allison added, "I heard a rumor that you're dying to tell your friends how much you love my dress."

"Jenny, Letitia"—Messy Bun's and Purple Lipstick's real names, Allison knows now—"Look at Allison's amazing dress. I just *had* to tell you how much I *love* it."

Jenny and Letitia turned to Allison as though they were seeing her for the first time.

Quickly, Allison said, "I heard a rumor you love my dress, too."

"Oh my god, so retro," Jenny squealed. "I love it."

"Me, too," Letitia agreed. "I love it even more. Where did you find it?"

"A thrift shop," Allison answered, leaning forward on the couch, closer to the other girls.

Jenny wrinkled her nose. "It's *used?*"

But this time, Allison had an answer ready. "It's so much less wasteful to buy clothes that were previously owned. Fast fashion is destroying the planet, and I heard a rumor that it's really important to you."

"Oh my god," Letitia said. "Fast fashion is totally destroying the planet."

Maybe this is getting out of hand. Allison only meant to be included in their conversation. No, that's not true. Allison wanted to feel better about her dress, about the fact that she was wearing something both inappropriate and out-of-date, the sort of thing that only Klaus could pull off; he can make anything look good.

Klaus, who said that Allison used her powers to get literally everything she wanted.

Well, Klaus doesn't know what he's talking about. Before tonight, she's never used her powers for anything other than a mission.

Right?

The phrase slips out from between her lips so easily tonight, her very own magic words, like other children are taught to say *please* and *thank you.*

Allison recalls her first magazine cover, back when the

press couldn't get enough of the Umbrella Academy. The photographer started out shooting Allison alongside her siblings (except Viktor, obviously), but at some point, he pulled Allison aside and did some shots of her alone. She can't remember now whether she was surprised to discover that she was on the cover by herself, without her siblings at her side, her arms folded across her chest, uniform blazer flying out behind her like a cape. Was she surprised by her next solo cover, or the one after that? How about by the magazine with the fold-out poster of Allison standing with her hands on her hips, her smile wide, showing off her missing baby teeth?

Maybe she rumored those photographers and journalists without realizing it. Maybe her siblings knew all along, even if she didn't.

Or maybe she did realize it at the time; she just forgot about it in the years since. Almost as if she'd rumored herself into only remembering the things she wanted to. She doesn't like the way it feels—being uncertain of her own memories. Who'd have ever guessed Klaus might remember something Allison forgot?

She'll ask Luther; he'll tell her the truth.

But suddenly Allison isn't sure she wants to know the truth, and that makes her feel even worse.

So instead of thinking about how she may or may not have used her powers, Allison tries to imagine a future with these three girls—May, Letitia, and Jenny—as her friends.

They could take a road trip together, like the friends she's seen in the movies. Stay up all night in their dorm rooms, sharing their deepest, darkest secrets.

But thinking about deep, dark secrets has Allison squirming in her seat once more. Have her siblings been angry at her for years, knowing that she'd rumored her way on to one magazine cover after another? Did Luther make them promise to keep their anger to themselves?

She shakes herself out of it. Surely she's not the only person who's done something she's ashamed of. Right?

"Hey," she says to May. "Have you ever done anything you, like, immediately regret? Or maybe you didn't realize you were doing it at the time, but later, you felt bad about it?"

May looks at Allison like she's speaking a foreign language. "Sorry, but we just met. I'm not about to tell you all my secrets."

"But you do have secrets?" Allison prompts. Surely that's what May means, right? Although, an ordinary person's idea of a secret is probably nothing like Allison's.

The words are out of her mouth before she can stop them. "I heard a rumor that all three of you are going to tell me your deepest, darkest secrets. Tell me one thing you're ashamed of."

"I throw up half my meals," Jenny says.

"I sneak into other people's dorm rooms and steal their clothes," May says.

Allison turns to Letitia for her answer.

"I cheated on my algebra exam in tenth grade," Letitia admits. She says it easily, without hesitating. Of course she did—that's the power of Allison's magic words.

"Why?" Allison asks.

All three girls answer at once: Letitia cheated because she was scared she wouldn't get an A, which would've destroyed her grade point average, which would've kept her out of honors classes, which would have ruined her chances of getting into this college.

Jenny throws up because she hates the way she looks: She hates her messy hair and her aquiline nose and her front teeth that are still crooked because her parents couldn't afford braces. She can't control any of that, but she can control is her weight.

May steals other people's clothes because she can't afford to buy the latest styles. She had to take out massive student loans and works two on-campus jobs in between classes. There's just enough money to cover tuition, food, and books, but nothing left over for anything as frivolous as new clothes.

"You do what you need to fit in," May says. "Do you think these girls would've been friends with me if I'd been wearing the wrong clothes?"

"Yeah," Jenny agrees. "I mean, *literally*, my clothes wouldn't fit if I didn't make myself throw up." She laughs as though she's made a joke, but looks sad, and the other girls don't crack a smile.

"Wouldn't you rather have friends who accept you for who you are?" Allison asks. She thinks about Luther, the only person she's ever been able to really be herself around. She always thought she preferred his company to anyone else's because of who *he* is, but maybe it's also because of who *she* gets to be around him.

"I mean, it's not just about fitting in," Letitia adds. "It's standing out, too. Getting into a college like this meant fitting in with the smart kids, but I also stand out in my family. No one in my family had ever gone to college before."

Jenny and May nod in agreement, and Allison finds herself nodding along with them. If she rumored her way on to those magazine covers, she was using her powers not only to fit in, but to stand out.

"You guys really get it," Allison says, her voice filled with awe. Even Luther doesn't know about this part of her—this part that's as desperate to stand out as it is to fit in.

Allison wants more of this closeness, so she turns to May and says, "I heard a rumor you want to tell me more."

"I hooked up with Jeff last semester," May answers. She looks over at Jenny when she says it.

"What?" Jenny jumps to her feet.

"You guys were fighting!" May explains, wringing her hands. "I thought for sure you had broken up. He told me you were breaking up."

"So which is it, you thought we had already broken up or that we were going to break up?" Jenny shouts so loud that the people around them turn to stare. "Scratch that—what did it matter? Even if we were broken up, you shouldn't have been hooking up with my boyfriend!"

"If you were broken up, he wasn't your boyfriend!" Now May's on her feet, too. "You don't own him just because you guys went out for like five minutes."

"Five minutes!" Jenny shouts incredulously. "We've been together for five months."

"It hadn't been that long last semester!"

"You've got to be kidding me!" Jenny says. "You're trying to justify what you did? Clearly you know it was wrong, or you wouldn't have kept it a secret."

"I knew you'd be upset!"

"Then why did you say something now?"

May blinks in confusion. "I don't know." She glances at Allison like she knows Allison has something to do with it but can't figure out how.

Suddenly, Jenny lunges for May. The two girls fall across Allison's lap and then onto the floor, Jenny's hair slipping out of its messy bun as she wrestles with May.

"Stop it!" Letitia begs. "You guys are best friends."

"Not anymore!" Jenny's out of breath as she and May tumble across the floor. The crowd around them parts, making space. Allison can't help noticing how quickly people accommodate the fight; she wonders if this kind of thing happens all the time.

Letitia tries to come between the other girls. "Stop!" she shouts again, thrusting her arm into the middle of the fray.

Jenny surfaces from the fight long enough to say, "Careful, Letty! You almost got me."

Letitia steps away, holding her hands up as if to say she's done coming between May and Jenny.

Allison shakes her head in confusion. She may have rumored these girls into talking to her tonight, but they still have years of shared secrets and inside jokes that she doesn't understand.

"You be careful, too, Jenny," Letitia says with a wink. "You gotta watch what you say."

"Right," Jenny agrees.

"And May, don't want to mess up your hair." Letitia winks again.

The girls continue to fight, but Allison can tell they're being somehow more *careful* now. Allison knows, once again, that there's some secret between the girls that she doesn't understand. She tries to imagine what it would be like to fight while holding something back, but that kind of hesitation isn't allowed in the Umbrella Academy, not even when the siblings are practicing against each other.

There's a sudden shout, and Allison thinks the crowd is cheering for the fight, but then she realizes there's another struggle on the other side of the room. Out of the corner of her eye, she sees Diego moving swiftly. The crowd gets louder and louder.

"What now?" Allison moans. She tries to figure out how long she and her siblings have been here. It can't have been more than an hour or so. They've been trained for combat practically since birth. Send them out into the world—whether to a party or on a mission—and that's what they do. Maybe it doesn't matter if they use their powers or not.

Maybe they never had a chance at being normal not just because of their powers, but because of the way Hargreeves raised them.

Allison crouches beside May and Jenny.

"I heard a rumor you guys stopped fighting and made up!" she tries, but the girls can't hear her voice over the din of the crowd. "I heard a rumor you stopped fighting!" she tries again, but her new friends roll away from her.

Allison turns to Letitia. "Can't you stop them?" she begs.

Letitia shakes her head. "I gotta be careful about getting caught between them."

"But they're your friends!"

"You wouldn't understand."

Allison understands one thing: Out here in the real world, surrounded by normal kids, she's utterly powerless to stop what she started.

KLAUS

It starts out well enough. A half dozen college kids—plus Klaus—sat on the floor in a circle, the only light coming from flickering candles. Klaus could tell them that there's no need for candles or the soft, plinky-plunky music coming from a set of speakers in the corner—that sort of thing never makes a difference—but Klaus is nothing if not a showman, and music and candles add a certain something to the show.

Klaus sits cross-legged, folding the pleats of his kilt across his lap. He joins hands with Chris and a girl who's chewing gum that smells like cough medicine.

"Nice ink," Chris says, noticing Klaus's umbrella tattoo through his long mesh sleeves.

"This old thing?" Klaus preens.

"My dad would bust a gut if I got one," Chris says longingly.

Klaus considers telling Chris that *his* father actually required this tattoo, but then Chris would inevitably ask why, and Klaus doesn't feel like explaining. Instead, he closes his eyes and tips his head back, inhaling deeply.

"Who do you want to contact?" he asks.

"My grandma," a girl sitting across from him whispers. "She died last year." The girl is kneeling like she's going to pray. Or maybe it's because the black miniskirt she's wearing is too tight to sit any other way.

Before Klaus knows what's happening, he sees the shadow of an elderly woman holding knitting needles in the middle of the circle.

"Tell my Bianca she looks like a slut in that outfit," the old lady says curtly.

When Klaus doesn't immediately comply, the old woman starts to shout.

"Tell her, tell her now! If I were still alive, I could've convinced her parents not to send her so far from home. I could've kept an eye on her. Tell her I know what she's been doing with that boy Cole every night this week. And I don't approve. They named her *Bianca* after me"—the woman spits the name—"even though my name is Bertha. But no, such a plain name wasn't good enough for their fancy little girl. And here she is at this hoity-toity college miles away from home. Tell her, tell her. *Grandma Bertha does not approve.*"

"I'm not going to slut-shame your granddaughter," Klaus says finally.

"What?" the girl—Bianca, apparently—asks.

Klaus opens his eyes and smiles, "Your grandmother says she's happy you and Cole found each other."

"How did you know about that?" Bianca asks, her eyes wide. She steals a look at a boy sitting on the other side of the circle with spiky hair and a nose ring. "We haven't told anyone we're hooking up."

"I haven't exactly broken up with my ex yet." Cole explains, running a hand through his hair. Klaus notices that he has a tattoo of the moon on the back of one hand and the sun on the other. Now he's the one saying, "Nice ink."

"Cole!" Bianca wails. "You told me you'd do it last week."

"I'll get to it, I promise, baby."

"That's not what I said!" Bianca's grandmother screeches to Klaus. "You tell that girl she better keep her knees together—"

"All right, who's next?" Klaus says, shouting in an attempt to drown out the judgmental old woman's voice.

"My cat," a guy to his left suggests. "He got hit by a car last month."

"I can't contact animals," Klaus says irritably. Someone always asks to talk to a beloved dog, parakeet, gerbil. Klaus never understands why people want to communicate with creatures who couldn't even talk when they were alive.

The boy looks disappointed but resigned. He nods.

"We're supposed to be reaching out to Jason Wright," Bianca says finally. "That's why Chris told us all to meet here."

"Wait, who's Jason Wright?" Klaus asks.

"Man, you don't know this story?" Chris asks incredulously. "Dude, where you been living, the moon?"

Klaus thinks of the Umbrella Academy, just across town but so isolated it may as well be another planet. If Ben were here, he'd remind Klaus that the moon isn't another planet. But luckily Ben's not here.

Where is Ben, anyway? And the rest of Klaus's siblings? Klaus feels bad that he left them to fend for themselves. He was supposed to be showing them the ropes, wasn't he? How to navigate a party and all that. No, he only offered to get them here. He never said he'd babysit once they arrived. Not that spending the night with his siblings is babysitting. He wanted to hang out with them, didn't he? One last hurrah before he leaves the Umbrella Academy for good. Or before one of them does. Wait, was that it? He wanted them to see the world? Yes, but that's not all. There's an itch at the back of Klaus's head, like he's not supposed to be in this room, conducting this séance, though he can't for the life of him remember why.

"Enlighten me," Klaus finally says to Chris. "Who's Jason Wright."

"Well, apparently, twenty years ago, Jason Wright was a freshman here, rushing this very fraternity. And one morning, his body was found on the street outside. They said he'd jumped off the roof, killing himself."

"Yeah, but no one believed it," someone breaks in. "The autopsy showed his blood alcohol level was through the roof. Everyone thinks it was really a hazing ritual gone wrong."

"But the coroner's report said he died by suicide," Chris continues. "Half the campus thinks it was a cover-up. The fraternity must've been responsible for what happened, and they made it look like a suicide so they wouldn't get in trouble and lose their charter."

"Some alum could've paid off the coroner's office," Bianca suggests. "You know we've had at least one president who was a member of this fraternity in college? No telling how high the conspiracy goes."

"Aren't *you* a member of this fraternity?" Klaus asks Chris. He thought this was Chris's room.

"Hell no!" Chris says. "I'm just here to find out the truth about Jason so we can get these assholes kicked off campus. This is my friend's friend's friend Eddie's room. Rumor has it, it was Jason's room back in the day."

Klaus thinks about the drugs he nicked from the desk drawer. He'll have to find Eddie and thank him later.

"Fair enough," Klaus answers, closing his eyes again. He tries to find the ghost who started shouting when he stepped inside the room. That must have been him. "Jason Wright, are you here with us?"

But instead of one ghost's voice answering his question, now the room filled with the shouts of dozens of dead people—though no one but Klaus can see how crowded it's become.

"Young man, I joined this fraternity in 1952," a man in a suit says condescendingly. I lived in this very room. And let me assure you that nothing untoward ever happened here."

"You mean other than the time you tried to force yourself on me, and I had to stab you with a pencil to get away?" a woman says.

"Your attack was certainly not the responsibility of the fraternity."

"Except you and your so-called brothers launched a campaign to get me kicked out of school for being—what did you call it?—'a clear and present danger to the fine young men of this institution'?"

"What did you need a college education for anyhow?" the man scoffs. "You got married and never had to work a day in your life. Anyway, you died two years later."

"And you died five years after that. Drunk driving, if I recall correctly."

"How I died is none of your business!"

"Don't talk to me like that! If I hadn't died, I would've gone back to work once my kids were in school."

Klaus shakes his head vigorously, trying to ignore the ghosts' escalating argument.

"Jason Wright," he says again. "I'm looking for Jason Wright."

"I know what happened to Jason Wright," another voice offers, and Klaus turns his head. He can see a sickly looking young man. "The same thing that happened to me. They hazed me my freshman year. It was 1986, but the rituals haven't changed much. Alcohol poisoning." He draws a finger dramatically across his neck. "You know, they could've saved me if they'd taken me to the hospital to have my stomach pumped. I thought they were going to. I was still alive when they dragged me down the stairs and out the door. But they dumped me back at my dorm room and left me alone to die. Because as long as I wasn't found on fraternity property, they knew they wouldn't be blamed for my death."

"Man, that sucks," Klaus offers sympathetically.

"It did suck," the man agrees. "With poor Jason Wright, they were too lazy to even take him that far."

Meanwhile, the man and woman from the 1950s have started screaming at each other.

"Jason!" Klaus shouts. "Jason, are you here?"

"Man, are you okay?"

Suddenly, Chris's face is right next to Klaus's. Gently, Chris pulls Klaus's hands from over his ears. Klaus hadn't realized he'd been covering his ears. His eyes are screwed shut so tightly that his head hurts.

What was he thinking, summoning spirits? He can't even control the ones that come uninvited.

"You need to chill out," Chris offers.

"I do," Klaus agrees. Chris's face is so close to his that Klaus can feel his breath. "I *really* do."

Chris holds out a pill. Klaus doesn't hesitate. He doesn't care what it is, he's taking it. Chris offers him a beer to wash it down, but that would take too long. Klaus smashes the pill on the hardwood floor and bends over to snort it. He doesn't care that dust bunnies and dirt might be entering his nose along with it. Who can be bothered with those sorts of details? He feels the drugs entering his system almost immediately; the voices fade away and grow quiet.

"This séance has become kind of a drag, don't you think? Besides, I've got a better idea," Klaus says, leaping to his feet, wiping the residue of the pill from his nose.

"What?"

"I can prove that Jason didn't die the way the fraternity said he did."

"How?"

"To the roof!" Klaus shouts triumphantly. He spins in place, his kilt billowing out around him. "Follow me!"

VIKTOR

The Bach winds to its conclusion, and once again Viktor can hear the louder, harsher, faster music coming up from downstairs. Most people might not find a link between the classical music on the turntable and the rock music blasting from the party, but Viktor can tell that the singer downstairs was accompanied by a full orchestra when they recorded the album.

"My friend Tish was supposed to find us some beer," Ryan explains as he carefully lifts the record off the turntable and returns it to its sleeve. "But judging by how long she's been gone, she must've gotten sidetracked." Ryan raises an eyebrow. "What do you say, Viktor—up for a little bit of larceny?"

"Larceny?" Viktor echoes nervously. It's the sort of crime his siblings were trained to fight against. Then again, they all stole their clothes tonight. But still, Viktor imagines his siblings coming after him the way they've gone after so many criminals over the years.

"Relax!" Ryan chuckles. "Stealing beer from some frat bro's bedroom isn't an injustice. Think of it as a redistribution of resources."

Ryan grins. Something about his smile sets Viktor at ease, and he finds himself following Ryan out the bedroom door.

"What year are you?" Viktor asks as Ryan leads the way down the stairs to the third floor.

Now that they're in the brightly lit hallway, Viktor notices more details of Ryan's appearance: He's nearly as short as Viktor, though not quite as slim. Before they left his room, Ryan pulled a plaid flannel button-down, unbuttoned, over his T-shirt. His hair is so short that in the light, Viktor can see Ryan's pale scalp. There's the tiniest bit of stubble on Ryan's white cheeks, which are flushed pink in the warm fraternity house. Ryan doesn't actually necessarily look older than Viktor, even though Viktor and his siblings are too young for college.

Ryan shrugs. "I haven't exactly been keeping track. I'll just keep taking classes until they tell me I'm done, I guess."

Viktor nods. He thinks that's a good approach to college, and the exact opposite of Hargreeves's approach to any kind of education. Hargreeves doesn't believe in learning for learning's sake. He's results-oriented. Viktor and his siblings were taught math, literature, and foreign languages by their mother. Hargreeves updated her software every year with a new set of lesson plans. If Viktor or his siblings ever had questions or interests that deviated from Mom's programming, she'd short-circuit, so Viktor quickly learned not to ask too many questions.

As Viktor descends from the fourth floor to the third to the second, the music coming from downstairs gets louder, along with a chorus of voices singing along it.

"God, I hate this music," Ryan moans. He doesn't seem to care that anyone might hear him. "I don't mean to be, like, a traitor to our generation, but doesn't it just sound like *noise?*"

"Yes!" Viktor agrees, nodding enthusiastically. He thinks of the pop music that's forever wafting from Allison's room, down the hall from his back at the academy. Or the heavy metal that Klaus plays so loud it drowns out pretty much every other sound. (Viktor guesses that's exactly what Klaus has in mind.)

"I knew I liked you, Viktor," Ryan says with a wink. Viktor tries to remember if anyone's ever told him that they liked him. He doesn't think so. He thinks of the adulation and cheers his siblings have received over the years. *Strangers* love them—or loved them—and Viktor's own family barely notices when he enters a room anymore. Ryan's only known him for the length of one Bach concerto, and he already likes him.

"I like you, too," Viktor says, and Ryan smiles.

On the second floor, Ryan tries one door, then another, until he finds one that's unlocked. Inside, a group of kids are strewn across two beds and a couch, making out with each other in various degrees of undress. Viktor expects them to yell at Ryan to get out, but instead they look up and cheer.

"Ryan!" they shout, nearly in perfect unison.

"Friends!" Ryan shouts in response.

Friends? Viktor thinks incredulously. How can Ryan be an outsider like him and still be popular? Is this a room full of outsiders? Is there such a thing as a room full of outsiders? Once there's enough of them, do they become *insiders*? Maybe there are different ways to be popular, different places where you can fit in.

The idea makes Viktor feel warm, like when that person called him *dude* earlier.

Ryan makes eye contact with one of the half-dressed girls and raises an eyebrow. "So this is where you disappeared to, Tish."

"I'm so sorry!" Tish scrambles to her feet, pulling her wrinkled tank top down over her stomach. She dives for the cooler of beer in the corner of the room and holds two bottles out, apologizing the whole time.

"Don't worry about it," Ryan says, taking the drinks from Tish's hands. "Viktor and I were happy to come down to grab these."

Ryan says Viktor's name like they're old friends, not two people who just met.

"Do you want us to change the music?" Tish asks. "We know it's not really your thing."

"But it's all of yours," Ryan says. He makes it sound like the music is a gift he's giving the party. Tish flushes with gratitude.

Ryan leads the way back out the door. Viktor follows. As he closes the door behind him, Ryan leans in to whisper,

"Do you think those guys in there are having more fun than we are?"

Viktor considers the question. For as long as he can remember, he's assumed that his siblings are always having more fun the he is. He glances around the crowded hallway . . . so many people laughing and shouting and pressed together, singing along to bad music with nonsensical lyrics. For the first time, he thinks he's having more fun than anyone else. With Ryan. A new friend who likes him.

"No way," Viktor says.

Ryan pops open a beer and passes it to Viktor.

"I used to live with a family that had a seriously warped idea of what qualified as a good time," Ryan confides. "They made me feel like a freak because I didn't, I don't know, fit in."

"I know exactly what you mean," Viktor says. "My family's like that, too."

"Yeah," Ryan says. "I thought you'd understand. Families, right?"

"Seriously," Viktor agrees. It's the closest he's ever come to actually criticizing the Umbrella Academy out loud. He thinks of the stories he could tell Ryan about his family, the myriad ways he's been left out for as long as he can remember. Would anyone ever be interested in his stories? About the ordinary sibling in an extraordinary family?

"Let me tell you something, Viktor," Ryan continues. "Things have gotten a lot better since I've been living here."

"What do you mean?" Viktor asks, thinking of Tish and the rest of the friends who greeted Ryan so enthusiastically.

If those people are so great, then why was Ryan holed up in his room alone?

"When my family kicked me out—"

"They kicked you out?" Viktor interrupts. The Umbrella Academy has never exactly made Viktor feel *welcome*, but he can't imagine being forced to leave either.

"Let's say it was mutual. I already had one foot out the door."

"Can I ask why?"

"I was sick of their rules, and they were sick of my refusal to follow them."

Viktor thinks of the countless rules at the academy. Klaus has been breaking them for months; tonight, they're all rule breakers. He knows they'll be in trouble if Hargreeves finds out, but he can't imagine Hargreeves ever kicking anyone out. And if he did—well, Viktor imagines that his siblings would stick together. At least for a little while.

"That sounds terrible," Viktor says finally.

"The people I grew up with," Ryan replies after a moment. "Let's just say they don't forgive mistakes."

Viktor thinks of all the mistakes he's seen his siblings make over the years. One of Diego's knives not hitting quite the right target—to be fair, usually because Klaus thought it would be hilarious to move the target after Diego released a throw. Ben's tentacles knocking over a glass case when he was still learning how to control them. Klaus conjuring ghosts he never meant to call on.

Viktor's never thought of Hargreeves as *forgiving*, but it occurs to him for the first time that maybe their dad isn't that bad. Or that he isn't as bad as he could be. He could've sent Viktor back to his birth mother when it turned out he was powerless, but he never did.

Viktor hasn't ever felt luckier than anyone else. But at this moment, he feels luckier than Ryan. Or anyway, luckier than Ryan was before he came here.

"Living here is nothing like it was at home," Ryan continues. "Trust me, Viktor, you just need to find people who appreciate your talents."

"What if I don't have any talents?"

"*Everyone* has a talent," Ryan insists. "Even outsiders like us. You just have to find the people who recognize them for what they are."

Viktor nods, thinking of the way Ryan was greeted when he walked into the room. Not like a bother for interrupting their fun, but part of the fun.

Ryan takes a long drink of his beer. "I promise you, Viktor, things get so much better when you find your people."

Ryan is speaking quietly, his stance unassuming. He's nothing like Luther—making an announcement with open arms, shouting to be heard. But something about him is irresistible; something makes Viktor want to listen to everything he has to say.

"How do you know if they're your people?" Who could be more *his people* than his family?

And yet, Ryan left his home—his family—behind.

"You'll know when you're part of a community where everyone truly appreciates the things you can do." Ryan grins.

Viktor considers this. Living at the Umbrella Academy has only ever made him aware of the things he *can't* do, not the things he can. But maybe other places—place like this, with people like Ryan—could be different.

Viktor smiles back, a smile so wide his jaw aches.

CHAPTER
21

KLAUS

Klaus breathes in the fresh air like a drowning man emerging from the water. He led Chris and the others up to the roof—from which Jason supposedly leaped to his death. According to the ghost who'd been abandoned by his would-be fraternity brothers, Jason was thrown from the roof to cover up that he'd really died of alcohol poisoning.

"What are we doing up here, Klaus?" Chris asks.

"Jason's ghost wasn't cooperating," Klaus explains. It's not exactly the truth. Jason's ghost might have shown up if Klaus kept looking for him. But now, with the booze and the drugs coursing through his system, the ghosts have gone quiet. Which means he can't find Jason. Which means Klaus has to think of another way to entertain his new friends.

"We can't count on Jason to tell us the truth about what happened that night. So we're going to have to resort to other methods." Klaus looks around, his eyes landing on the ledge that rings the roof. At once, he has an idea.

Klaus could just tell them what the other ghost said about Jason's death. But that wouldn't be particularly entertaining, would it?

"How?"

"You said that the fraternity claimed Jason died from jumping off the roof, right?"

"Right."

Klaus hops onto the ledge of the building, balancing like a gymnast on a beam. His new friends gasp.

"Careful!" Chris shouts.

Klaus continues, his arms held out for balance. "This building's only four stories high. It's hard to believe that a fall from this height could actually kill a person."

"I mean, maybe, but wouldn't that depend on how the person fell?"

"What do you mean?"

"Like, if someone jumped feet first, maybe they'd break their legs, but they'd survive. But if they dove headfirst, and their head went crashing into the sidewalk, that'd be enough to kill them, right?" Chris shudders, like he's horrified by the thought of someone landing on the sidewalk below.

Klaus hadn't given it that much thought. Klaus never gives anything that much thought.

He looks down over the edge. "But there are bushes. Wouldn't they have broken Jason's fall?"

"Maybe." Chris reaches an arm out. "But Klaus, seriously, come down. You're freaking me out."

Klaus laughs. Normals *freak out* so easily. If they saw or heard half the things that he sees and hears, he's pretty sure their normal minds would explode.

"Don't be a killjoy, Chris. You're just like my brother." Klaus tries to sound serious, but it's hard when he's having this much fun. "I've jumped from higher places than this, and I've been fine. No way did this fall kill Jason."

Klaus hops from one foot to another. Chris looks worried but also—Klaus can tell—intrigued.

And Klaus likes that.

"What do you mean, you've jumped from higher places than this?" Chris asks after a moment.

Klaus waves his hands like the details aren't important. Just this afternoon, Klaus leaped from a building on the verge of collapse. Though he's not exactly sure how high up he was. And he doesn't actually remember what happened after the jump. But here he is, standing on two feet and right as rain, so it must have been okay.

Klaus keeps hopping from one foot to the other. Chris and his friends gasp, then clap. Klaus bets he can spin just like the gymnasts on TV. He attempts a pirouette.

"Klaus!" Chris shouts. Though his form isn't perfect, Klaus does manage a full rotation.

What else do those gymnasts do? Klaus wonders. He jumps again, spinning in the air. Again, imperfect form, but he lands with just the littlest bit of a wobble.

Next, a front handspring.

Klaus keeps his eyes open as he rotates, arms over head. Klaus can feel his kilt billowing in the breeze as he moves. He can't explain why he isn't afraid. Someone else might think it had to do with the drugs and the booze, but Klaus doesn't fear death even stone-cold sober. Maybe that's what happens when you grow up talking to ghosts. Death loses its mystery. Every other human on Earth doesn't know what happens after they die. They may believe in heaven or reincarnation, but even the most fervent believer holds a little seed of doubt. Everyone suspects that there's a chance that after they die, there will be *nothing*. That's it, the end, oblivion. And that scares the shit out of them, obviously. But Klaus knows—he's always known—that whatever else there is, it isn't oblivion. So death doesn't hold the same dread for him that it does for everyone else.

The dead are another story. Klaus can remember being locked up in that mausoleum for hours on end, ghosts screaming all the while. He couldn't drown out their voices by covering his ears; even his own sobs weren't loud enough. Hargreeves told Klaus he needed to control his fear, but Hargreeves doesn't know what it's like to be hounded by the dead every day of your life. If Hargreeves had asked, Klaus would've explained that there was no need to lock him up in that tomb. The dead follow him everywhere.

Hargreeves, Klaus thinks, *had no idea what the hell he was talking about.*

His hands make contact with the stone ledge, and he pushes himself over, his legs splayed out behind him.

One foot lands on the ledge; the other dangles in the air, wobbling. Out of the corner of his eye, Klaus thinks he sees his new friends reaching for him, but he's already too fargone.

Crap, he thinks as he goes over the edge. *I shoulda stuck the landing.*

Klaus can hear his new friends screaming as he goes flying. *They wouldn't scream*, he thinks, *if they knew how lovely it felt to freefall.*

He really does think he's jumped from higher than this—if not today, then on some other mission, or during one or another training exercise. Time and time again, Hargreeves pushed Klaus past what he thought he was capable of, until Klaus realized he was capable of just about anything. The human body isn't nearly as fragile as people seem to think it is. Or at least, Klaus's body isn't.

He's jumped from the third floor of the academy several times, and this is only a teensy bit higher than that. It was his go-to escape before he figured out how to navigate the sewers. (The key is to leave a window open *before* Pogo sets the alarm. Easy-peasy.) He almost suggested they leave that way tonight, but he knew Ben would've put the kibosh on that before Klaus would have a chance to finish explaining how harmless it is, how lovely the fall.

At once, Klaus realizes what it was—that nagging feeling he had before he began conducting the séance. He and his siblings promised not to use their powers tonight. He completely forgot. *Oops.*

Before he has a chance to feel bad about it—not that he *would've* felt bad about it, it's not as though he can really *control* his powers, something his siblings and Hargreeves never seemed to understand, or maybe they just don't believe him—Klaus hits the ground.

He bounces to his feet triumphantly. He can hear his new friends cheering from up on the roof. Much to his surprise though, Chris is crouched beside him.

"How'd you get here so fast?" Klaus asks. "Did you jump down after me? Did I miss it?"

"Dude, I ran down the stairs. You were unconscious. We were about to call for an ambulance."

Klaus furrows his brow, trying to make sense of the time he lost. He doesn't remember being unconscious. Then again, he wouldn't—isn't that the whole thing about losing consciousness? Which reminds him, whatever happened to Luther and that unconscious stranger on the street?

"Well, no need. As you can see, I'm just fine. Must've hit the old noggin"—Klaus knocks on his skull for emphasis—"but otherwise, good as new. And proof that Jason didn't die the way they said he did," he adds, but Chris doesn't seem interested in Jason anymore.

"Man, we have to introduce you to Ryan!" Chris exclaims, clapping Klaus on the back.

"Who's Ryan?" Klaus asks.

"You're gonna love him," Chris promises.

From up above, Chris's friends spill their beer as they pump their arms into the air. Liquid hits Klaus like raindrops. He opens his mouth to catch them.

"It's like you came back from the dead!" Chris shouts.

"Don't be ridiculous," Klaus says. Of all the many, many, many ghosts he's met—among all the different ways they died, and the different things they'd had to say about the world they left behind—there's one thing every single one of them has had in common, and Klaus yells it now, as loud as he can:

"A person can't come back from the dead!"

CHAPTER
22

LUTHER

Luther makes his way toward the raging frat house, the deafeningly loud music like a beacon drawing him closer. It's one of the ugliest building he's ever seen. Narrow and cramped, the windows thrown open. There's a crowd of people crouched around someone on the ground. Luther guesses someone just partied a little too hard, but he doesn't have time to stop and play hero, as Diego would say. He has to get inside and tell his siblings what he saw—Mateo's black hands, the earthquake, the dust.

As he gets closer to the house, Luther's eyes start to water. The house looks fuzzy, like it's encased in fog, but Luther shakes his head and rubs his eyes. No, not fog—dust. The air is thick with dust. This is more than detritus from his encounter with Mateo, he's sure.

And then there's the ugly house itself. Luther could swear he sees it sway like it could be knocked over by the breeze. Or wait—is it the house that's moving, or the earth beneath his feet? Could there be *another* earthquake?

Luther has to find his siblings, and fast. If they put their heads together, they can figure out what the hell is going on.

Inside, Luther looks around, expecting to find the rest of the Umbrella Academy in the center of the room, holding court, sticking together, but instead all he sees is a heap of kids piling on one guy. The room is dim, the only light coming from tall lamps over which someone has tossed red scarves, giving the air a haunted look. It takes Luther a second to recognize that the guy in the center of the heap is Diego.

Of course it is. Of course everything went to hell without Luther in charge. That's why the Umbrella Academy needs a Number One.

Okay, but that doesn't explain why the rest of the Umbrella Academy is standing back while Diego is fighting a multiple people on his own. *Where are they?*

Luther makes his way toward the makeshift boxing ring in the middle of the room. It's obviously not a real boxing ring, but a circle of kids surrounding Diego and the six guys currently piling on top of him. Luther reaches into the pile and pulls one kid off his brother, then another. A girl jumps on Luther's back, locking her legs around his waist.

"That's my boyfriend!" she shouts, but Luther shrugs her off, losing his balance. Luther feels his feet sliding over the hardwood beneath him, slippery with spilled drinks.

Soon, Diego and Luther are alone in the center of the circle. Diego turns on Luther, fists in front of his face, like he thinks Luther is another opponent. Diego's wearing only a black T-shirt with his tight black pants; he must've lost his jacket in the fray.

"What the hell is going on?" Luther asks, and Diego scowls.

The thing Luther's siblings don't seem to understand is that tonight *is* a mission. Their mission was to go to a party, act normal, have fun. And as far as Luther can tell, they're failing miserably. But now, Luther is here to get things back on track.

Or he would be, if the mission hadn't changed. *Now* their mission is to figure out what the hell is going on—with Mateo, with the dust in the air, with this house, with the earth beneath their feet.

"I was handling it just fine," Diego says, which isn't really an answer.

"Looked like it," Luther says. They're still surrounded by a circle of partygoers who are practically foaming at the mouth. *What did Diego do to piss them off this badly?* Luther wonders, but they really don't have time to get into it. "Where is everyone?"

"What are you talking about?" Diego asks. "This place is packed."

"I meant the rest of the Umbrella Academy," Luther explains.

"Oh my god!" someone from the crowd shouts. She points to Luther's jacket with the crest embroidered on the pocket.

"I recognize you!" She shifts her gaze from Luther to Diego. "You, too!"

She shouts again, but this time she's not addressing Luther or Diego but the whole room.

"Everybody!" she yells. "These guys are from the Umbrella Academy!"

Luther relaxes, expecting that he'll have to give an autograph or two, be asked how many people he can lift up at one time, that sort of thing. Everyone will listen when Luther tells them they need to evacuate the house while he and his siblings investigate. But instead, there's a murmur across the crowd that sets Luther's teeth on edge.

"I remember the Umbrella Academy!" someone else shouts. "They were those freaks that went around fighting crimes like a miniature police department."

Luther opens his mouth to explain how much more effective the Umbrella Academy was than the local police. Hargreeves kept a record of the crimes they solved and compared it to the stats of their more official counterparts—according to him, the academy won out every time. But something makes Luther close his mouth. He doesn't think this crowd is likely to be impressed with statistics.

"I dressed as them for Halloween last year!" someone adds.

"I almost did, too, but then I wanted to pick something cooler."

Diego has his fists up once again, but the crowd doesn't seem to be itching for a fight anymore. They're not shouting or even murmuring now. It takes Luther a second to recognize it, but the overriding sound coming from the crowd is something else entirely.

Laughter. They're *laughing.*

The Umbrella Academy is a *joke* to these kids.

"Man, you just had to wear that jacket, didn't you?" Diego mutters with a scowl.

"The one Allison picked out was too small."

Diego rolls his eyes. "Of course it was." Diego spins on his heel to face his brother. "You couldn't let it go for one night, could you? Had to swoop in and play the hero, like always?"

"What are you talking about? You were getting pummeled by a half dozen people when I got here!"

"What about the guy on the street?"

"You're blaming me for the fact that some guy passed out?" Luther asks. Which reminds him of what he's really doing here. It's just as dusty inside as it was outside. Why haven't his siblings noticed?

"Haven't you been paying attention?" Luther demands. "Or have you been too busy picking petty fights to notice anything *important?*"

"You sound just like Hargreeves," Diego says gruffly. "Barking commands like a drill sergeant."

"Someone has to take charge," Luther says firmly. "You're Number Two. When I'm not around, you're supposed to take the lead. And instead, I get here and find you goofing off—"

Before Luther can finish, Diego's fist lands squarely against his jaw.

"What the hell—" Luther says, but Diego's winding up for another punch. Luther moves, but he isn't fast enough to avoid the hit entirely. Instead of connecting with his jaw, this punch lands on his shoulder. Luther roars in protest.

He doesn't intend to hit his brother back, but his body's so well trained that it reacts on reflex. He punches Diego, an uppercut that connects with his brother's chin.

Diego runs headlong into Luther's chest, but Luther's bigger than his brother. He pulls Diego off his feet, turning him over so that his legs are in the air.

"Put me down!" Diego yells, his voice muffled.

"Not until you cool off," Luther insists. He flips Diego over his shoulder and starts walking toward the door. Clearly, Luther and his siblings need a quiet place to regroup outside and come up with a plan—but before Luther can make it to the door, someone's hands are pressed against his chest. Luther tries to step forward, but the person is strong enough to stop him.

Luther looks down, expecting to see someone huge—a person would have to be muscular and tall to stop Luther in his tracks—but standing in front of him is someone half his size and incredibly skinny.

"What now?" Luther growls.

"No fights in the house," the guy says. "Fraternity rule."

"Well, you're a little late for that," Luther points out. "Besides, we were just leaving."

"Good," the guy says with a nod.

Once he's out of earshot, Diego says, "We were not just leaving." His face is turning red from being held upside down.

Luther prepares to argue, but he realizes that Diego's right. They can't go anywhere until they find their siblings. He puts Diego down. Diego plants his feet on the floor like he thinks he can keep Luther from lifting him again.

"We have to find the rest of the team," Luther says, then turns back to the kid that stopped them. "How'd you—" he begins, but whoever it was has already disappeared into the crowd.

"Stay here," Luther says finally, his hands on Diego's shoulders.

"I'm not following your orders," Diego huffs. "You're not Number One tonight, remember? No powers."

"Someone has to take charge," Luther insists. "There's weird stuff going on tonight and I'm going to get to the bottom of it." Things were a mess when he got here. But now he's going to get the night back on track. A track that will solve the mystery of the guy on the street and the dust in the air and the shaky ground. A track that will lead them back home where they belong with another successful mission behind them.

CHAPTER
23

BEN

Of course Diego got into a fight. Ben guesses he should be grateful that at least his brother hasn't pulled a knife yet. Maybe he would've if Luther hadn't shown up when he did.

Which started an entirely different sort of fight.

The pool table is in the center of the room. Directly in front of Ben, his brothers were just fighting. Ben tries turning around—maybe if he ignores them, they'll magically disappear; stranger things have happened—but facing the other direction is another fight, this one with Allison at the center.

"You guys, calm down!" Allison shouts. "You're best friends. I heard a rumor—" she begins, and Ben winces. So much for not using their powers. Still, he thinks maybe it doesn't count if it doesn't work. It seems like the fighting girls can't hear Allison's voice over their own mayhem.

Ben turns again, this time to face the front door, where Klaus is walking in—when did he leave? *how* did he leave?—greeted with cheers, his arms overhead like he's just won a race. His shirt is torn, his lip is bloody, and his bare knees are scraped raw, but knowing Klaus it's not because he got into a fight. Klaus got into some other kind of trouble all his own.

Ben's not surprised. He's not even angry. Just . . . disappointed.

It's not entirely his siblings' fault. How could they expect to blend in like normal when they were raised to be anything but?

Ben sighs heavily and puts the pool cue down. Someone has to get everyone out of here in one piece.

He extricates Allison from her pile of girls first.

"Ow!" she shouts as Ben tugs her arm, pulling her upright. She crouches like she's about to fight him off (another fight, just what they need), but stops when she realizes it's Ben.

"What are you doing?" Allison straightens her dress as she stands. The puffy purple sleeves have fallen down over her shoulders, and her hair has fallen out of the half up, half down style she twisted it into at the thrift shop.

"What are *you* doing?" Ben asks.

Allison looks distraught. "Apparently destroying a three-way best friendship."

"How'd you manage that?"

Allison looks ashamed, and Ben knows that she'd been using her powers long before he overheard her.

"Allison, really? Did you even try?" Ben moans.

"I did! But you don't understand, I *had* to use my powers," she pauses. "It was harder to fit in than I thought it would be. Those girls were totally ignoring me—"

Ben rolls his eyes. Only Allison would think rumoring someone was the only solution to being ignored. He suspects she doesn't even realize just how often she uses her powers to get her way.

"I managed to fit in just fine without my powers." It's the truth, but it feels like a lie. Part of the reason he's good at pool is because of all that practice managing his tentacles over the years. Maybe he was using his powers in a way, even if he didn't mean to. Maybe it's impossible for him not to. For all of them not to.

"Then why are you here with me instead of hanging with your new normal friends?"

"In case you missed it, our siblings are causing chaos." Ben gestures toward their siblings. "We've got to get out of here."

He drops Allison's arm and moves toward his brothers next. Luther and Diego are facing each other, looking dumbfounded, the circle of kids around them having dispersed.

"Glad to see you guys made up," Ben says. Now that there's not a crowd cheering on their fight, Ben can hear the music again. He's never heard this song before, but he already likes it: the bass thump, the rhythm of the drumbeat.

"We didn't," Diego grumbles.

"Some guy *stopped* our fight," Luther sounds like he can barely believe the words coming out of his mouth. "Did you see who it was?"

"You'd hauled me over your shoulder, dude. All I could see was the back of your stupid sport coat."

"Did you get hurt?" Allison asks Luther with genuine concern.

"No," Luther answers. Ben can hear the pride in his brother's voice. Luther loves showing off for Allison.

"I'm fine, too, thanks for asking," Diego interjects.

Luther turns back to Ben. "I swear, Ben, there was no way this guy should've been strong enough to stop us. He was, like . . . *scrawny*. But he put his hand on my chest and I swear, I couldn't move."

"Weird," Allison says.

"Yeah," Ben agrees, feeling uneasy.

"And it's not the first weird thing to happen tonight," Luther says. "Did any of you notice when you got here that the house is practically coated in dust?"

"It's a frat house, Luther," Diego says. "I don't think these guys put that much effort into cleaning up dust bunnies."

"No, like, not normal dust. This is more like the dust upstate. Like, construction dust. It's everywhere."

"Maybe they're building some new structure on campus," Allison suggests with a shrug.

Ben has to admit, he'd been ignoring the dust, but the longer the night's gone on, the harder it is to overlook. The air is growing thick with it. But none of the other partygoers seemed to mind, so Ben didn't either. It wouldn't be fitting in to be bothered by something that didn't bother anyone else.

"Okay, but what about the earthquakes?" Luther asks.

"One by the thrift shop and the other upstate," Ben supplies, but Luther shakes his head.

"Haven't any of you noticed that the house is shaking?"

Ben hadn't noticed. He thought it was the loud music making the walls vibrate all night. But now that Luther points it out, he realizes—there's something in the air that's vibrating a whole lot harder than a drum solo.

Before Ben can try to make sense of it, something *whooshes* past him, literally making his hair stand on end.

"What the hell was that?" Allison shouts.

"I better get Klaus and Viktor—" Ben starts, but Luther interrupts.

"Before I forget," Luther says. "Look!" He pulls a wallet from his pocket. "That guy on the street was a student here. Mateo. I wanted to see if someone here knew him. Could get this back to him."

"Always a Goody Two-shoes," Diego mumbles.

"It's not Goody Two-shoes not to steal someone's wallet," Luther insists.

This is like herding cats, Ben thinks miserably. It'll be a miracle if he can get his siblings out of here before dawn. Luther will never leave now that this feels like a mission. He's practically programmed to fix problems instead of walk away from them, even problems that are none of his business.

Whatever it was that *whooshed* past the siblings before *whooshes* past them again.

"What is that?" Allison asks.

This time, Ben makes out the shape of a person speeding past them.

And it all clicks into place.

"Oh my god," he says. "The scrawny guy who was strong enough to break up your fight. This girl speeding past us—don't you see?"

They all look at him blankly. He sighs. Sometimes he wonders how his siblings have survived this long without simple common sense.

"These kids must be like *us*," Ben says finally.

"No one's like us," Allison points out, flipping her messed-up hair over one shoulder with such aplomb Ben wonders how she ever had trouble fitting in with the mean girls. "We're the only members of the Umbrella Academy."

"Yeah, but there were other kids born the day we were born, born the . . ." He hesitates, trying to think of the right way to say it. "Born the *way* we were born. Dad only got seven. There were more."

"What are the odds a bunch of them would end up here tonight?" Diego asks.

"What are the odds Dad ended up with the seven of us?" Ben counters with a shrug. "Think about it. What else makes sense?"

"Didn't you guys notice anything weird at this party before I got here?" Luther asks. The siblings look at each other, blinking. Luther throws up his hands in exasperation. "Dad always said to take note of our surroundings the instant we step into a room."

"He was talking about missions, not parties," Diego complains. "That was the whole point of going out tonight. To have a night off. Apparently, everyone except Luther under-stood that."

"Well, I'm not sorry that I've been paying attention," Luther counters. "Someone has to."

"Oh my god, you've never sounded more like Dad!" Diego rolls his eyes.

"That's not—whatever, just, look," Luther holds up Mateo's student ID. "It says his birthday right here—July 1, 1988. He's older than we are. And his hands were black and like . . . smoky."

"Smoky?" Ben echoes.

"I thought it must've been from the lightning strike, but—"

The superspeeder *whooshes* past them again, but this time, Ben's ready. He darts out with just one of his tentacles—there's no point in trying to be *normal* anymore; the cat's out of the bag—and catches her. The clothes he took from the thrift shop don't have openings like his uniform does, and Ben can feel the fabric of his T-shirt ripping. At least he's not wearing his jacket. The speeder spins on her heel.

"Hey!" she shouts. She seems more irritated by being stopped than surprised about being grabbed by a tentacle. Another clue: The kids at this party are used to weird.

"Can I ask you a question?" Ben says.

"You're literally holding me against my will. It's not like I can stop you."

"Sorry." Ben retracts his tentacle. He tries to be polite to make up for grabbing her. "Would you mind telling me when your birthday is—the day and the year?"

The superspeeder raises an eyebrow. "Didn't anyone ever tell you it's rude to ask a lady her age?"

"I'm sorry—" Ben begins, but she laughs.

"I'm kidding. Screw that ageist patriarchal BS. My birthday's April 8, 1988."

She speeds away before Ben can ask another question.

"How is that possible?" he asks.

"Well, of course they're older than us," Allison explains. "They're in college. We haven't even graduated high school yet."

"We never went to high school," Diego points out.

"Okay, but I meant if we had gone to high school, we wouldn't have graduated yet."

"So I should come to you for my hypothetical diploma this spring?" Diego starts marching in place, humming the graduation song.

"Don't talk to her like that," Luther breaks in.

Ben rolls his eyes. Are they really going to start fighting again?

"You guys are totally missing the point!" Ben shouts. His siblings look at him in surprise. It's not like Ben to lose his temper.

"What's the point, mon frère?" another voice asks.

Ben flinches with surprise as Klaus drapes his arms around Ben's shoulders from behind.

"And where the hell have you been?" Ben asks. He has to stop himself from brushing the blood off his brother's lip.

"Careful there, Benny, add a 'Number Three' and you'll sound exactly like dear old Dad."

"Number Four," Allison corrects. She's Number Three.

"We thought there had to be other October first kids here, but everyone's older than us," Ben explains.

"Not everyone," Klaus answers, his voice drawling. Ben can tell his brother's high.

"What are you talking about?" Ben asks.

"Rumor has it there's a kid upstairs who's been camping out in the frat house for weeks even though he's still in high school."

"What?" Ben asks.

"Yeah, after I jumped off the roof, everyone was like, *We have to introduce you!*"

"You jumped off the roof?" Guess that explains why Ben saw him coming back in through the front door. Ben isn't the least bit surprised.

"Jumped, fell . . ." Klaus shrugs. "I don't like to get caught up in semantics. Let's just say I was on the roof, and now I'm back on solid ground."

"Why haven't they kicked this guy out?" Allison asks, trying to get them back on track.

"What's with all the questions?" Klaus whines. "This is a party!"

"It's turned into a mission," Luther answers seriously, and Klaus stomps his foot.

"That is not what tonight was supposed to be about!"

Ben can't remember the last time Klaus sounded this invested in anything. "What are you so upset for?" Ben asks. He gets the feeling it's more than a mission destroying his buzz.

Instead of answering, Klaus blinks, looking confused, but for once, Ben gets the sense that Klaus is faking his spaciness.

"Whatever," Klaus shrugs. "Apparently, this kid is the life of the party."

"Then what's he doing upstairs instead of down here?" Allison asks.

"Who is he, anyway?" Luther asks.

"Yeah," Diego agrees, flexing his knuckles like he's itching for yet another fight.

"Didn't catch his name. Oh wait—I think it was . . . Brian? Ryder? Rain? Something like that."

"Ryan?" Ben guesses.

"Eureka!" Klaus plants a kiss on Ben's cheek. "Johnny, tell the boy what he's won!"

Ben glances around the room, catching sight of the feminist superspeeder, searching for the scrawny guy with superstrength who broke up his brothers' fight. Across the room, a girl holds her fingers up and electric sparks come out of the tips. Someone else has snakes instead of hair coming out of the top of his head, and several of the snakes are swiping beer bottles from other people's hands. Another person appears to be levitating off the ground.

"You guys?" Ben begins. Finally, he has his siblings' undivided attention.

But before he can make the most of it, the ground beneath their feet begins to shake. Again.

"Does anyone know where Viktor is?" Ben asks.

24

VIKTOR

Viktor follows Ryan back up to the fourth floor, but instead of leading the way into his room to play more records, Ryan keeps walking until they're on the roof. Viktor breathes in the cool, crisp air. Up here, he can't hear any of the music from the party below. The sky above is clear, but the city never gets dark enough for the stars to be very bright.

"Do you ever miss living in a small town?" Viktor asks. "I mean, I know you had to get away, but don't you ever miss being able to see the stars?"

Ryan doesn't hesitate before shaking his head. "Nope," he answers firmly. "I hated it there."

Viktor never allowed himself to question whether he loves or hates his home. Until tonight, it never occurred to him that it might not be his home forever.

A group of kids dressed in black are crowded at one edge of the roof, looking down at the ground below.

"Ryan!" one of them shouts. "Some guy fell off the roof! But he was *totally fine*."

"Yeah, he got right back up, like falling off the roof was nothing," another adds, a girl wearing a tight black skirt and ripped-up fishnet stockings. "Ryan, you've gotta meet this guy!"

"Sounds good, Bianca," Ryan answers with an easy smile, as though someone jumping off the roof—and then surviving it—doesn't faze him at all. "You know I'm always happy to meet new people."

Viktor's used to weirdness, having grown up at the academy—a talking chimp, a robot mother, six superpowered siblings—but he's surprised that Ryan barely bats an eye at the strangeness of someone who can jump off the roof and bounce back up without a scratch. He wonders how Ryan got so good at handling weird.

Before Viktor can ask, the girl named Bianca adds, "Not that this guy really needs your help. I swear he can, like, commune with the dead."

Inwardly, Viktor groans. Of course this girl—Bianca—is talking about Klaus. It was only a matter of time before everything became all about Viktor's siblings. As usual.

But still, Ryan seems unimpressed. At least, he's not rushing after Bianca's friends to meet Klaus downstairs. Instead, Ryan keeps his focus on Bianca, still lingering on the roof, looking at him hopefully. Her fishnet stockings are tucked into thick-soled boots. Her eyes are rimmed with thick liner. *It's similar*, Viktor thinks, *to the makeup*

Klaus put on tonight. Bianca's bleached blonde hair is stick-straight and parted down the middle, dyed red on the ends. She's wearing wine-colored lipstick and has a hoop through her lower lip. There are black tattoos running up and down her arms. Viktor makes out the shape of a mermaid, an eagle, a horse, a butterfly, like the girl has her own private menagerie.

Viktor wonders what it would be like to permanently mark up his skin. Until tonight, he never had the freedom to pick out his own clothes. He can't imagine Hargreeves letting any member of the Umbrella Academy do something as drastic as getting a tattoo—except for the one he sanctioned, an umbrella and their arms. Viktor watched his siblings get inked, at once relieved not to be forced into getting a tattoo *and* jealous of his siblings; the tattoo was another thing that set Viktor apart from them.

Maybe there will come a time when Hargreeves isn't in charge of what Viktor wears, how long his hair is, whether his skin is clean or inked. Maybe there will come a time when no one will remember that his father called him Number Seven and his mother called him Viktor. Ryan said he left his family behind and found his people. Viktor tries to imagine himself living somewhere far from this city, just like how Ryan packed up his life and never looked back at Dobbsville.

The name is like an itch in Viktor's brain. Why has he heard of it?

And what did Bianca mean when she said that Klaus didn't need Ryan's help? Ryan's helped Viktor tonight just by befriending him. But Klaus has never needed that kind of help.

Before Viktor can work out the answers, Ryan is talking to Bianca again.

"Why were you trying to commune with the dead, Bianca?" Ryan's voice is soft and slippery, different from how he sounded when he and Viktor were alone in his room, listening to music together.

"Well, you know, the whole mystery around Jason's death . . ."

Ryan cocks his head to the side. "Was it really Jason you were hoping to speak with?"

Bianca suddenly looks at her feet. Her toes are pointed inward, her shoulders slumping, like she's a little kid being scolded instead of a college student in a miniskirt.

"Not exactly," she mumbles.

Ryan crosses the roof and places his hand under Bianca's chin. When Bianca looks up, her eyes are very bright.

"My grandmother died last year," she begins.

"I know." Ryan's voice shifts again; now, he sounds like he's never cared about anything more. It's the same way he sounded when he told Viktor he needed someone to play Bach with. The sort of voice that makes the person on the receiving end of it feel important, as though they're the only person in the room. (Or on the roof.)

"I mean, I really did care about getting to the bottom of what happened to Jason!" Bianca insists. "It's just that I thought, maybe we could solve the mystery of Jason's death and while we did, I could say goodbye to my grandmother, too."

Tears spill over onto Bianca's cheeks.

Viktor wonders whether Ryan's voice is about to change again. Will he admonish Bianca for lying about her motivations? For being stuck in the past instead of living in the here and now? For crying? That's what Hargreeves would do. Viktor shivers, thinking of his father's reaction, reminding himself that Ryan isn't Hargreeves; Ryan is a teenager, just like Viktor.

But there's something about Ryan that Viktor can't quite put his finger on. He calls himself an outsider, like Viktor, but his voice holds the same kind of magic Klaus's has—like there's not a room he can't captivate. But then, Ryan's voice can also hold authority the way Hargreeves's does. When he speaks, people listen. But there's something else, too. Hargreeves's voice can make you feel small and insignificant even as it's entirely focused on you. Ryan's voice takes that focus and makes the listener feel *bigger*.

It reminds Viktor of the violin; how one little instrument can make so many sounds—it can sound thin and reedy, or rich and wild. Still, despite its infinite variations, a listener can always tell exactly which instrument they're hearing. Viktor never knew that a *person* could do that, too.

Viktor notices that he isn't the only person on the roof paying attention to Ryan and Bianca's conversation.

In fact, it seems to Viktor that everyone on the roof is

watching Ryan, taking steps closer to him, drawn to him as if he's a magnet.

Viktor can't help himself. He moves closer to Ryan, too. He thinks Ryan might be the most special person he ever met—despite having grown up in a house of spectacularly gifted people.

"Our friend Bianca is suffering," Ryan announces to the crowd. His voice is different once again, loud and clear. Everyone nods and murmurs in response. No one cracks a joke to break the tension. No one dismisses Bianca's pain. No one laughs at her for crying or criticizes her for lying.

Ryan takes Bianca's hands in his own. Quietly, he asks Bianca a question Viktor can't hear, but he thinks he hears her answer.

Voice shaking, she responds, "I want the power not to feel grief anymore," she says.

"Are you sure?" Ryan asks. Bianca nods quickly.

"Really sure?" Ryan repeats.

"I'm positive," Bianca answers, loud enough that Viktor is sure he hears every word correctly.

The small crowd that's gathered around them seems to hold its breath. Viktor's holding his breath, too, though he can't figure out why. It feels as though something important is about to happen.

Where Ryan and Bianca's hands meet, Viktor sees a faint flicker of light, as if there's a candle burning between their palms. The ground beneath their feet begins to shake. Viktor swears he can feel the building itself swaying, as though it's been hit by a strong breeze. Suddenly, the air is thick with dust. Viktor's eyes water, and he starts coughing.

The crowd around him doesn't seem the least bit troubled by the dust in the air or the unstable ground beneath them. Instead, they burst into cheers.

"Ryan! Ryan! Ryan!" They chant his name.

Viktor finds himself joining in. Ryan catches his eye and smiles slowly. Viktor glows under the attention. For once, he feels like he's part of something bigger than himself, instead of watching something so much bigger than him from the outside looking in. It feels good, participating from the *inside* for a change.

VIKTOR

The crowd surges toward Bianca—slapping her on the back, shaking her hand, giving her high-fives. Someone musses her blond hair. Static electricity in the air makes it look like it's standing up straight.

Someone says, "Congratulations!."

Then another person chimes in, "Way to go!"

And another, "My sister died last year. Wish I'd thought of that when it was my turn."

When what *was your turn?* Viktor wonders. What did Ryan whisper to Bianca before she asked for the ability not to feel grief anymore?

No—she didn't ask for the ability. She asked for the *power.*

Bianca says, "Maybe Ryan will give you another chance," Bianca says.

"Do you think it's possible to have more than one?"

More than one what? Viktor almost asks. But the answer hits him before he can form the words.

Ryan isn't ordinary, like him. And not because he has a voice that shifts and slithers like a shape-shifter—people without powers can do that, if they try. But ordinary people don't have friends who talk about powers.

Viktor takes a step back, then another. His teeth start to chatter. Wasn't he wearing a jacket earlier? The old bomber jacket that smelled faintly of someone else's cologne. He must've left it downstairs. That's right; he took it off in Ryan's room, when they were discussing Bach. He better go get it. He doesn't want to lose it. It's his favorite thing he's ever worn. He's almost toward the door leading back downstairs when he feels a hand on his shoulder.

It's Ryan. With the crowd focused on Bianca, he must've managed to slip away.

"Where are you going?" he asks. His voice is friendly and warm once more.

"I'm gonna get my jacket," Viktor explains. "I'm cold."

"It's not that cold out," Ryan insists. Ryan's face glows with sweat, as though he's just run a race.

Viktor nods toward Bianca. "What was going on there," Viktor gestures at the crowd around Bianca, "with that girl?"

"It's hard to explain." Ryan smiles, but the smile doesn't quite reach his eyes.

Viktor sighs. He's used to people dismissing his questions. But much to his surprise, Ryan takes his hands.

"It'd be easier," Ryan says, his voice barely a whisper, "to show you."

"Show me what?" Viktor asks. He isn't entirely sure that he wants to know the answer yet but he wants to be shown more than anything. How is it possible to feel both ways at once?

Instead of answering, Ryan squeezes Viktor's hands tightly in his, just like he did with Bianca moments earlier. Like Viktor, Ryan is small and skinny, but his grip is stronger than Viktor expected, his fingers long and thin, his skin pale and smooth. Viktor's own fingers are scarred and callused from practicing his violin. Viktor tries to pull away, but Ryan holds fast.

"You're shivering," Ryan says.

"I told you I was cold."

"And I told you it wasn't that cold." There's suddenly an edge in his voice, the same one that was there when he asked Bianca about talking to the dead. Ryan stares intently at Viktor, but this time, Ryan's gaze makes Viktor feel like he's the only person in the world, and Viktor doesn't like it. He wishes Ryan would break eye contact.

Viktor can't explain why he's suddenly scared of his new friend. Just a few minutes ago, he'd never felt more comfortable with anyone else.

"I know what it's like to be the odd man out, always on the outside. Let me help you," Ryan says softly, his voice oily and smooth. "Let me help you."

Ryan squeezes Viktor's hands. "Sometimes I let people choose, like with Bianca," Ryan explains. "But sometimes, I can tell what someone needs better than they can."

"Do you think you know what I need?" Viktor asks. "You haven't known me very long."

"It doesn't take long." Ryan's grip remains firm.

"Is it so obvious?" Viktor feels like his uselessness must be written on his skin. He might as well be holding up a sign that says his siblings are special, and he's not.

"You're special, Viktor," Ryan says. It feels as though Ryan is reading his mind. "Just because other people don't see it, doesn't mean I can't."

"And now," Ryan continues, "I'll make sure everyone knows just how special you are."

Yes, Viktor thinks, his heart pounding in his chest. *That is what I most want. For my siblings, for Hargreeves, to see I'm special, just like they are.*

Viktor waits for a flicker of light, some kind of surge of energy, but nothing happens.

"What the hell?" Ryan mumbles. A bead of sweat drips from his forehead down his cheek, and his face looks strained, as though he's trying to lift a weight that is too heavy. But he holds fast.

"Let me try that again," Ryan says, louder this time. Viktor can't help noticing that the same crowd that was looking at Bianca earlier is now staring at him. All these eyes on him make Viktor's skin crawl. He thinks of the flash of camera bulbs and shouted questions that used to follow his siblings from one place to another.

"I don't want anything," Viktor says abruptly. If Ryan weren't holding his hands, Viktor might reach for a pill to calm himself.

"You're lying," Ryan says, his voice as sharp as a razor's

edge. "Everyone wants something. Everyone wants to be more than they already are."

Is that true? Viktor wonders. He doesn't think his siblings want to be anything more than what they are. But tonight, Ben practically leaped at the chance to be normal. Klaus couldn't get out of the house fast enough. Allison was so determined to find the perfect outfit; Diego practically itched with energy. Viktor has spent his whole life comparing himself to his siblings, wishing he could have the gifts they had, wondering what unique power he was supposed to have been born with. Over the years, Viktor never imagined that his siblings might have wished to be something else, too.

Ryan squeezes Viktor's hands tighter. The ground rumbles gently beneath his feet, as though the earth itself were letting out a deep breath. Viktor's throat tickles; he can't stop coughing. There's so much dust in the air that his eyes burn. As his hands grow slick with sweat, Viktor's finally able to free himself from Ryan's grip.

Suddenly, Viktor knows exactly the right thing to say. "When is your birthday?" he asks.

"October 1, 1989," Ryan answers. Ryan smiles, and Viktor knows that Ryan understands why Viktor asked. "When's yours?" Ryan demands. His face isn't relaxed into a smile. Instead, his lips are pressed into a straight line.

"It's not important," Viktor answers quickly, and he means it. Even if his birth was miraculous, he doesn't have the sort of powers other October first children do. "I mean, I'm not supposed to be here. I'm too young for college." *So are you*, Viktor thinks but doesn't say. Ryan isn't supposed to be here any more than the Umbrella Academy is. "We crashed this party," Viktor adds. Maybe Ryan will have Viktor and his siblings kicked out. Maybe they can go home and Viktor will be able to forget he ever met this guy.

"*We*?" Ryan echoes. He sounds intrigued. "I thought you were alone."

Viktor shakes his head. "I mean, I *was* here alone. But I didn't come here alone."

"Who did you come with?"

"My siblings," Viktor explains. "They're probably wondering where I am." Can Ryan tell he's lying? Viktor isn't even sure his siblings remember he's here. He tries to recall what each of them were doing when he last saw them: Klaus didn't notice Viktor following him up the stairs (and then he apparently swan-dived off the roof); Allison, Diego, and Ben disappeared into the crowd on the first floor; and Luther stayed behind at the thrift shop. They've probably made a million friends. Wherever they are, they're probably the life of the party. They don't want to hear that their useless sibling has gotten himself into some kind of trouble on the roof.

"Siblings?" Ryan echoes.

"Yeah. We're the Hargreeves," Viktor answers instead of saying *We're the Umbrella Academy*. He wants to make them sound like an ordinary family; an ordinary family would say their last name, not the name of their academy, right? Of course, an ordinary family wouldn't be part of an academy.

"*Hargreeves?*" Ryan echoes. He spits the name like it's a dirty word.

Viktor can see recognition crossing Ryan's face. His stomach drops. What was he thinking? Of course their name is as abnormal as the academy itself. Hargreeves, as in *Reginald Hargreeves*. As in their mother who's a machine, their butler who isn't a human being, their house that isn't a home but a training facility.

"I thought there are only six members of the Umbrella Academy," Ryan continues, incredulous. "Five, since your brother died."

"He didn't die." Viktor feels defensive. He's heard Ben interrogating Klaus each and every day since Five disappeared. According to Klaus, there's been no sign of Five among the dead. After years of watching his siblings, Viktor can tell when Klaus is lying, and he's never lied about that. Not yet.

Ryan continues as though Viktor hadn't said anything. "So the great Umbrella Academy deigned to grace my party with their presence."

"*Your* party?" Viktor is confused. Then he remembers how Ryan said the fraternity gave him his choice of room. At the time, Viktor was so excited that he and Ryan would have chosen the same room that he hadn't stopped to question why Ryan had first choice. And the way Tish apologized for forgetting their drinks and offered to change the music—as though Ryan's experience mattered more than her own.

Ryan folds his arms across his chest. "And they sent you

upstairs to gather intel." His voice has changed again, into an almost growl. Viktor thinks Ryan sounds angrier than Hargreeves ever has. His voice is more frightening somehow because he isn't yelling, because there isn't spittle forming at the edges of his lips, because he isn't gesticulating wildly. He seems completely calm.

"No—" Viktor breaks in, but Ryan continues.

"Was that your brother who fell off the roof?" Ryan continues. "The one who can commune with the dead? Klaus, right?"

When Viktor nods, he realizes how much he's shivering. The air is thick with dust, but no one on the roof moves to go inside. Viktor supposes that shouldn't be surprising; they weren't disturbed by the earthquake even though they're unheard of in this part of the country.

Almost as if they were expecting it.

Before Viktor can put the pieces together, Ryan continues, "Your team must've gotten wind that there was a new act in town. Someone even more powerful than the Umbrella Academy."

"What are you talking about?" Viktor asks. No one's more powerful than the Umbrella Academy. Despite Hargreeves's endless criticisms, they've yet to fail at a single mission. Not entirely, anyway.

"The Umbrella Academy is limited by the powers they possess."

Viktor shakes his head. This doesn't make any sense. His siblings' powers aren't *limits*. Quite the opposite.

"But my powers? Mine are unlimited," Ryan explains,

spreading his arms wide. "What could be more unlimited than the ability to empower *others*?"

Ryan waves his hands like a magician performing a trick, and the crowd cheers.

Behind him, someone sprouts wings, scaled and leathery, like a dragon's. Someone else's eyes radiate red, boring an actual hole into the roof beneath their feet. These college kids may be older than Viktor and his siblings, but they seem to be imbued with the same sorts of gifts. The earth shakes every time one of them displays their new powers.

For the first time, Viktor appreciates Hargreeves's strict rules. Without them, the Umbrella Academy might have used their powers irresponsibly—to get their own way, instead of to help people.

Ryan raises his voice as he announces and turns to address the crowd, "The Umbrella Academy came here tonight to take your gifts away!"

"No!" Viktor yells, but his voice isn't nearly as loud or commanding as Ryan's. "We didn't. We were just trying to be *normal*—"

At the word *normal*, Ryan and his acolytes burst into laughter. The sound makes Viktor want to cover his ears.

"That's the worst lie I've ever heard," Ryan says. "Who among us would choose to be ordinary when they could be *powerful*?"

Viktor squeezes his hands open and shut. Why didn't Ryan's power work on him?

What power was Ryan going to choose for him?

What power would he have chosen if he'd been given the chance to choose?

Before Viktor can make up his mind, the crowd is headed straight for him. No, not for *him*. They're moving toward the stairs. Ryan grabs a tall girl's hand. "Your bite is poisonous," he announces, then grabs the hand of someone wearing an oversized hoodie: "Everything you touch turns to stone." He's granting powers like he's giving out candy.

The earth beneath the fraternity house shakes.

Of course no one was surprised when the earth shook earlier, Viktor realizes. *They were* expecting *it. Whenever Ryan's acolytes use their powers, the earth shakes.*

His siblings thought the earthquake outside the thrift shop tonight was an aftershock from the one upstate.

Viktor starts coughing again as dust fills the air. His siblings were covered in dust when they arrived back home this evening.

Earthquakes, dust.

They thought it was a corrupt oil company.

But what if it was Ryan and his followers—Viktor can't think of them as friends anymore—all along?

But how? The mission this morning was so far from the city.? There's no time for Viktor to put the pieces together, to connect all the fragments connected like a puzzle, the same way he breaks down the notes and puts them back together when he's learning a new piece of music.

Viktor has to get to his siblings before Ryan and his friends do.

CHAPTER 26

LUTHER

As the ground beneath them heaves and shifts, rather than running for cover, the kids around them erupt into cheers.

"Ryan!" they shout, like he's the star of their favorite team and he's just scored another point.

"What's going on?" Luther shouts.

"It must be Ryan," Diego answers. "His power is probably the ability to cause earthquakes, right?"

Luther shakes his head.

"That doesn't explain everyone else." Mateo's black hands, the gifted people around them.

Luther thinks of the ID in his pocket. "How did all these other people get powers?"

"Maybe ours isn't the only miraculous birthday," Allison tries.

"You think if there were some other magic birthday Dad wouldn't have collected those kids, too?" Diego says, and as much as Luther hates to agree with Diego, his brother is right.

"Besides," Ben points out reasonably, "no way do all the kids at this party have the same birthday. We already know that Mateo and the super-speeder don't."

"What else do we know?" Luther begins. "We know that people at this party have powers. We know that upstairs, there's one kid—"

"Ryan," Klaus supplies proudly.

"Ryan," Luther continues, "who *does* have an October 1 birthday."

"We think," Ben says.

"Right, we think," Luther agrees.

"But what if, what if . . . what if Ryan has something to do with everyone else's powers?" Luther asks finally.

"You think Ryan made Mateo collapse on the street?" Allison asks. "How could he, if he was here at the party?"

"We don't know if he was here," Ben says. "If his power's teleporting, maybe he beamed himself from the party to the thrift shop and back again."

Allison looks skeptical. "Why would he have done that?"

"Maybe Ryan hated that Mateo kid," Diego suggests.

"Yeah, but if his power is teleportation, it's not *also* making other people collapse," Luther points out. "And anyway, Mateo didn't collapse. He was knocked out by debris from a falling building that was struck by lightning."

"But why was there lightning at all?" Ben asks. "Maybe Mateo . . . *made* the lightning. Maybe *that's* his power."

"He said . . ." Luther pauses, trying to grasp the memory of what Mateo said before the ambulance took him away. "He said he was *practicing*."

"Practicing using his powers?" Ben suggests.

That would explain things: Mateo made lightning—which comes with the sound of thunder—and that lightning struck the side of a building, causing it to crumble. The power must come from his hands—hence his black and smoky palms.

"But *how* does he have a power?" Luther asks, frustrated.

"How do any of these people?" Ben asks.

"Look around," Allison says gently. "These people are celebrating. They're chanting Ryan's name. They obviously love him."

"Maybe that's his power—he can get people to love him?" Klaus tries.

"And also to celebrate earthquakes?" Diego says. There's mockery in his voice, but Luther tries to ignore it.

"They're cheering Ryan's name like he just won the championship or something," Allison insists. "Their powers, the earthquakes, Ryan—it's all connected. And whatever the connection is, they love it."

"What if . . ." Luther starts, then stops. "No, that can't be it."

"Tell us," Allison begs.

"No, it's too out there," Luther insists.

"We don't need to hear another stupid idea," Diego scoffs. Luther knows that his brother is trying to undermine his authority. "Let's just split up again. I was having a lot more fun when I was on my own."

"Oh yeah, getting the crap beat out of you looked fun," Luther says.

"I was not getting the crap beat out of," Diego insists. "I was winning a fight!"

"Either way, tons of fun," Ben says witheringly. "Luther, please tell us your idea."

"What if Ryan's power is—the ability to give out powers?"

Diego laughs. "Who ever heard of the power to *give* powers?"

"Would you believe it if anyone other than Luther had come up with it?" Ben asks, exasperated. "Seriously—can you think of a better explanation for everything that's happened tonight?"

Diego opens his mouth to say something, but he must not come up with anything good, because no words come out.

"It's not fair," Luther says suddenly.

"What's not fair?" Allison shouts above the din.

"We had each other. We had Hargreeves teaching us how to use our powers. Ryan probably didn't have anyone. And the rest of these kids definitely don't have anyone."

"So?" Diego asks. "Maybe some of us don't need anyone else."

"So, they probably don't know how to use their powers properly."

"Ryan seems pretty aware of how to use them," Ben suggests reasonably. If Ryan didn't understand his powers, how could so many of their fellow partygoers be so gifted?

"I mean, do any of us really know how our powers work?" Klaus adds with a shrug. He's slurring his words. Luther's surprised he's still paying enough attention to make a relevant point. Concentration isn't exactly Klaus's strong suit.

"Yeah, but if he were one of us," Luther continues, "he'd be able to harness his powers. Just think—Dad could build an entire Umbrella Academy army with someone like him."

"You think there should be *more* of us?" Diego mumbles.

It occurs to Luther that Diego's probably worried that this Ryan guy could become the new Number Two, taking Diego down a notch.

Actually, Luther thinks, *that doesn't sound so bad.*

"I don't know, Luther," Ben adds. "The idea of an Umbrella Academy army kind of makes my skin crawl."

Luther shakes his head. None of them are seeing the big picture like he is.

"They're not lucky like we are," he insists. "They didn't have Dad."

"Lucky?" Diego scoffs. "To be raised by *Hargreeves*? Luther, it's clear this Ryan guy is dangerous. I'm with Ben. An Umbrella Academy is not a good idea." Diego continues, "We should take this guy out, not invite him home like a stray cat."

"You guys, this isn't what tonight was supposed to be," Ben protests. "We should go home—"

"And tell Dad about Ryan," Luther finishes. "You're right. Dad'll know what to do."

"That's not what I was going to say," Ben explains through gritted teeth. "If Dad knows about Ryan, he'll want to add him to his collection."

"We're not his *collection*," Luther insists. "We're his *kids*."

"Not sure Dad knows the difference," Ben says, so quietly that Luther isn't sure he heard him correctly.

But Allison is nodding in agreement. Before Luther can ask her what exactly she's agreeing with, Ben continues.

"Anyway, we're supposed to be normal tonight," he says, louder now. The crowd around them is getting rowdier. Even though Luther and his siblings are standing close, they have to shout to hear each other. "There's nothing *normal* about confronting someone else with powers, whether it's to destroy him or bring him home."

"Listen," Luther takes a deep breath, puffing out his chest. "I'm in charge here. And I say we bring him home."

"You're not in charge of anything," Diego counters. "This isn't a mission."

"It turned into one," Luther insists.

"No!" Ben's almost shouting now. "It didn't. It *isn't*. We're finding Viktor, and we're going home."

"Not without Ryan. Someone could get hurt." Luther starts for the stairs, but before he gets far, he feels something tugging on his shoulder, pinning him to the wall. He looks down and sees that Diego has used a knife to attach Luther's Umbrella Academy jacket to the closest wall. Thanks to Mom's perfect stitching and Hargreeves's insistence on superior materials, the jacket doesn't rip beyond the hole Diego's knife made.

"What the hell, Diego?!" Luther spins around, struggling to pull his brother's knife from the wall.

"If this is a mission, then we're free to use our powers." Diego speaks calmly, as though restraining his brother is was an everyday occurrence.

"Come on, you two." Allison moves to stand between the brothers. Luther's hands curl into fists. Diego grabs another knife, this time pointing it in Allison's direction.

Before he knows what he's doing, Luther's running headlong into Diego. They're falling, but before they hit the ground, Ben's tentacles grab them and set them back on their feet.

"One night!" Ben moans. "Is one night without having to use these things too much to ask?"

"Sorry!" Luther says quickly. Beside him, Diego apologizes, too.

The ground beneath them starts to shake again.

"Another earthquake?" Allison groans.

"One emergency at a time," Luther insists. "We have to take care of Ryan and these other kids."

"We have to neutralize him before he does some real damage," Diego says firmly. "If this guy can give out powers, can you imagine what kind of abilities he's given *himself*?"

"Maybe Luther's right. We should get Dad," Allison suggests, looking nervously between them.

"I'm not going running home to *Daddy*," Diego huffs. "We can handle this guy on our own. Like Luther said, we've been trained, and he hasn't."

That definitely wasn't what Luther meant to say. He didn't mean to suggest that, because the Umbrella Academy is obviously trained, they're equipped to take this Ryan guy out without so much as breaking a sweat. But he meant to say that Ryan deserved to be trained, too. Still, this is the closest Diego's ever come to agreeing with him.

"Fine," Luther says. "But just, you know, restrain him. Don't *hurt* him."

"I'll do whatever it takes," Diego insists, and he makes his way toward the stairs.

Luther runs after his brother, determined to stop Diego before he hurts their new brother. In his imagination, he pictures Dad offering Ryan one of the spare rooms back home. Ryan running drills with them every morning, Ryan coming along on missions. Maybe he'll give powers to local law enforcement so they can help out during missions, too, the earth shaking beneath their feet.

Then again, Dad would hate that, so probably not.

DIEGO

L eave it to Luther to turn their supposedly fun night out into a mission. And leave it to Luther's holier-than-thou, glass-half-full attitude to see this as a *rescue* mission instead of what it really is. At best, they could call it an extraction: Get Ryan out of here and back to the academy so Dad can take charge.

At worst—and maybe this is actually best—it's a catch-and-kill mission.

If Diego were Number One, he could've been the one to decide exactly what kind of mission it was. But even if he'd made the call, Ben would've insisted on having a vote, and Allison, too, and even if Luther were at the bottom of the heap, he'd want a say in things. (Klaus can't pay attention long enough to have an opinion, and Viktor doesn't count.) Maybe being Number One wouldn't fix that.

Diego liked being able to decide all on his own to dance with that redheaded girl; he liked fighting on his own, too, seeing just how many people he could defeat all by himself. It was fun. Until Luther came in and made that all about himself—again.

Actually, now that he thinks about it, Diego was having plenty of fun before Luther showed up to insist they all work together.

Okay, so it wasn't exactly *fun* when he first got here. Diego was so nervous he didn't think he'd be able to keep still, and the only thing that let him plant his feet on the floor was the feel of his knives pressing into his skin. He's bleeding a little, he can tell. One of the knives nicked his right thigh just below his hip bone. But he doesn't mind. Sure, it hurts, but it's also a reminder of just how close his knives are. How easily he could reach for one if he needed it.

And he's definitely going to need one now.

What if he'd kept dancing with that girl, though? What if he'd had another beer instead of picking a fight?

What if, when Luther showed up, Diego and his dance partner had disappeared into one of the rooms upstairs, completely oblivious to all the mischief that some random guy named Ryan had caused?

Maybe they'd have gotten out of here entirely. Maybe she'd have taken him across campus to her dorm room, and Diego would've had an entire night off from his siblings and their mayhem. A night on his own. An adventure all his own. And at no point would he have been Number Two relegated to do whatever Number One decreed.

Maybe all that would've happened if only Diego hadn't picked a fight on the dance floor.

But what was he supposed to do when that boy bumped into him? Just walk away?

That's not how he was raised. And more to the point, he doesn't *want* to. It's not in his nature to walk away from a fight.

It's not like he can walk away *now*, not with some kid upstairs handing out powers and making the earth shake and who knows what else.

Diego pulls a knife from each side of his waistband, twirling the blades between his fingers as he makes his way up the stairs.

He may have been nervous when they first got here tonight, but he's not nervous anymore.

ALLISON

Allison follows her brothers upstairs. All her life, every time the Umbrella Academy embarked on a mission, Allison's gotten a rush of adrenaline: They were off to save the day, use their training, display their powers. Most of all, people watched them doing it. People cheered. Allison has always thought there was no feeling better than that. The applause, the adoration. What was that, if not love?

But taking one stair after another tonight, Allison's legs feel like they weigh a thousand pounds. Rather than a rush of adrenaline, there's a tug of reluctance.

She doesn't want to ascend the stairs. She doesn't want to engage in battle. What she wants, more than anything, is to sit down on the couch with her new friends. She wants to go back in time, before they were fighting and continue gossiping about love interests and fashion trends. That sounds so much more exciting than saving everyone here from whatever sort of havoc this Ryan person is wreaking.

It hits Allison suddenly that Luther wouldn't understand if she told him that. And Luther's always understood everything about her. But she's certain he wouldn't be able to make sense of *this*. She can hardly make sense of it herself. Sitting with those girls—before everything exploded into a fight—felt so good. It felt even more meaningful to be *one of the girls* instead of the crime-fighting machine she was raised to be. And when Jenny, Leticia, and May laughed at Allison's jokes, it felt more like love than all the applause in the world, all the photographers snapping her photo, the fans crowded outside her house calling her name. Even if she'd had to rumor them to get her friends' attention— once she had it, it was *incredible*.

Allison's purple dress swishes with each step she takes. It was designed for dancing, not fighting. The skirt is meant to twirl out wide when her dance partner spins her around in circles, not when she spins around to meet an adversary.

Allison wonders: What if she'd been like Ryan—born with powers, but raised outside of the Umbrella Academy? Raised by a real family. Of course, Allison has no idea how Ryan was raised, but in her imagination, she sees him with two parents, living in an ordinary house with a yard and a driveway in the suburbs, a couple of younger siblings. All of them wear knapsacks to school, and they eat lunches they carry in brown paper bags: peanut butter and jelly and juice boxes. Ryan cheers at his younger siblings' Little League games; he groans when his parents force him to babysit on a Saturday night, but secretly he loves spending time with them.

Allison's feet slide around in her purple high heels. She'd known they were half a size too big when she tried them on at the store, but she didn't think it mattered much. She hadn't expected to be running, to be on a mission.

Maybe if Allison had been raised like the Ryan in her imagination, she never would have discovered her power. What are the odds she'd have used just the right phrase at just the right time? Certainly, she'd have learned how to interact with other people without relying on her powers to get them to listen to her. Wouldn't she?

One thing's for sure: She never would've trained in combat. She wouldn't have been forced to get a tattoo. Her siblings would be her *siblings*, not her teammates. And sure, that means her face wouldn't have been splashed on magazine covers, and she'd never have met Luther, but—

There are other ways to meet people. Other ways to be famous. Other reasons to be praised.

"C'mon, Allison!" Luther shouts. He's taking the stairs two at a time, several steps ahead of her. She puts her head down and runs after him.

The adrenaline finally makes an appearance, humming beneath her skin, pushing her up the stairs more quickly. She feels a sheen of sweat rising on the back of her neck, behind her knees. Regardless of how she feels, her body knows how to do this.

KLAUS

ood lord, where are his siblings running to now? And why were they fighting before? He's never seen Ben use his tentacles to pull Luther and Diego apart. Has he? Come to think of it, it's a miracle that hasn't happened before. You'd think it would happen every day, multiple times a day, the way Luther and Diego bicker.

"I'm Number One."

"Well, I should be."

"Nah-nah, nah-nah, I'm Number One."

Like they're members of a team instead of a family. Klaus envisions himself as a cheerleader holding pom-poms, cheering his brothers on from the sidelines. He'd look *amazing* in a cheerleading uniform. And it would make a nice change from his Academy uniform. And he would totally be at the top of the pyramid, given the chance.

Give me a U!

Give me an M!

Give me a B!

Give me a . . .

Klaus shakes his head. Too much spelling.

The fighting, the running, the spelling—it's all ruining the good vibes! Seriously, Klaus's siblings have no idea how to behave at a party. He wanted them to experience it for themselves, to figure out their party personas all on their own. Because if there's one thing Klaus understands, it's that there are about a zillion different ways to party. Some people are wallflowers, and some people (like him) are the life of the party, and some people want to get lost in the crowd. Until tonight, Klaus didn't think there was a *wrong* way to party, but turns out, there is. Because the rest of the Umbrella Academy are definitely doing it wrong.

And now there they go, up the stairs, calling some name— *Ryan!*—like he's their mortal enemy.

Everyone here *loves* Ryan. Don't his siblings know that if they turn against Ryan, the rest of the party will turn against them? *Against* us, Klaus thinks, remembering that he's one of them. One of *us.*

Us is the Umbrella Academy. The greatest crime-fighting-team-slash-family the world has ever known!

Other people join teams when they're in high school: basketball, soccer, rugby. Other people are born into their families. Somehow Klaus and his teammates-slash-siblings found their team-slash-family differently from literally every other person on the planet. He can't quite make sense of it now. Though he finds himself wondering if he'd even be able to make sense of it sober. He's not sure. Most people who join a team get to choose their sport; they have to try out, and some coach decides whether they're good enough. Klaus guesses Hargreeves is kind of like a coach. Viktor is kind of like someone who didn't make the team and got relegated to equipment manager or something—still always hanging around, but not really a part of things.

But when normals don't make the team, they can try out again. Or they can join some other team, try some other sport. They don't have to keep living with their coach and their would-be teammates.

Most of all, normals can leave their team behind anytime they want.

Actually, Klaus thinks, *that's not a privilege exclusive to regular people.* He doesn't need to be a normal to be a dropout. He just has to pick the right time. And tonight isn't the right time.

So Klaus follows his sibling-teammates up the stairs. Though his pace is a bit more lackadaisical than theirs.

Lackadaisical. That's a funny word.

Word is funny word, when you think about it.

Word. Wooord. Wooooord.

Just a hop, skip, and a jump to *whooooo* or *whooosh* or any of those other sounds that people who don't know any better associate with ghosts and spirits.

At least he has a break from all *those* voices for now, thanks to the booze and the drugs—it's good shit, whatever it is. Unfortunately, Luther is shouting nearly as loudly as the ghosts do.

"Let's go!" he calls.

And Diego adds, "Outta my way!"

Klaus hears Allison's breath quickening as she breaks into a run, the taffeta of her purple dress flying out behind her like a cape.

Ben looks at him from a couple stairs above. "Keep up, Klaus!" Ben sounds worried, not pumped the way Luther does. Like he isn't sure what will happen to Klaus if he lets him out of his sight.

The only teammate-sibling voice missing is Viktor's. Where is he, anyway?

Guess it makes sense, Klaus thinks hazily, remembering that Viktor never comes along for missions. *But he did come tonight. So where does that leave him in this team-slash-family?*

This is way too complicated for a night out. The next time he sneaks out, he's not asking his siblings to come with him. They have no idea how to party.

All they know is how to carry out a mission.

CHAPTER

30

BEN

I t was too much to hope for an ordinary night—Ben knows
that now. He barely breaks a sweat as he runs up the stairs,
his body conditioned for combat. Beneath his skin, he can
feel his tentacles twisting and stretching around his internal
organs. At least some part of him is excited.

What would happen, he wonders, if his tentacles were
amputated? People live without arms and legs all the time;
feet are removed at the ankles, fingers lost to frostbite and
gangrene. Could he survive without his tentacles? What if
they got terribly damaged in a fight, injured beyond repair?

He's heard of phantom limb syndrome, the phenomenon
that occurs when an amputee continues to feel the append-
age that's been removed. Would he continue to feel his tentacles if they were gone? Maybe they would grow back, the
way a starfish's points can regenerate if it's lost. He shudders
at the thought; it makes him feel less human.

Sometimes, even when his tentacles are tucked away, he can feel them. Not only the way they move beneath his skin; he can feel the weight of them, like a backpack he's never allowed to take off. He knows Luther is technically the "strong one" among his siblings, but he bets that his shoulders are even more powerful than Luther's, given what he's had to carry all these years.

Even tonight, playing pool and doing his best to ignore his tentacles, Ben was never unaware of them. They shifted beneath his skin, twitching to be set free. That's something else no one could possibly understand: His tentacles hate being tucked away. If they had their way, they'd never retract. They have desires entirely separate from the rest of Ben's body and mind. His siblings assume that his tentacles are *part* of him, but Ben's always experienced them as something *other*: some foreign object that's been stitched into his muscles and bones. He's never told anyone that it hurts every time they break through his skin. He nearly told Klaus once, but he knew that Klaus wouldn't be able to keep it to himself. Klaus would never *intend* to break Ben's confidence, but he can't be trusted to remember that he'd promised to keep anything secret in the first place.

Tonight, Ben came the closest he ever had to forgetting about his tentacles. Or anyway, he did the best job of ignoring them that he ever did. But then Diego and Luther got into it and he didn't even have a chance to hesitate before his tentacles made their grand entrance.

And now they're more excited than ever, knowing that a fight is forthcoming as Ben follows his siblings up the stairs. Only Klaus is behind him. Ben glances back like he thinks his brother might have wandered off, but Klaus is making his way up the stairs, albeit more slowly than the rest of them.

Klaus is the only one of his siblings who Ben guessed would be more interested in parties than powers, and even he used his gift tonight. (As expected, Klaus couldn't be trusted to remember a promise.) And he made a spectacle of himself—though Ben guesses that's inevitable. He isn't sure Klaus knows how to avoid making a spectacle of himself.

So now Ben's running up the stairs. The way is narrow, and the hardwood beneath his feet is sticky, as though someone spilled a beer earlier and never bothered to clean it up. On the railing there are forgotten jackets and scarves. They fall to the ground as Ben and his siblings race upward, the stairs shuddering beneath them. Ben can't tell anymore if the floor is shaking because of another earthquake or because of his siblings' footsteps. Luther and Diego practically looked like they'd won something the instant they realized they could turn tonight into a mission, even if they didn't exactly agree about what the mission should be. It's like they were *relieved* when something went wrong.

Ben supposes he can't blame them. *This* is what they've been trained for, all of them. To recognize the things that aren't right, and then to beat those things into submission. Even Allison sprang into action. It's a reflex, a muscle memory. Almost as if their brains have been hardwired for missions.

Actually, maybe they *were* wired this way. Ben imagines surgeons opening up their skulls while they slept, adjusting their neurochemistry like they're living, breathing science experiments.

It's possible. Ben wouldn't put anything past Hargreeves.

CHAPTER
31

VIKTOR

Viktor can't quite figure out the exact moment Ryan turned from his friend—the first friend, the only friend Viktor had ever made—into something else, someone with a voice like a snake and anger in his eyes. Viktor stumbles down the stairs, trying to catch up to Ryan, but there's a crowd of people in between them. Viktor shouts, but no one's listening. The only person they're listening to is Ryan, and Ryan told them that the Umbrella Academy is their enemy.

Viktor's almost hurt that no one in the crowd bothered going after him, but he's not surprised. Even at a moment like this, with a crowd of people racing to destroy his siblings, Viktor's not enough of a threat to demand attention. Even these strangers know that they'd be wasting their time fighting him.

The stairs are narrow but surprisingly bright after the moonlight up on the roof. Viktor keeps his eyes focused on the back of Ryan's thin frame, even though there are at least a dozen people between them. Ryan's black T-shirt is stretched over his shoulders; Viktor takes in Ryan's short, light brown hair, his faded blue jeans, his beat-up sneakers. Viktor thinks he can make out a sheen on sweat on the nape of Ryan's neck, though he can't be sure whether it's from excitement or fear. Viktor's own palms are damp from Ryan holding them just a few minutes ago.

Was it really only a few minutes ago that they were friends? Just a few minutes ago that Viktor thought Ryan understood him better than his siblings—people who'd known him his whole life rather than just a single evening—ever could?

Viktor imagines what his siblings would say if they knew how easily Viktor fell for Ryan. Of course, Viktor's siblings would've known better. They've had more experience; they've faced enough enemies to recognize one standing in front of them.

On the third-floor landing, Ryan nearly runs headlong into Diego, who picks the smaller boy up by the neck of his T-shirt.

"You must be Ryan," Diego growls, lifting his feet off the ground. Just as Viktor expected: Diego recognized an enemy on sight.

"Diego, don't hurt him!" Luther shouts, coming up from behind. Viktor's surprised to hear Luther say that. Isn't the point of the Umbrella Academy to take their enemies down? Isn't that what Dad's been training them to do all along?

"I'll do what I have to do," Diego says. Luther puts his hands over Diego's, forcing his brother to let go of Ryan. But Luther and Diego plant themselves on either side of Ryan, keeping him from going up or down the stairs.

"Remember," Luther says, "he's one of us."

"He's not one of us," Diego insists.

"But maybe he could be," Luther counters. "We have to give him a chance."

Diego looks skeptical, but he stands down.

"Do I need to be here for this conversation?" Ryan drawls, sounding bored, like they're talking about the weather rather than what to do with him.

Viktor realizes that there's not a doubt in Ryan's mind that he and his friends will overcome the Umbrella Academy, so arguing with the Hargreeves would just be a waste of his time.

Luther digs something out of his pocket and holds it out in front of Ryan. Viktor squints. It looks like a student ID.

"Do you know this boy?" Luther asks. His voice is calm and friendly.

Viktor's siblings have no idea what Ryan shouted on the roof—that he told his friends that the Umbrella Academy is their enemy.

But there's no time for Viktor to explain before Luther continues. "His name is Mateo. He was sent to the hospital—"

"The Umbrella Academy are here to take control!" Ryan's shouts so loud it makes Viktor jump.

"No, we're not," Luther begins. He still sounds cheerful, but Viktor detects the slightest edge to his voice, like he's surprised to find this isn't going according to plan. "We just want to talk to you. I don't know if you realize what you're capable of—"

Ryan knows exactly what he's capable of, Viktor thinks. Viktor saw it on the roof.

Now Ryan shouts over Luther's attempt at peacemaking. "They want to lock us up in their academy until we agree to join forces with them."

"No, we don't," Luther insists.

"Tell me, then, what are your plans for me and my friends?" His voice is icy as he stares Luther down. "How exactly did Hargreeves train you to follow his commands like a puppy?"

"I'm no one's puppy," Diego mutters, but Viktor can tell Ryan hit a nerve.

"They're threatened because together," Ryan laughs, "We're so much more powerful than they could ever be!"

Allison, Ben, and Klaus join their brothers on the third floor. Viktor looks down at his siblings, his heart pounding. They crouch, ready to take on a fight.

The seam of Allison's purple dress tore as she took the last few steps two at a time; it was designed for slow-dancing, not hand-to-hand combat. Viktor wonders if she's upset that her dress is ruined.

Klaus's eyes are barely open; he's definitely high on something. Still, when someone lunges toward him, Klaus parries deftly, so well trained that his body knows what to do even when his brain is foggy.

Ben looks like he might burst into tears, his shoulders slumped. Viktor doesn't think he's ever seen Ben look so disappointed.

Luther's planted in front of Ryan. He smiles crookedly—like half of his face is still hoping to make peace, while the other half knows he may have to fight. He presses his lips together and thrusts his shoulders back like he's determined to at least *look* like he's in control of the situation.

Diego's face is twisted into a scowl. Viktor can't tell whether his brother is angrier at Ryan or Luther for stopping him just when he was about to take Ryan out. *Together,* Viktor thinks, *Luther and Diego look like one of those good cop/bad cop pairings that I've seen on TV.*

For an instant, everything appears almost frozen: Viktor's siblings, Ryan, his horde of friends and followers gathering above and below. Viktor holds his breath, wondering what is going to happen next.

Then, Ryan breaks the silence.

"Don't let them destroy us!" Ryan shouts in the voice Viktor recognizes from the roof, the one that really scares Viktor. "This is what you've been waiting for. Use your powers! Go!"

The crowd of superpowered college students surround the Umbrella Academy—half come from the stairs above them, half from below. Viktor's never seen so many gifted people in one place. He thinks that probably no one ever has, not even Hargreeves. After all, Hargreeves was only able to find seven children to adopt, and one of them doesn't even have powers.

"Why is this happening?" Luther shout.

Viktor knows that Luther expected Ryan to embrace him, because he thinks everyone wants to be like him. Not in an obnoxious, self-satisfied way. Okay, maybe he's a little self-satisfied, but Viktor can't blame Luther for that. For most of Luther's life, everyone *has* wanted to be like him. Number One in the Umbrella Academy, the star of every mission, handsome, tall, strong. It's as though Luther was built to be a mannequin for an old-fashioned "teen boys" section at a department store. *If they'd gone to a regular high school,* Viktor thinks suddenly, *Luther and Allison would've been homecoming king and queen.* Star of the football team and head cheerleader. (Or whatever passes for that kind of status these days. Everything Viktor knows about high school, he learned from eighties movies in their library.) Viktor feels a pang of frustration; there should be more than one way to be the model teen boy. Or girl. Or person altogether.

Instead, Viktor's sure that in a regular high school, he'd be considered the misfit. The kid shoved into lockers between classes, the butt of every joke, so pathetic that even the teachers make fun of him.

Then again, Ryan and his friends didn't make fun of him tonight. They treated him like he belonged.

Until they didn't.

Viktor hates himself for still aching for that feeling of

belonging when it came from the crowd of people about to attack his siblings. He feels torn between the only family he's ever known and the people who were actually kind to him for a few hours, the first people to be nice to him in as long as Viktor can remember. Sure, his siblings let him tag along tonight, but only because they thought he knew something about being ordinary. And to them, ordinary might as well be invisible. Ryan might be gifted, and he might be attacking Viktor's siblings, but at least he *saw* Viktor—at first.

Now Viktor thinks that Ryan looks so small, cowering between Luther and Diego. And suddenly Viktor understands: Ryan can *bestow* powers, but he doesn't *have* any powers himself. If he had, he'd have used his powers to throw Diego off, to make Luther back away. Instead, he had to call for his friends to come to his rescue.

Viktor recalls Ryan's frustration when he couldn't gift Viktor powers. He imagines Ryan must've felt the same way when he tried and failed to bestow powers on *himself*. Viktor wonders how many times he tried before he gave up. Despite himself, Viktor feels a tug of sympathy for Ryan. He knows what it feels like to wait for a gift that never materializes, to be surrounded by people whose powers you can only imagine.

Maybe there's still a chance to talk some sense into Ryan, to stop all of this before it gets worse. If Viktor could only explain that he knows exactly how Ryan feels. Ryan's acting out—telling his friends to attack the Umbrella Academy—because he's tired of being the only person without powers.

Because he sees everyone who has powers as a threat. Viktor thinks of all the time he wasted, sitting alone in his room, imagining what he could be if only he'd been born as gifted as his siblings. The fantasies he had of being Number One instead of Number Seven—the one on the cover of magazines, giving out autographs, answering questions from the press, saving the day.

Ryan must have felt like that his whole life, too. Giving powers and never receiving them. Viktor wonders what became of all the people Ryan must've given powers to before he arrived on this campus. Did they all leave him behind when they realized they could do so much that Ryan couldn't? Is it only a matter of time before all of Ryan's friends here at the frat house leave him, too?

Ryan needs to come back to the academy with Viktor.

They can be powerless together.

Viktor just has to make his siblings understand. He has to make *Ryan* understand.

And if he can, then Viktor will be the hero for once—the one who stops the fight, the one who saves the day.

DIEGO

Luther's still standing beside Ryan, poised to spring. Diego suppresses the urge to roll his eyes; Luther is still *protecting* this kid! They could end this now if Luther would just let Diego take charge. But Luther would never do that.

Fine. Let Luther guard Ryan, the singular reason why they're currently under attack. Diego will take on everyone else.

He's ready when the horde descends. Where did he hear that phrase before? In one of Mom's lessons about the history of epic battles? Some ancient army was known for its great horde or warriors—is that it? No, that doesn't sound right. Hargreeves would scold him for not being able to remember a simple history lesson, but Mom would understand that he's got more important things to think about.

Especially right now.

The kid with snakes for hair is running toward him. The snakes are black and so tiny that if they were still, they could probably pass for strands of hair. Right now, however, they're sticking out in every direction, fangs bared. Diego suspects that one bite could incapacitate him. He shifts to the side, and Snakehead goes tumbling over the banister.

"Should've wished for wings instead of scales!" Diego calls with a laugh. Given the choice, Diego definitely wouldn't have chosen a headful of snakes.

"Be careful, Diego!" Luther shouts. "Remember, these are kids just like us! We want to neutralize them, not kill them!"

Diego shakes his head. Luther always wants to see the best in everyone, but Diego knows better. Another history lesson with Mom comes to mind: *Absolute power corrupts absolutely.* Diego can't remember who said that or what they were talking about, but he gets the meaning.

Ryan has too much power. And too much power twisted him into something evil. Which means the people he made are evil, too. And evil things have to be destroyed.

"Diego!"

He looks up and sees Viktor standing on the landing above.

"Don't let them touch you!" he shouts.

"Who?" Diego calls back, but before Viktor can answer, someone runs down the stairs toward him, arms outstretched. They're wearing a hoodie pulled up over their head, but Diego can see that beneath the hood their skin appears light gray, more like gravel than skin.

"Don't let them touch you!" Viktor repeats, and Diego spins instinctively out of the way, graceful as a jungle cat. Whoever it is loses their balance and tumbles down the stairs. As they get to their feet, Diego sees why Viktor didn't want them touching him. Their hands hit the banister, and it turns from wood into rock.

"Holy shit!" Diego yells as Rock Person comes running back up the stairs.

How did Viktor know? Where has he been all night? Why is he coming down from behind Ryan and his horde?

Even Luther would understand why this person has to be more than just neutralized. Diego pulls a knife and hurls it downward, but Rock Person brushes it away with their hand as their hood falls away from their face. As he suspected, their skin is fully made of rocks. Diego knows that when his knife hits the floor, it's no longer made of metal. He winces as it cracks in two.

"That was my favorite knife!" he shouts, swinging over the banister and touching down on the second-floor landing. Rock Person swings around to face him, hands still outstretched.

He can hear Hargreeves in his head: *Don't give up the higher ground, Number Two.* And he just jumped to a lower floor willingly.

The Hargreeves in his head adds, *Number One would never make such an obvious error.*

Well, screw Hargreeves. The real one, and the one in his head. Diego pulls another knife and takes aim, sending the blade into the narrow crevice between Rock Person's open palms, careful to throw a curve that won't bounce against their stony sternum. He's not aiming to kill, just to knock Rock Person out, but the hit sends Rock Person tumbling to the ground.

Diego throws his arms up in the air, but there's no one around to see his good work. He grabs a crumpled sweatshirt off the floor and heads toward where Rock Person is curled on the ground.

"Don't worry, I didn't hit anything vital," he promises, careful to avoid touching any pebbly flesh as he ties Rock Person's arms behind their back.

Then Diego springs back to his feet, ready to take on the next foe. It's hard to keep his balance: The ground beneath him is rolling, just like it did upstate this afternoon.

Diego doesn't have to struggle to keep still for long. Someone else leaps from the stairwell above, but instead of falling, this person floats down toward him slowly.

It's the girl he was dancing with earlier—the redhead with the easy smile and the freckled cheeks.

When she gets close enough, she shifts so that her heavy boots are aiming for Diego's head, and then she picks up speed. He dives out of the way, catching her by the ankle as he does, and spinning her around like a top.

"You're a better fighter than you are a dancer," she says as she regains her balance.

"Well, you're a better dancer than you are a fighter," Diego quips, lunging for her feet once more.

He spins her again, and again, and again.

"Actually," he says, "this is kind of like dancing." There's still music coming from the party down below, and Diego sways in rhythm with the beat.

"Can I have the next dance?" he asks, as he spins her

again. He hums along with the tune, then grins. "Seems like I can fight and dance at the same time."

"Quite the multitasker," the red-haired girl answers, and Diego thinks he hears the tiniest hint of a smile in her voice. Under other circumstances, she might actually be charmed by his banter. *Maybe even under these circumstances. After all, the fight can't go on all night, can it?*

"I never did get your name," Diego says.

"You never asked," the girl pants, out of breath.

"I'm asking now," Diego says, loosening his grip.

The girl smiles widely, but instead of offering up her name, she lands another kick, knocking the wind out of him.

So much for his attempt at flirting.

Diego grabs her, spins her one final time, and then lets go, leaving his former dance partner so dizzy that there's no way she'll be able to hit anything on purpose. Diego sends her careening toward a group of her friends on the first floor. She knocks them down like bowling pins.

Diego turns his focus back up the stairs. He has to get to Ryan. He'll fight Luther (again) if he has to. But no way is he letting this go on any longer. Get rid of Ryan, and end the war. It's as simple as that.

Or at least, he thinks it's as simple as that. Diego doesn't know for sure that taking Ryan out will rob everyone of the powers he's given them. But it's worth a try.

Diego spins on his heels and starts running up the stairs. The air is thick with dust, and Diego finds himself coughing more with each step, his eyes watering. He rubs them vigorously, clearing his vision. He can feel his knives beneath his pants. He'll use them against Ryan if he has to. He pulls out a short, sharp blade to be ready. But before he reaches the second floor, he's confronted by a girl with long blond hair, a floor-length black dress, and swirling, spinning blue eyes.

"You're getting very sleepy," she says in a low monotone.

Diego lifts his arms to throw his knife, but it feels like his limbs weigh a thousand pounds now. For the first time in his entire life, when he lets go of his knife, he doesn't have any control over it. It just lands on the floor with a clatter. He wants to bend down to retrieve it, but for some reason, he can't look away from this girl's spinning, swirling eyes. He tries desperately to turn his head away, to look at something—anything!—else. But he can't.

"Very, very sleepy." The magic-eyed girl giggles. "Who knew it would be this easy to take down the famous Umbrella Academy?"

She says their name like it's the punchline to a joke. Diego opens his mouth to argue, but his tongue feels like it's swollen to ten times its usual size. He can't make his mouth cooperate.

"Go to sleep, knife boy," she croons.

"Diego," he tries to correct, but a nonsensical mumble comes out. Nothing makes him angrier than not being able to say the words he wants to. He tries to lunge for the girl, but he collapses to the floor.

BEN

"D iego!"

Ben looks up and sees Viktor pointing and shouting from the landing above. Ben follows Viktor's finger to see Diego lying in a heap at the bottom of the stairs, his eyes shut, a blond girl in a long dress standing over him menacingly. Someone who looks like they're made of stone is limping toward Diego, struggling to free their arms from what looks like a sweatshirt tied around their wrists.

Ben doesn't hesitate. He releases his tentacles and reaches over the banister to grab his brother and pull him back to the third floor, up through the center of the stairwell. Ben uses his tentacles to hold Diego in front of his face, feet dangling a few inches above the floor. Over the din of the fighting, Ben can hear his brother snoring.

"Diego!" he shouts, but Diego's eyes stay firmly shut.

"Wakey wakey, sleepyhead," Klaus purrs, standing beside

them. Klaus reaches out and pinches Diego roughly on the arm. When that doesn't work, he slaps him across the face.

"Wake up!" Klaus shouts as he gives their brother another slap. "Rise and shine!"

Diego opens his eyes with a start.

"What the hell happened?" Ben asks.

"Some girl literally hypnotized me into falling asleep." Diego looks shocked that such a thing is possible. Klaus doubles over laughing, which makes Diego scowl.

"And the person you tied up with a sweatshirt?" Ben asks.

"Turns you to stone! Don't let them touch you."

"Noted." Ben puts his brother down, maybe a little less gently than he could have.

Ben knows he shouldn't be angry at his siblings. It's not as though any of this is Diego's fault, any more than it's Luther's or Allison's or Klaus's. And nothing is ever Viktor's fault. But still, this is the last thing he wanted to do tonight.

It's Hargreeves's fault, Ben realizes suddenly. When Hargreeves created the Umbrella Academy, he set them up against every other gifted child on Earth. Ryan saw the Umbrella Academy as adversaries, because that's how Hargreeves wanted them to be seen: as the greatest set of adversaries the world has ever known.

Ben reaches out a tentacle and smacks the person Diego tied with a sweatshirt. He's careful to touch them through their clothing rather than making contact with any skin (if that's the right word for it). The truth is Ben's not sure he'd mind if one of his tentacles turned to stone anyhow. Maybe it would crumble into a thousand pieces and disappear. Maybe all of his tentacles could. Maybe then Hargreeves would kick him out of the Umbrella Academy forever. (Probably not; Hargreeves never made Viktor leave.)

Ben takes a step backward, his own thoughts taking him by surprise. He wanted a normal night *tonight*, not a normal life *forever*.

Right?

The person made of stone tumbles down the stairs and lands in a heap, taking the blond girl with the power of hypnosis with them. At least Ben and his siblings won't have to worry about those two for a little while.

And not a second too soon, because when Ben turns around, the tallest person he's ever seen is looming over him. This guy's feet are on the ground floor below, but his body is snaking up through the center of the stairwell, so tall that his face is hovering over Ben's while he stands on the third-floor landing.

"Really, man?" Diego shouts. "Ryan made a giant?!"

Diego leaps from the stairs onto the giant's back. He drives one of his knives into the giant's shoulder, but it barely seems to register—Ben guesses that Diego's cut is a mere scratch for someone that size. The giant reaches one of his long arms behind his back and pulls Diego from his body like he's picking a piece of lint off his sweater. He flings Diego to the ground.

"Ben!" Diego shouts.

It would be easy, Ben knows, to release his tentacles and reach them toward his face. The giant wouldn't even have a chance to know what was coming before Ben gouged his eyes, blinding him.

Ben knows what he has to do. Instead, he releases his tentacles, sending the longest ones down to the ground floor, where they snake between the giant's legs. He sends two tentacles toward the giant's face, intending to gouge his eyes, then pauses.

Ben can't help it: He wonders who this kid was before he was a giant. Maybe he'd been bullied in school. Maybe he was the sort of guy who volunteered during his summer vacations. Maybe he's the sort of person Ben would've wanted to befriend. Maybe, if things had gone differently tonight, Ben would've ended up playing pool with him. He wonders if his siblings ever feel this same reluctance when taking down a bad guy.

Ben recalls a bank robbery years earlier where they sent him into a glass room despite his protests, certain that he could release his inner monster to take out the bad guys and save the day. And yeah, he could. He *did*. But in a perfect world, those robbers would've been arrested, put on trial, sent to prison for their crimes. Instead, Ben was judge, jury, and executioner.

Hargreeves is always saying that the Umbrella Academy exists to make the world safe, but Ben can't help wondering whether the Umbrella Academy actually does the exact opposite. They turn routine crime scenes into spectacles. Earlier, what started as an earthquake turned into exposing a corrupt oil company. Ben knows it was the right thing to do—but did it really make the world safer? Won't that company simply pack up, change their name, and do the same thing again somewhere else? And then the Umbrella Academy will have to save the day again, and on and on—it's never-ending.

Ben retracts his tentacles without touching the giant's face. Instead, he curls the longer ones around his knees, causing the giant to lose his balance and fall to the ground. Not as effective as gouging his eyes, but it's enough for now.

Tonight, Ben and his brothers turned a party into a battle The ground is rolling beneath their feet, and dust is filling the air, so thick that Ben can barely see six feet in front of him anymore.

If they'd never shown up, Ryan might have continued handing out powers like party favors—but he wouldn't have led his army into battle. Had the Umbrella Academy never shown up, Ryan and his army wouldn't have had an opponent to fight.

Then again—Ryan's power seems to cause other problems. The earth beneath their feet, the dust in the air.

Just like earlier today, upstate in Dobbsville.

Wait—

But before Ben can finish his thought, Diego is shouting "Way to go, Ben!" as the giant falls to the floor with a crash, taking half the staircase along with him.

A handful of Ryan's acolytes fall with the debris. Diego

dives out of the way to avoid being buried in the rubble. The giant shrinks back down to his former size.

Ben hardly has a second to retract his tentacles before a girl with braids and a plaid kilt leaps onto his back, baring fangs like she's a vampire. Ben feels the heat of her breath; when her saliva drips on his neck, it stings.

Holy hell, this girl's poisonous. Ben has to get her off him before she can bite him. He tries to release his tentacles again, but the girl is clinging to him like a human knapsack. If he released his tentacles now, they'd drive straight through her, killing her instantly. Ben doesn't want to do that; he doesn't want to be a monster, even if it could save him. In fact, he never wants to kill anyone ever again, Ben realizes as he spins around frantically. He imagines how Hargreeves would react to such an announcement. Ben's father would mock him, say he's gone soft. Even his siblings might agree. Ben can see Diego rolling his eyes, calling him a Goody Two-shoes.

But Ben doesn't care.

He reaches his arms up, lacing his fingers between the poisonous girl's around his neck, trying to loosen her grip. He moves in circles, trying to make her dizzy, but he only makes himself lose his balance. He tumbles to the ground, falling on his back, rolling down a few steps. The impact is so hard it must knock the wind out of the venomous girl, because she loosens her grip enough that Ben can get free. He wriggles out from between her arms and legs and crawls across the floor, squinting through the dust and debris, trying to take inventory of where each of his siblings is.

Luther is still planted in place in front of Ryan. The siblings still don't know exactly how Ryan bestows powers, but Luther is standing between Ryan and the remaining partygoers, holding both of Ryan's wrists in one hand. Unless Ryan can give out powers telepathically, Ben guesses that Luther's hold is enough to keep him from doing any more damage. In fact, Ryan looks so helpless and small beside Luther that Ben almost feels sorry for him.

There's Diego, climbing over the rubble below to get back upstairs.

And Allison, battling the mean girls she was befriending not so long ago.

Viktor is pointing and screaming from above. *What is he trying to say?*

And Klaus . . . Where the hell is Klaus? He was right here a second ago.

KLAUS

His siblings can manage the battle. Six of them—no, five of them. Or actually, four of them, because Viktor isn't much help against . . . Klaus tries counting the super-powered college students racing up and down and all around the stairs, but he loses count after twenty, and he can't be sure he isn't counting some people more than once because they're all moving so fast, and he's pretty sure that he accidentally counted Allison among their opponents so he should really start the counting over again, but who is he kidding, he'll never get the number quite right.

The point is, Luther, Ben, Allison, and Diego are more than equipped to take on Ryan and his friends—however many of them there are—without him. His siblings will barely notice he's gone.

Or anyway, that's what he tells himself as he tiptoes through the crowd, sidestepping the fight, inching his way back to Chris's room on the third floor.

Whatever happened to Chris, anyway? Klaus lost track of him after he jumped—fell?—from the roof. Or no, Chris was there when Klaus woke up after his magnificent descent. Klaus didn't lose him until he got pulled into his siblings' argument on the first floor. He'd always intended to go find Chris again, but then . . . well, things took a bit of a turn, to say the least.

Klaus turns the doorknob, stepping inside Chris's room. Maybe Chris will be waiting for him inside? No, it wasn't Chris's room, was it? Chris said he was using this room for the séance, but really, he'd crashed the party tonight. Is that right? Klaus can't keep track. Certainly, he'd imagined that if/ when he and Chris hooked up—the way they'd been flirting, it was only a matter of time—it would be in here, though Klaus supposes it could have been anywhere. This fraternity house is chock-full of bedrooms and nooks and crannies and closets and kitchens and bathrooms—there's plenty of places for doing plenty of things. Unfortunately, his siblings are using most of those nooks and crannies for fighting. Klaus sighs, thinking of what better use those places could be put to.

So much has happened since they arrived here tonight. A little séance here, a fall (or was it a dive?) off the roof there, and suddenly his siblings are picking a fight with the host. If Ryan's their host. Klaus can't be sure. Is he a member here or just a guest?

Klaus can only pay attention so much before it's all the same thing, over and over again: *blah blah blah blah blah* bad guys.

Blah blah blah Diego's fighting with Luther.

Blah blah blah Allison's taking Luther's side (again).

And always, always, *blah blah blah* Ben asking where Five is, where Klaus is, where Klaus has been, when is he coming back, how did he get out, how much did he have to drink, what did he take, *blah blah blah blah blah.*

Tonight was supposed to be a break from all those *blah blah blah*s, but no such luck. His siblings are single-minded in their pursuits; getting them out of the house and away from Hargreeves wasn't enough to change all that. So much for their perfect night together. So much for showing them how exciting the world outside the Umbrella Academy could be.

At least Klaus is still high. Otherwise, ghosts would be breaking in among the *blah*s, and that's more than Klaus has the bandwidth for right now. Bad enough he's got his siblings' voices floating around in his brain at all times.

"There's only room for so much chatter up in here," Klaus mutters, tapping his head as he opens the door to Chris's (?) room. Klaus doesn't turn on the overhead light; a few of the candles they left earlier are still burning, and that's more than enough light to get what Klaus came here for.

"Oh, *drugs*," he whispers like he's calling someone's name as he riffles through desk drawers and sock drawers and empty pockets. "Where are you, drugs? Come out, come out, wherever you are!"

Jackpot! A little baggie filled with pills tucked into a left-behind sneaker. He kisses the plastic bag, then pulls a face as he realizes it smells like a dirty shoe.

"Have a little decency," he says to the drugs. "No one will want you if you stink of athlete's foot." Then, in a soothing voice, as though he's worried he hurt the pills' feelings, he adds, "Don't worry. I'll always want you."

He breaks into song: "*I will always love you . . .*" he croons, clutching the baggie to his chest and spinning in a circle.

Maybe he's being too loud, because the next thing he knows the door to the room is flung open, and light floods the room.

"Crap," Klaus says, tucking the baggie into his sock before kicking out his left leg, sweeping his mysterious visitor's legs out from under them.

This person gives a shout—sounds like they're female, Klaus observes—as they fall to the ground. The door closes shut behind them, plunging the room into candlelit darkness. One candle, then another burns out. Only one is left burning, and its flickers don't give off much light. Klaus can hear his opponent huffing and puffing as she pulls herself up to stand.

Klaus prepares to land another kick, following the sound of her breath, when suddenly, he sees something. Two somethings. Two beady red dots in the darkness.

Suddenly, the red light spreads in two narrow straight lines. Klaus jumps away to avoid the heat emanating from the narrow red beams. They land on the desk, igniting a pile of papers and books.

"Holy shit—she's got laser eyes!" Klaus shouts to no one in particular. He hears the girl laugh with delight.

In the light from the fire, Klaus can see his opponent more clearly: She's wearing an oversize flannel shirt over jeans with scuffed Doc Martens boots. Her hair is cut close to her skull, practically a buzz cut. Her eyes are lined with thick eyeliner, and her lips are stained a deep burgundy. He can't tell what color her eyes are beneath their red glimmer, but under different circumstances, Klaus would be complimenting her look.

The eighties song "Bette Davis Eyes" gets stuck in Klaus's head as he propels himself off the wall behind him, trying to misdirect his opponent's gaze so he can topple her safely. Her eyes ignite Chris's bed (is it Chris's? Crap, it doesn't matter anymore), his bookshelves, a pile of dirty laundry.

Klaus starts coughing as smoke fills the air. But not just smoke—in the light from the fire, Klaus can see dust particles floating, so many that the air is thick with them. And when Laser Eyes takes aim, it's not just where her gaze lands that ignites but the air itself.

This dust, whatever it is, is *flammable*.

Overhead, the smoke detector goes off, deafeningly loud. A second later, sprinklers burst open, water raining down on everything.

Including Laser Eyes. When the water hits her, her beady red eyes fade to brown. Klaus sees his opening. He dives toward her, wrapping himself around her knees so she slides down onto the wet hardwood floor.

"Nice kicks," Klaus finds himself saying as they fall. No reason to be rude just because she's trying to set him on fire.

This time when she hits the ground, she doesn't get up.

"You'll have a hell of a headache in the morning," Klaus says apologetically. Reluctantly, he reaches into his boot and procures two of his hard-won pills. "These should help," he offers, tucking them into the pocket of her damp jeans. The fires she set are already dying down. Klaus steps over her body to get to the door and emerges into the brightly lit hallway. The sprinklers are raining down in the hallway, too, and Klaus can hear that the fight between his siblings and Ryan's pals is ongoing. He feels confident that his brief absence didn't make any difference.

"Still cheaper than buying pills," Klaus finishes as he closes Chris's door behind him.

Klaus slides across the hardwood floors like he's ice-skating. He can't help noticing that the air in the hallway is thick with dust, just like it was inside Chris's room. Which means that it's not just Laser Eyes making the dust to set things on fire.

Something else is. Maybe lots of somethings.

CHAPTER
35

ALLISON

It hadn't occurred to Allison that the girls she'd befriended—tried to befriend?—downstairs were among those Ryan gifted with powers. They didn't use any powers when they fought, and what's the point of having powers if you don't use them? In training, Allison and her siblings use their powers against each other all the time. How else, Hargreeves always said, would they learn to master their powers before they face a *real* enemy?

But now May, Jenny, and Letitia are headed up the stairs and straight for Allison with the confidence only superpowers can bestow. Ryan must've given them their gifts before Allison met them. Allison realizes that it never occurred to them to use their powers against each other when they fought. Unlike Allison and her siblings, no one ever encouraged them to practice on the people to whom they're closest.

May reaches up to her hair. Allison thinks the other girl is about to tuck her perfectly straight hair behind her ears—getting it out of the way for combat, perhaps—but instead May sticks her fingers into her thick hair and emerges holding what looks like a needle. Allison recalls that earlier, Letitia told May to be careful when flipping her hair. It's not because Letitia was worried May would mess up her style—it's because May's hair is a *weapon*.

May puts the needle to her mouth and blows.

Allison feels the sting when the needle makes contact with her bare shoulder. Why did she have to pick an off-the-shoulder dress? Why did she have to pick a *dress* at all? Much as she's come to loathe the Umbrella Academy uniform—it's nearly impossible to express herself when she has to wear the same thing every day—she has to admit, Hargreeves knew what he was doing when he designed them. Or when he programmed Mom to design them. It's easier to fight in the uniform than it is in a dress and heels. Allison kicks off her shoes.

May reaches for another needle from her hair and blows it in Allison's direction again. This time, Allison's prepared, and she ducks out of the way. The needle lodges itself into the wall behind her. Allison plucks the first needle from her shoulder, wincing in pain. It's thin, but somehow as sharp and strong as Diego's knives.

How did Ryan come up with this? she wonders. Turning someone's hair into needles, turning a fashion choice into a weapon?

She feels a tiny bit of admiration. Luther might be right. Maybe Ryan *would* make a good addition to the team.

Before she can reach Luther to tell him as much, May flings another needle in her direction. Allison isn't quite fast enough, and this one pierces her cheek.

"Ow!" she shouts. "That really hurt, May!"

May grins. And Allison realizes her rumoring wasn't enough to inspire true loyalty. May didn't use her powers against her real friends downstairs; she didn't want to cause serious damage. But Allison's not one of her best friends, so the same rules don't apply.

Suddenly, Allison feels as mad as she ever has. The image of taking a road trip with these three girls dissolves in her imagination, along with the image of sneaking into each other's dorm rooms late at night to share secrets. There was never a chance that any of those dreams would come true.

Allison leaps, colliding with May and knocking the other girls to the floor.

"I heard a rumor you wanted to use your superpower against your very best friends."

May turns on Jenny and flings needle after needle in her direction.

"No, May!" Jenny shouts. Her shout echoes through the room, each repetition growing louder, until it's enough to make the walls shake. Allison loses her balance, falling to the floor.

May appears to be frozen in place. Jenny's shout *paralyzed* her. That's what Letitia meant when she said Jenny had to watch what she said—the inside joke Allison didn't understand. Well, she understands it now.

Allison turns just in time to see exactly what power Ryan gifted Letitia with. Tiny little spikes of metal peek through her shirt.

Ryan gifted Letitia skin made of knives. This is why she couldn't get in between her friends during their fight—she could have hurt them. Allison scrambles to her feet, planting them firmly beneath her. She's going to have to fight Letitia without making contact with her spikes. Easier said than done. But Allison knows she can do it. Unlike these girls, she's been in training all her life. There may be more of them, but Allison's more skilled.

Allison leads with a kick to Letitia's legs. She winces as her bare foot grazes Letitia's jeans, discovering that there are spikes on the lower half of Letitia's body, too, sharp enough to poke through denim. But Allison can handle pain. Over the years she's lost track of the places on her body that have been split open during one fight or another. So far tonight, it's been her shoulder, her cheek, and now her foot.

Allison has to think before she can make another move. How can she take Letitia down without risking injury? Finally she realizes that Letitia's face doesn't appear to be spiky like the rest of her. Allison spins around, her bloody foot making contact with Letitia's cheek. She's right—the skin is smooth and soft.

Allison backs up and takes aim again, this time landing a punch directly on Letitia's jaw. She can feel it when one of Letitia's teeth cracks beneath the pressure of the hit. Allison grazes Letitia's ear and discovers that it's razor-sharp. She backs away slightly. Now her right hand is bleeding, too, the deepest cut yet.

Jenny opens her mouth, and Allison knows she has to take Jenny out before she can shout at Allison to stop.

"I heard a rumor," she begins, but Jenny has already begun to yell. Allison won't be able to finish her sentence before the shout lands.

So Allison spins on her bleeding heel like a ballerina. In another life, maybe she'd have been the sort of little girl whose parents sent her to ballet lessons, long tights under a black leotard, baby-pink slippers on her feet. Maybe she'd have giggled with her classmates as they scrambled late to class, some French-accented teacher scolding them as she commands them to take their places at the barre, *maintenant!* That alternate life flashes before Allison's eyes as she spins, every bit as vivid as the imagined road trip was less than an hour ago. Finally, Allison kicks her leg out one more time. She feels her heel make contact with Jenny's stomach, knocking the wind out of the other girl, Jenny's mouth slamming shut before she can let out a shout. When Jenny opens her mouth again, it's filled with blood. She bit down so hard that she sliced her own tongue almost in two. Blood bubbles up over her lips, and she looks to Allison in horror.

Letitia crouches by her friend. "Oh my god, we've gotta get you to the hospital!" she screams, helping Jenny stand. She acts as though Allison's an afterthought, which, Allison guesses, she is.

May is still paralyzed beside the other two girls with her hands in her hair, but Allison can tell that May desperately wishes she could go with them, to help her friend.

Suddenly, Allison isn't angry anymore. In fact, she doesn't want to fight these girls at all. The air is thick with dust, and Allison's throat is burning. She thinks she can smell smoke; is there a fire upstairs? She hopes that her kicks haven't caused any permanent damage. She takes a step closer to May, whose eyes—the one part of her that can move—widen with fear.

Allison's voice is hoarse when she says, "I heard a rumor you didn't want to hurt your best friends anymore," then adds, "Oh! And you can move, too."

May drops her hands immediately and takes Jenny's other arm.

"Let's go," she says.

The three girls wind their way through the crowd and toward the front door. Allison watches them. May turns back and mouths the words *Thank you* before they leave.

Allison hopes that the doctors are able to repair Jenny's tongue and Letitia's teeth. Helping those girls felt so much better than fighting with them or even rumoring them into befriending her.

Allison finds herself tempted to follow them out the door—she could rumor the doctors at the ER into giving them the very best care—but there are shouts coming from the floor above her, and the dust in the air is making her eyes water. That alternate life—the one with ballet lessons and road trips—will have to wait.

LUTHER

Luther hasn't left his post in front of Ryan. *He's Ryan's guardian*, he thinks, *his bodyguard*. It's like he's the Secret Service, and Ryan is the president. A dangerous sort of president whose wrists Luther has to hold to keep him from using his powers.

Maybe Hargreeves will give him an assignment like this someday. Guard some very important (non-dangerous) person and keep them safe. Luther thinks he'd be good at that. It's a big part of his job already—being Number One means keeping an eye on his siblings during a mission, ensuring that everyone makes it out alive. And he's succeeded so far. When Five disappeared, it wasn't during a mission but in a fight with Hargreeves. Luther can't be held responsible for that. Though he can't help feeling guilty about it either.

Yes, he would make an excellent bodyguard, if Hargreeves ever chose that sort of mission for him. After herding all of his siblings, being in charge of just one person would be like taking a break. It's almost enough to make him laugh.

But Luther has to stay focused on Ryan. All of his muscles are clenched, ready to leap into action in case someone tries to get to Ryan, in case Ryan tries to squirrel away. Luther wouldn't blame Ryan if he did—Ryan doesn't know that their real plan isn't to hurt him or his friends. When things calm down, Luther will share their plan—that they're not here to harm him; they want to bring him home. Things escalated before he could explain, but everything will work out once he clears the air. *And this air needs literal clearing*, Luther thinks, coughing.

He doesn't understand how his siblings didn't notice the dust the minute they walked inside. Maybe they just attributed it to the party—cigarette smoke and sweat and perfume and god knows what else in the air. Unlike Luther, they didn't approach this fraternity house on high alert. They didn't know something weird was going on before they even stepped inside.

Leaving the academy to go to a party tonight was supposed to be *fun*. Luther knows that a night without a mission, for once, is what his siblings wanted. But for Luther, nothing feels better—or more fun—than leading a mission. It's what he knows best. That's why he's Number One, right? Even though every mission is different from the one before, it's like his body knows exactly what to do each time—like muscle memory in reverse, if such a thing exists.

Luther can't wait any longer to explain. Even as the fighting swirls around them, he tells Ryan, "You're gonna love it at the Umbrella Academy." Luther tries to make it sound like Ryan isn't being held hostage, like they won't be dragging him home against his will. "You have no idea what it's like to be surrounded by people who are just like you."

Ryan shakes his head, his eyes steely. "You have no idea what I know. No idea what sort of people I've been surrounded by my whole life."

"Okay, sure," Luther admits. He has to shout to be heard over the sound of his siblings' fighting. It's strange to be standing still when they're whirling around everywhere. Usually he sees more action than anyone else. "You've given your friends superpowers, so it feels like you're surrounded by other gifted people. But believe me, it's not the same thing."

"How would you know?" Ryan asks through gritted teeth. "The powers I've given out are better than the ones you and your siblings have."

This time, Luther does laugh. As though anyone could be more powerful with a gift they just received than he and his siblings, who had trained every day their whole lives long. "Look at your friends fight," Luther adjusts his grip so that he's holding both of Ryan's wrists in one hand and uses the other hand to gesture to the crowd around them. "You have, what, two dozen people out there that you've given gifts? We've only got four people fighting them, but we're still winning. That's because we're highly trained. Just you wait."

"You're not winning," Ryan counters. "My friends will take you down. They'll save me."

A lightbulb goes off in Luther's brain.

"None of them tried to save you tonight," he says suddenly. "None of them have even made a move for you."

Ryan throws back his shoulders like he's trying to look taller than he actually is, but Luther can tell he hit a nerve.

"You're not sure if they are your friends," Luther says gently. "You're worried they all came here tonight to get powers from you—not to actually be around you."

For the first time, Ryan lunges at him, struggling to get his wrists free. Luther restrains him easily.

"It won't be like that at the Umbrella Academy," Luther promises, his voice still calm and optimistic. But Ryan doesn't smile in return. If anything, Luther's gentle demeanor makes him even angrier. Luther thinks that he must not have explained everything well enough for Ryan to understand, so he tries again.

"All of us already have powers we wouldn't trade, so none of us will ask you for anything. Well, except for Viktor. He doesn't have powers. And Ben would probably trade in the ones he has for something else if he could. And Klaus, well, he's never really learned to control what he can do. And Diego would give just about anything to be powerful enough to be Number One. But seriously, other than that . . ." Luther trails off, realizing that "other than that" means only Allison and him.

Luther tries to explain, but the truth is he's finding it hard to breathe. The air is thick with dust. Luther thinks of the way he coughed when they took Mateo's body away.

"What's up with this dust?" he asks Ryan.

"What's a little collateral damage when you're building an army?" Ryan growls.

"An army?" Luther's voice comes out hoarse. "I thought you just wanted friends."

"I can want more than one thing," Ryan scoffs.

Luther's throat feels like it's on fire. As he doubles over coughing. he must loosen his grip without realizing it, because suddenly Ryan is grabbing one of the partygoers caught in the melee, a short girl with black bangs cut across her forehead.

"You can breathe fire!" Ryan shouts before Luther can stop him. That's all it takes, Luther realizes, for Ryan to bestow powers—he merely needs to touch someone and declare their gift.

The girl opens her mouth, and fire comes out. It seems to ignite the very air around them. Wait, it *does* ignite the air around them. *Crap*, Luther thinks, *the dust is flammable*. He takes off his blazer and throws it over the blaze—luckily, it's wool—snuffing it out as best as he can.

"What is wrong with you?" Luther shouts. "Didn't you know what fire would do in here?"

Ryan smiles slowly. "Looks like the tide is turning in our fight, Number One."

The ground beneath them rumbles and shakes. Luther recalls the earthquake upstate. Could this be *another* aftershock?

No, that earthquake was miles away. Aftershocks are centralized. Even if they're the kind that are linked to illegal fracking, like the one upstate. No one's drilling for oil this close to the city.

So why is the ground shaking now? Why has it been shaking, on and off, all night?

Luther loses his footing, tumbling down the stairs. *Shit—* Ryan's out of his reach now. Above, he sees a crack spreading across the ceiling of the fraternity house.

This place is going to collapse. They have to get everyone out of here. *Now.*

Luther tries to shout, but his throat is as dry as sandpaper. He rips the bottom of his shirt and creates a makeshift mask to tie around his nose and mouth. He stumbles up the stairs, reaching blindly for Ryan, intending to drag him down the stairs with him—while there are still stairs to drag him down—but the ground rolls again. Through the dust, Luther sees Allison and Diego losing their footing below him.

"Get out of here!" he shouts desperately.

He turns around to grab for Ryan once more. But Ryan has disappeared.

Maybe he'd be a terrible bodyguard. Luther supposes that's why Hargreeves is in charge of selecting their missions, not him.

VIKTOR

Viktor pulls Ryan into an empty bedroom, coughing harder than he's ever coughed in his life. Under other circumstances, he wouldn't have been able to get past Luther, but the latest earthquake caught Luther by surprise, sending him down the stairs away from Ryan. Viktor tears a strip from his T-shirt to cover his nose and mouth.

"Ryan," Viktor says, panting. "You have to make them stop."

Ryan shakes his head. "Why should I?" Ryan's voice doesn't sound slippery, or harsh, or friendly anymore—instead, it sounds hoarse and desperate. Viktor wonders just how many voices Ryan has. He wonders which is the authentic Ryan.

"Ryan," Viktor begs. "You know that the more they use their powers, the worse it gets. You're killing them!"

"I'm not killing anyone," Ryan insists. "I gave them their powers. How they use them is their choice."

"You told them to attack my siblings! You told them we were here to take their powers away from them."

"Weren't you?"

"No!" Viktor insists. "We didn't even know about you when we came here tonight."

"That's a pretty wild coincidence if you ask me," Ryan points out, and Viktor can't argue with that.

"Why does it do this?" Viktor asks finally. "The earthquakes, the dust?"

"I don't know." Ryan shrugs as though the shaking earth and toxic air aren't important. "But I do have a theory," he adds casually, as though he's been mulling over the idea. "When I give powers to someone who wasn't meant to have powers, it causes something to shift. Like, literally, the gases in the center of the Earth churn."

"Causing earthquakes and releasing poisonous dust?"

"Exactly!"

"Has it ever been this bad before?"

The superior look on Ryan's face falters for just a moment, and Viktor knows: It's never been like this before.

"Have you ever given this much power to this many people before?" Viktor asks.

"No," Ryan admits. In a single syllable, his voice sounds small, confused. Viktor thinks maybe *that* voice is the real Ryan: a scared kid in over his head.

"So when all these people use their powers, it literally turns the air into toxic fumes. It's causing earthquakes in parts of the world where earthquakes never happened before—"

Viktor pauses, thinking of the mission his siblings completed earlier today.

"Have you ever given powers to people outside of the city?" Viktor asks.

"Yeah," Ryan admits. "I mean, I lived upstate before I escaped down here. There were people where I grew up. Some of them are still there."

"In Dobbsville?" Viktor asks. Suddenly he remembers why the name of Ryan's hometown was so familiar.

"Yeah."

Dobbsville is where the Umbrella Academy went on their mission this afternoon.

"So when the people you left in Dobbsville use their powers, they cause earthquakes?"

Ryan shrugs, like all that potential destruction isn't important.

Viktor's got to tell his siblings. Whatever they thought happened upstate, they've got it all wrong. It wasn't illegal fracking. It was *Ryan*—or some empowered person Ryan left behind up there.

"The kids in Dobbsville weren't like the kids here!" Ryan shouts, and Viktor suddenly realizes that Ryan has no idea what happened in his former hometown this afternoon. "Here it was different. Here people just showed up, knocking on my door at all hours. I mean, they let me move in even though I'm not even a student—that's how much they like me! Everyone kept coming to my room, telling me how magical I am—"

"Instead of judging you because you don't have any powers of your own," Viktor finishes.

"*Exactly.* You get it." Ryan's light brown hair is messy, and his face is streaked with sweat. Dust clings to his damp skin, and Viktor can see that he's breaking out in a rash beneath it. *It must burn*, Viktor thinks, but Ryan seems to ignore it. When Ryan speaks, his voice is smooth and silky once again. "*You* know how it feels to be a freak. You understand why I couldn't go on living like that."

Despite himself, Viktor nods. Ryan may be attacking Viktor's siblings, but Viktor does understand how it feels to be alone, to think that no one in the world will ever love you—will ever see you and appreciate who you are, even if that is someone completely ordinary.

Viktor thinks of all the time he's spent wishing that his powers would spontaneously materialize. He's imagined himself with tentacles like Ben's, with strength like Luther's, with the ability to control people's actions like Allison. Finally, he would prove his worth and finally, his family would embrace him. Of course, it never happened. For the first time, Viktor wonders if his family would embrace him even if he did miraculously develop a magic power. He's not certain they'd recognize a superpower if it was *his*; after all, they've never looked closely enough to see what he's already capable of.

"You knew what I wanted most," Viktor says softly. "You could tell just by looking at me." He feels like he told Ryan his deepest, darkest secret. Then he realizes—he's not the only one Ryan saw. "And Bianca—she asked for the ability not to feel grief. Imagine how much pain she must've been in to ask for that, when she could've asked for anything. She trusted you."

"She's my friend," Ryan says. "Of course she trusts me."

"Do you trust her?"

Ryan doesn't answer.

"I'm not sure that's friendship," Viktor says. He's hardly an expert on the subject, but he feels certain that he's right. "*Are* these people your friends, Ryan? Do they love you? Or are they using you? Is all of this"—Viktor waves at the mayhem beyond the closed door—"about you, or is it about what they wanted *from* you?"

"I don't care," Ryan answers. "It's better than the nothing I had before."

"Is it?" Viktor asks. Viktor doesn't want to be loved like that. It's not real love; it's a transaction. Viktor adds, "Ryan, I liked you. I wanted to be your friend—not because you could give me powers, but because you and I had the same taste in music, and we both needed a break from the party. I thought I'd found someone like me when I met you. Someone who understood me. I didn't have to tell you what I most wanted—you *saw* it all on your own."

Out in the real world, Viktor thinks, *it's the people* with *powers who are the freaks*. Viktor never would've guessed that someone who grew up outside of the Umbrella Academy would get it backward, too.

"Please, Ryan," Viktor pleads. "Stop giving out powers.

Not just because it's dangerous. But because it's a crappy way to make friends. Think about it: You couldn't give me powers, and I'm still here, trying to help you."

Viktor wonders again why Ryan's gift didn't work on him. Maybe it's because he was born on October 1, 1989. He's *supposed* to have powers. No one can *give* him what he was supposed to have been born with.

"You think I should go about life completely powerless?" Ryan says it like he can't imagine such a thing, even though it's how he's been living his whole life.

"Maybe we're not completely powerless," Viktor answers. "Maybe we need to stop comparing ourselves to people with actual superpowers to figure out where our own powers lie."

"I do understand you, Viktor," Ryan says, narrowing his eyes and lowering his voice. "*You're* the one who doesn't understand *me*."

"What?" Viktor asks, but he catches the meaning from the look in Ryan's eyes, the harsh sound of his voice. Viktor hasn't gotten through to him any more than Luther did.

At once, the bedroom door is flung open. Ben is standing in the doorway, Diego behind him with his arms raised, ready for combat. Their faces are streaked with tears, their eyes watering from the poisonous dust in the air. Like Ryan, their skin is covered in burns where the dust has accumulated. Viktor can see that on the stairs, people are passing out. He can smell smoke, and on the stairs beyond the open door, Luther is using his jacket to snuff out flames. But the in the distance, someone is breathing fire into the flammable air more quickly than Luther can contain it. If the dust spreads, it could take out half the city.

And that would be just the beginning. Even if Ryan vowed never to use his powers again—and that's a big *if*, Viktor knows—the people he's gifted powers to will scatter, spreading dust and causing earthquakes wherever they go.

"Viktor!" Ben shouts. "We have to get out of here. The building's gonna collapse."

Diego charges into the room and grabs Ryan by the shirt. "It's all because of him!" Diego drags Ryan out the door. Viktor follows helplessly.

What made Viktor think he'd be able to talk sense into Ryan, neutralizing the danger he poses? Viktor's siblings are the ones who run missions, taking down the bad guys. Tonight, Viktor only made things worse: falling for Ryan's friendly warmth from the start, then alerting him to the fact that the rest of the Umbrella Academy was there. If Viktor had only kept to himself, maybe none of this would have happened. Or at least, it wouldn't have happened like *this*.

His siblings would've known better than to be taken in by Ryan. They would've recognized the threat he posed on sight. They've been training to recognize bad guys their whole lives.

Viktor understands violins, not villains.

LUTHER

The building is crumbling, and Luther can't keep the flames under control. He's not sure whether the girl breathing fire can control herself; like everyone else, she's coughing in the smoke and the dust, and with every cough, she sets the air ablaze. Ryan's horde starts running for what remains of the front door. The air is a viscous mix of dust and smoke. Luther winces as he watches a group that was working together turn on itself. In their rush for the door, people fall to the floor, and rather than help their compatriots up, people scramble over crumpled bodies. He even sees a few people using their powers to overcome the people in front of them—oblivious to the fact that every time they use their powers, they're actually making things worse.

This is what happens, Luther thinks, *when people with powers aren't trained the way me and my siblings were.* Hargreeves taught them to work as a team, to work in tandem, and to never leave a teammate behind.

He taught them *loyalty*. But these people—Ryan's so-called friends at this fancy college—Luther doubts they know the meaning of the word.

It's not just Ryan he needs to bring back to the Umbrella Academy. It's all of these people. He and his siblings will have to track them down, one by one. Left to their own devices, these people will rip a hole in the world, filling the sky with toxic dust until no one can breathe. Luther doesn't think they can join the team—not if they spew poison every time they use their powers—but he's sure Hargreeves will figure out another way to keep them safe.

Diego's still holding on to Ryan.

"Come on!" Luther shouts, heading toward the stairs. They have to get out the front door before the building collapses. He grabs Viktor and flings him over his shoulder.

Viktor pants as they head downstairs, explaining breathlessly: When the people to whom Ryan has gifted powers use those powers, it changes the Earth itself. "He's never given power to this many people in one place before," Viktor says. "I don't think he knew it would cause all this."

"Do you think it would've stopped him, if he did?" Luther asks.

"I don't know," Viktor admits, and Luther's face falls with disappointment.

"So you're telling me when Ryan's friends all use their powers at once, it could literally change the rotation of Earth or something?" Ben asks, rushing down the stairs behind Luther and Viktor.

"I don't know," Viktor says. "Nobody knows! Not even Ryan."

"It doesn't matter what he knew," Luther insists as they reach the second-floor landing. "All that matters is getting everyone out of here in one piece. We'll figure out the rest later."

For once, none of Luther's siblings argue with him.

Up ahead, Luther sees the boy with snakes for hair struggling on the floor. It looks like he fell and broke his leg. He can't make it out on his own. Luther reaches for the boy to sling him over his other shoulder, but the boy must not realize the fight is over. Instead of accepting Luther's outstretched arm, the boy turns his snakes onto it. Luther recoils as fangs sink into his flesh.

At that very moment, the earth begins to shake again.

"It's the snakes!" Viktor explains. "He used his power, and then there was another earthquake."

There's a loud *crack*, and the stairs beneath Luther's feet give way. He cries out as he begins to fall.

He feels one of Ben's tentacles grab him, jerking him back. For a second, Luther swings in the air, Viktor holding on tight to him. Through the dust, he can see that another one of Ben's tentacles is wrapped around the fourth-floor stairs, miraculously still intact. Ben is dangling between his tentacles, outstretched in either direction.

"Look out!" Allison shouts. The fire that started on the second-floor landing is moving up, up, up. The stairs around

Ben's tentacles are ablaze. Luther can see panic on his brother's face.

Suddenly, Luther is falling again. Above him, it looks as though Ben is surrounded by flames. Luther hears his siblings screaming.

"We have to get out of here!" Diego shout as Luther hits the ground, the wind knocked out of him.

He's temporarily blinded by dust—not the toxic residue this time, but actual dust from the building collapsing around him. The sound is deafening. It takes him a second to realize that Viktor is trapped beneath him.

"Viktor!" he shouts, shifting his weight as quickly as he can. Through the dust he can make out the shape of the boy with the snakes on his head; the snakes are immobile, and Luther silently hopes that they're knocked out and not dead.

Viktor coughs as Luther pulls him to sit up. He's surrounded by bricks and dust, debris falling down from the bedrooms above: pages of books, scraps of clothing, feathers from down pillows, a lone teddy bear.

"I think I cracked your ribs," Luther explains. "I'm so sorry."

"I'm okay," Viktor says, but he winces when he speaks. "Where's Ryan?"

Luther looks up. Above them, Allison, Klaus, and Diego are scrambling down what's left of the stairs. Klaus screams Ben's name.

"Diego, where's Ryan?" Luther shouts.

"I lost him," Diego admits.

"There!" Viktor shouts, pointing. Ryan is still clinging to what remains of the landing above. "Ryan! You have to jump!"

"No way," Ryan yells.

"I'll catch you," Luther offers.

"And then what?" Ryan asks. "Take me home with you? Lock me up so I can never use my powers again?"

"It wouldn't be like that," Luther promises, but he's not entirely sure what it *would* be like. He doesn't know what Hargreeves would do with Ryan and his friends.

"I'm not leaving," Ryan insists. "This is my home. I live here with my friends."

The flames threaten to engulf him. Luther lunges forward—he wants to run up the stairs to grab Ryan, but the stairs are gone.

Where the hell is Ben? Luther thinks desperately. Ben could use his tentacles to grab Ryan and pull him out of here.

Then, two terrible things happen at once: The flames engulf Ryan, and the floor gives out beneath him. Luther watches his fall, still thinking he might be able to catch him, but before Ryan hits the ground, Luther's eyes land on someone else.

Ben.

CHAPTER
39

ALLISON

Ben is flying through the air. No, not flying—falling. He hits the ground so hard that Allison could swear she feels another earthquake. But really, it's the pounding of her heart that's making her shake.

Not Ben.

Klaus is on his knees, digging through the rubble. Luther and Diego race to meet Klaus so quickly that now it looks like *they're* flying. Allison rushes to follow, barely feeling her bare feet being nicked by the debris below.

It all happened so fast that Ben didn't have a chance to use his tentacles to grab on to something. Even if there'd been more time, Allison isn't so sure that Ben would've been able to find something to hang on to. Sheets of paper and mountains of books fall down from the bedrooms that were above them, some of them catching fire as they fall. Two walls of the building remain upright, but they don't exactly look steady.

Klaus is shaking Ben's shoulders, while Luther and Diego lift enormous pieces of rubble to free Ben's body.

"Klaus," Allison shouts, trying to pull him off of Ben's body. "Klaus, you have to move!"

Klaus is sobbing, but Allison's words must register, because he moves enough that Allison can crouch over Ben and begin CPR. It's hard to make out much of anything with the smoke so thick in the air. It's like being trapped in fog.

Tears stream down Allison's face, making the dust on her cheeks sticky. Luther takes over chest compressions. Diego pulls Klaus away—he was making CPR more difficult—but Allison can still hear his sobs. She counts in time with his raggedy breaths.

It feels like forever, but finally Ben's body shudders with life.

"Thank god," Allison says. She presses herself up to stand as Klaus drops to his knees, throwing his arms around Ben, who hugs him back gingerly. Allison can tell that the embrace is hurting him, but Ben doesn't tell Klaus to let go.

"Careful, man," Diego says softly. He reaches down to pull Ben to his feet. "That was close." Diego smiles just a little, which makes Allison grin.

Klaus lets go of their brother and starts laughing. Ben joins in. Soon, they're all laughing, so hard that Allison's sides hurt. Luther claps Ben on the back.

"Ow!" Ben shouts.

"Sorry," Luther says, which makes them all dissolve into giggles once more.

When their laughter finally dissipates, Luther says, "We have to get out of here." He gestures to the unstable walls, the flames, the dust.

Allison nods in agreement, turning toward the space that used to be the fraternity house's front door. Now it's just a gaping hole leading to the city street.

"Wait," Allison stops short. "Where's Viktor?"

"He was right here," Luther says. He looks surprised that Viktor isn't standing beside him.

Allison spins in circles desperately. Outside on the street, partygoers are streaked in dust so thick it's like their clothes have been painted white. She can't tell which of them are the ones Ryan gave powers to versus those that simply got caught up in the mayhem.

"There!" Allison shouts suddenly.

Viktor is crouched on the ground just outside the fallen fraternity house.

Allison rushes toward him. At Viktor's feet are the remains of a broken body—Ryan. There are burns on his skin, but it looks as though he fell from above before the fire could take him entirely. In all their missions, Allison's never seen a body so terribly mangled.

"Jesus," Luther breathes. "How did he get all the way out here?"

"I pulled him out of the rubble," Viktor explains. "I thought if I could get him away from the thickest dust, maybe—"

Viktor doesn't finish his thought. *He doesn't need to.* Allison knows he was hoping that Ryan might be able to breathe easier where the air was clear. But Ryan isn't breathing at all.

"So much for taking him home and getting him the training he needed." Luther sounds disappointed.

"He wasn't a stray dog you were going to bring home and put on a leash," Diego argues. "And anyway, what was your plan for the rest of them?"

"I thought," Luther hesitates. "I thought we could find everyone Ryan had given powers to and teach them, too."

Allison could tell that this plan made perfect sense in Luther's head.

"Speaking of the rest of them—" Luther spins on his heel, on guard for the next wave of attack from Ryan's friends. "Surely they're going to avenge the death of their leader now, right?"

But the kids they were fighting just a few minutes ago look every bit as defeated as their fallen leader. Allison sees the boy with the snakes struggle to get to his feet, balancing on his good leg; as he stands, his snakes shift, melting back into hair.

"Look," Luther says, holding his arm out to Allison. "That's where he bit me." Now the skin is smooth and unbroken, as though he'd never been bitten at all.

Allison sees the girl with the spinning eyes—the one who hypnotized Diego to sleep. Her eyes look perfectly ordinary now. The person made of stone's skin is smooth once more. Even the dust in the air appears to be dissipating. Allison takes a deep breath. The air is smoky, but she can breathe again.

"I was right," Diego says, unable to disguise his pride. "Cut off the head of the snake, and the body dies."

"What does that mean?" Klaus asks.

"It means that with Ryan dead, everyone he gave powers to went back to normal," Ben explains.

"He wasn't a snake," Viktor says softly. "He was a messed-up, lonely kid."

Maybe he was both, Allison thinks, but she keeps the thought to herself. Something in the way Viktor speaks makes Allison think he isn't only talking about Ryan.

BEN

The sound of sirens fills the air.

"Here comes the cavalry," Ben says.

"The cavalry?" Diego scoffs. "Where were they when the battle was raging? What good can they do now? We won already."

"There are a lot of injured people here, Diego," Ben says. "They need care." Ben isn't so sure that *he* doesn't need care too. His arms and legs ache. At the very least, he'll be covered with bruises tomorrow.

Firefighters start spraying the remains of the building with water as students from the adjacent town houses emerge. Ben notices that when Ryan's fraternity house fell, it took the wall of the house to the left along with it. He can see into someone's bedroom, their lights still on, a book still open on their bed, like they were having a relaxing evening in before all hell broke loose.

That person must've been studying, Ben thinks. *They thought they were going to have a quiet night in.* Maybe they'd never even heard of the Umbrella Academy and didn't know there was anything the least bit significant about being born on October 1, 1989.

The front-facing windows of the house on the right are blown out. Ben hopes no one got hurt when the glass shattered, but he knows it's unlikely. Ben sees people with gashes all over, arms and legs twisted into unnatural positions. He hears the sound of people crying: They maybe got out okay, but their home was destroyed.

Gently, Ben uses his tentacles to lift Ryan's body and lays it across the street where the sidewalk is clean and clear. It almost looks like Ryan is sleeping; it's hard to connect this small, still body with the havoc the person inside of it was wreaking mere moments ago. Luther is right about one thing: If Ryan had been adopted by Hargreeves like the rest of them, his life would have been different.

Still, Ben can't help wondering—different how? Once Hargreeves discovered the danger inherent in Ryan's powers, what might their father have done to control him? Ben wonders, if his own powers had come with a terrible price—like, if every time he released his tentacles it caused a flood in some other part of the world—what might Hargreeves have done to keep Ben from using them?

EMTs pour out of ambulances to attend to the wounded. Broken bones are set in temporary splints to be fixed properly at the hospital; people who breathed in too much dust are given oxygen, as though they're suffering from smoke inhalation. Ben was right: Injured people need the kind of care the Umbrella Academy can't provide.

But he has to concede that Diego wasn't entirely wrong to scoff when he heard the sirens. Had the police, the fire department, a crew of EMTs shown up just a few minutes earlier, they'd have been easily overtaken by Ryan's horde of college students. Even if they might not have been able to understand the true source of the threat.

Ben imagines police officers with their tasers and batons. The gifted students would've rendered those weapons useless in seconds. The giant could've stepped on them, crushing their guns to dust. The superspeeder could've run at them, disarming them.

Ben imagines firefighters directing a plume of water at the crumbling building, only to discover that the flames were coming from a fire-breathing student being fed by the air itself, filled with flammable dust. He pictures police officers coughing as noxious dust filled the air, never understanding where it was coming from or why it was present.

Of course, the police would've called for backup. Emergency response crews have systems in place for this kind of thing.

And the backup would've brought bigger weapons. The streets of the city might have been taken over by weapons of war: tanks, machine guns. Maybe even bombs.

Ben wonders how many students might have died if anyone other than the Umbrella Academy had been put in charge of containing the emergency.

At least with the Umbrella Academy in charge, only one student died.

And when he died, the emergency was contained.

Two EMTs load Ryan's body onto a stretcher.

"He was a friend of yours?" one asks Viktor, who shrugs.

"Not exactly," he says. "But I knew him a little bit."

"Do you know his parents' names? Their phone number? We need to let them know what happened."

"No," Viktor answers thickly. "I don't know anything like that." Ben can see that Viktor is trying not to cry.

"Don't worry about it," the EMT assures him. "We'll take care of it. You get home safe now. I'm sure your parents are worried sick."

They wheel Ryan's body away. Ben wonders what will become of it. Does he have parents waiting at home who'll be devastated to learn what happened to their son? Siblings who will miss their brother? Friends from school who will hold a memorial for him?

Ben can think of one way in which Ryan might have been better off if he'd been adopted by Hargreeves. There's not a doubt in Ben's mind that, if something were to happen to him, his siblings would show up at his funeral. He can picture Allison crying, while Diego tries to hide his tears. Luther would give the eulogy. Viktor would put flowers on his grave every week. Klaus would stay high and avoid contacting him. Ben smiles as he thinks of himself haunting Klaus every time he catches him sober. Ben catches sight of his leather jacket among the rubble; he digs it out and puts it back on, now so covered in dust that it looks gray instead of black.

A stranger limps up to them. It takes Ben a moment to recognize him: It's the boy who—until recently—had snakes for hair. "Sorry," he says, holding out his hand for Luther to shake. "Things were getting so out of control. I didn't know how to stop it. Thank you—all of you—for stopping it." He hesitates, then shifts so that he's hugging Luther instead of shaking his hand.

"You're very welcome," Luther says, beaming with pride.

After the boy lets go of Luther and limps away, Ben takes a deep breath and exhales. He turns to his siblings and says, "Good job, you guys."

Allison raises an eyebrow. "We may have helped that kid, but we also destroyed a city street and sent toxic dust into the air."

"*We're* not the ones who created the dust," Diego points out. "And anyway, the dust is more or less gone."

Firefighters have opened hoses of water onto the remains of the fraternity house, shrinking the flames down to embers.

"We contained the damage," Ben insists. "No one else could've done it without hurting more people."

He hates admitting that Hargreeves is right about anything, but maybe a world in which Ryans exist is a world that needs the Umbrella Academy.

So much for being normal.

"It's weird, though," Ben adds. "What are the odds that our one night out, we'd end up where someone with superpowers just happened to be wreaking havoc?"

"Actually," Viktor jumps in, "this wasn't your first run-in with him. Or at least, it wasn't your first run-in with his powers."

"What?"

"The earthquake in Dobbsville—that's where Ryan used to live. Before he came here."

Ben recalls their mission earlier today. Maybe it was yesterday—it must be after midnight now, right? Either way, it feels like a hundred years ago. There was that same dust in the air, the same rolling earth beneath their feet.

"You mean that upstate, there are more people he gave gifts to? People who could cause the sort of damage that was caused here?" Ben tries to put the pieces together.

"Not anymore," Diego says.

"No need to look quite so gleeful about what happened," Ben says, losing his train of thought. "I mean, job well done and everything, but—good or bad—someone *died* tonight. Maybe try being a little more sensitive?"

Diego shrugs. "Too sensitive, and a person could back down from a fight."

"Fighting is all you know how to do!" Viktor breaks in.

"He has a point there, brother," Klaus says. "Even before everything that happened with Ryan, you were fighting at that party."

"I can't help it if someone picked a fight with me," Diego insists, but it's obvious no one believes that Diego wasn't the instigator.

"Me either," Allison adds quickly, before Ben can remind her that *she* was fighting, too.

"Face it, brother," Klaus says, letting an arm drape around Ben's shoulders. "Our sibs were brought up to be fighters, not lovers."

"What about me?" Viktor asks. "What was I brought up to be? A fool who was tricked by the first person who was nice to me?"

"What do you mean?" Ben asks.

Viktor kicks the ground, looking at his feet as he says, "I didn't see Ryan for what he really was. If his powers had worked on me, maybe I would've been just like the rest of them—fighting *you* rather than risk losing my gift."

Ben thinks he catches Viktor's meaning, but he isn't certain. Gently, he asks, "What do you mean, if his powers had worked on you?"

"On the roof tonight—Ryan tried to give me a power, but it didn't work." Viktor kicks the ground. "I'm dud even out here in the real world."

Ben shakes his head. "No. No, you're not. You're a *Hargreeves*, even out here."

"Yeah," Luther agrees. "You tried to warn us when he sent his people after us."

"Plus," Allison adds, "you're the one who figured out

how his powers worked. You're the one who connected him to Dobbsville."

"You had our backs," Diego says.

"And you looked badass in your outfit tonight," Klaus adds.

Viktor sniffs, but he no longer looks like he's about to cry.

"Meanwhile Allison couldn't even find a decent pair of shoes." Klaus rolls his eyes in mock-derision.

"Hey!" Allison protests, elbowing Klaus in the ribs. "I *had* shoes—they just didn't survive the fight back there."

"No judgment," Klaus insists. "Bare feet walking through the city is a bold fashion choice."

"At least my dress fit," Allison says. "Diego's pants are so tight you can practically see through them."

Diego looks angry for a second, then admits, "Yeah, the seam split back there at some point." He points to a hole near his crotch that gets everyone else laughing.

Ben has never felt more *normal* than he does in this moment—laughing with his siblings; making fun of each other for their outfits, instead of arguing over which of them put up the best fight or took on the most bad guys.

"Come on," Ben says finally. "Let's go home."

He starts walking and doesn't turn to see whether his siblings follow. Klaus parked Hermes near the thrift shop, but Ben walks right past the car. He needs to clear his head; he doesn't feel like being crowded into the car with his siblings. Anyway, Klaus is the only one who knows how to drive, and he's too high to get behind the wheel right now.

Ben *should* know how to drive. Ben should get his license and his own car and the ability to go wherever he wants whenever he wants to go there. Suddenly, the house where he's lived all his life doesn't feel like a home, it doesn't even feel like a school or a training facility. It feels like a trap.

Ben can hear his siblings' footsteps behind him throughout the long walk back to the academy.

CHAPTER 41

ALLISON

She can be more than a fighter.

Allison thinks about Jenny, May, Letitia. They were her friends, however briefly. The coolest girls at the party: well-dressed, full of gossip and just the right amount of angst. Allison picked them out from across the room because they looked like they were having so much fun together, squashed on that couch, sitting so closely their legs were nearly intertwined, passing a drink back and forth between them, sharing like they'd known each other all their lives.

Their giggly, playful talk had turned into confessions, which turned into a fight. Would that have happened even if Allison hadn't been there, rumoring her way around the conversation? They'd been keeping secrets from each other; maybe the truth would've come out whether Allison had been there or not. And when they did start fighting, Allison tried to stop it. She didn't want to fight. Not tonight.

It wouldn't be true to say that she *never* wants to fight. Sometimes, on missions, it feels amazing: what her body can do, what she's capable of. Years of Hargreeves's required exercises have made her strong; his simulations have made her fast; his riddles have made her smart. She knows Luther never feels better than on a mission: his body moving exactly as it was trained to do. Perhaps as it was born to do.

Is that why she and her siblings were born when they were, the way they were, with the powers they each have? Maybe they're meant to be fighters. That would explain why their birth parents—mothers; there were no fathers, Allison supposes—gave them up so easily when Hargreeves came knocking. Maybe those mothers and their families knew they were ill-equipped to raise the babies they'd spontaneously given birth to.

Or maybe they were horrified by the magical phenomenon that took place within their bodies and wanted to forget it ever happened.

Allison's feet hurt. The walk home isn't short, and her bare feet are bloody and sore. Her hair is falling around her shoulders; she can see her curls out of the corner of her eyes, sticking out from her scalp. The sleeves of her dress are sliding down her arms, and the skirt is ripped and fraying. She finds herself longing for her uniform: flat shoes, fitted jacket, even the mask over her eyes. Her skin itches where the toxic dust touched it. She can't wait to go home and rinse it all away.

Still, something about fighting tonight felt *different*. Fighting those girls—her almost-friends—kept her on her toes. Tonight, she had to *think* before taking on Letitia—it was only because of their earlier conversation that Allison knew where to hit her. Maybe it was because she was wearing an outfit she'd picked out herself, maybe because she was fighting girls she'd so recently been giggling with, maybe because she was fighting someone with powers to rival her own, maybe because it wasn't a mission handpicked by Hargreeves—nothing about tonight's fight felt robotic. And that made it feel special; that made *Allison* feel special.

Luther's right: Ryan would've been better off if Hargreeves had adopted him, too. Allison wonders if Hargreeves tried and Ryan's birth mother turned down his offer. If she'd given him up, he'd still be alive.

Probably. What might have happened to Five if Hargreeves hadn't convinced his mother to let him go? Would he have gotten lost somewhere in the corners of the universe sooner without Hargreeves's supervision? Or would he have been less eager to go searching if he'd been raised in an ordinary home?

Allison sighs heavily. Luther and Diego and even Ben think that despite everything that went wrong, they accomplished something tonight. Not what they set out to do—have an ordinary night, as normal teens—but something else, something bigger.

"We saved the world tonight, Allison," Luther says, shortening his strides so that he can walk side-by-side with her. "Diego thought the threat was the fact that Ryan could build his own army, but that wasn't the most dangerous part.

Those kids would've ripped a hole in the world if we hadn't stopped them."

"Now they've only ripped a hole in one city block," Allison says, trying to sound as cheerful as her brother.

Luther laughs. "A few ruined buildings are a small price to pay for neutralizing a threat like Ryan."

"*Neutralizing* is a nice word for what happened to him," she says.

Luther nods soberly. "I wish we could've gotten him out of there, too, but he didn't want to leave. Still, there's no arguing it's safer this way. Everyone is safer this way."

Allison nods, but she's not so sure. Is the world really any safer tonight than it was this morning?

They thought they'd neutralized the threat upstate only to discover later that the origin of the threat had been just across town from the academy all along.

"Can it be a coincidence?" Allison asks, loud enough for all her siblings to hear. "The earthquake upstate—that was Ryan. And then we just happened to go to a party with him there?"

Diego shrugs. "Like they say, 'It's a small world after all.' I mean, look at us, we were born all over the planet, and we all still ended up at the same place."

They turn on to their block. Diego gestures to their house up ahead. His all-black outfit looks almost entirely white now, covered in dust. Allison thinks her purple dress probably looks less like a hideous prom dress and more like a hideous wedding dress. She can't wait to take it off.

"We all ended up in the same place because Dad made it that way," Allison says. She wonders what happened to the high heels she slipped off during the fight. Probably lost in the rubble. She imagines someone coming across them and throwing them away. Or maybe they're buried so deep in the detritus that they'll just build a new fraternity house over the top of them.

Allison shakes her head, dust sprinkling from her hair on to her bare shoulders. Something about all of these coincidences doesn't feel right.

"What do you think, Ben?" she asks. If anyone can make sense of this, it would be him.

Ben shrugs. "Frankly, I'm sick of thinking about it."

"Hallelujah!" Klaus shouts, raising his arms overhead. It's the middle of the night, and their block is dark and quiet. Klaus's voice echoes against the tall buildings like they're walking through a canyon. "Ben's never been sick of *thinking* about anything." Klaus's laugh sounds like a cackle.

"Cut it out," Ben admonishes. "You're gonna wake up the whole neighborhood."

"Who cares? They could use a little excitement!" Klaus spins in a circle, dancing to music only he can hear. Somehow, his outfit is covered in less dust than anyone else's. The white spatter on his kilt and sweater look intentional, like they were made that way.

Allison recalls the way paparazzi used to crowd their block, hoping for a peek of the famous Umbrella Academy.

But it's been quiet here for years. She can't remember the last time she saw their neighbors. Maybe Hargreeves bought up the whole block in a bid for more privacy, so no one would overhear what went on at the Umbrella Academy.

"Okay, but we don't want to wake up Dad," Ben points out. "We have to figure out how to sneak inside without raising the alarm." He glances at Klaus.

"What are you looking at me for?" Klaus asks, pausing mid-spin.

"You said you'd come up with a plan to get us back inside."

Klaus shakes his head. "That doesn't sound like something I'd say."

"Are you fucking kidding me?" Diego shouts.

"Shhh," Ben insists.

"Well, how the hell are we going to get back inside?" Diego throws up his hands helplessly. "Dad's gonna kill us if he finds out."

"I don't think you have to worry about sneaking inside," Viktor says softly.

"What do you mean?" Diego's hands curl into fists like he's looking for someone to punch. "Of course we have to sneak in. What, do you want us to just knock on the front door until Pogo opens up?"

"You're not going to have to wait," Viktor says, his voice calm. He's shivering in the cool night air; Allison wonders what happened to the jacket he picked up at the thrift shop hours ago. Viktor points at their front door.

It's open wide. Silhouetted against the light pouring out onto the street from the foyer is Hargreeves, standing up perfectly straight, as though he knew precisely the moment they'd come home.

"Crap," Klaus exhales.

We are so screwed, Allison thinks.

CHAPTER
42

KLAUS

C an I get you anything, sir?" Pogo asks as Klaus and his
siblings file into the living room. Pogo follows them,
his distinct gait ringing like a song in Klaus's ears. *A good
DJ,* Klaus thinks, *would sample the sound of Pogo's footsteps
and lay it over a bass rhythm and a sick drumbeat until the
whole club was shouting for more.* They'd make up a dance
called the Pogo, and it would sweep the nation. Klaus can
see it now: Pogo starring in his own music video, teaching the entire world how to dance. People would dress up
like Pogo: the jacket and tie, the tiny glasses on the bridge
of his nose, the chain across his waistcoat. They'd call
it *Pogoing.*

"What are you doing tonight?"

"I'm Pogoing!"

Klaus giggles to himself as he collapses on the dark
leather couch. He's starting to sober up, but he remembers
the pills tucked into his sock with a smile.

"I'd love a hot chocolate, Pogo," Klaus says with an exaggerated shiver. "It's chilly out there."

"Of course, sir," Pogo answers,

"And can I have five mini marshmallows?" Klaus adds.

"Indeed."

"And whipped cream?"

"Number Four!" Hargreeves's voice rings out before Pogo can answer. "This is not a restaurant, and Pogo is not your waiter."

"He offered," Klaus mumbles with a shrug. Louder, he adds, "Ordering hot chocolate isn't a crime."

"That's enough," Hargreeves snaps.

For what feels like the zillionth time, Klaus wonders why Hargreeves assigned *him* Number Four. Ben deserves to be higher than him; surely having tentacles is more useful than speaking to the dead. Seriously, when has that particular talent ever come in handy on one of their missions? Klaus trained his body like his siblings: He can land kicks and punches with the best of them. But unlike Allison, he can't rumor a criminal into sabotaging his own crime, and he can't stab the ringleader in the eye from a mile away like Diego. His powers are useless in a fight.

Five may have disappeared, but before that he had the ability to jump through space and time—surely that's enough to merit a place above Klaus in the hierarchy. Even Viktor . . . okay, maybe not Viktor, but assigning Klaus Number Six would've definitely made more sense than Number Four. Klaus shakes his head in disbelief. What was Dad thinking?

Of course, it's impossible to know what Hargreeves is thinking. He's never even explained why he created the Umbrella Academy in the first place. Sometimes Klaus thinks he was collecting children the way he collects art—more masterpieces to adorn his home.

"Well?" Hargreeves asks, settling into a dark leather club chair nestled between the couches where Klaus and his siblings are sitting.

"Well *what*, Daddio?" Klaus asks. "Well, I'm still waiting for my hot chocolate?"

It'll be the most delicious way to wash down his new pills. If he can just get back to his room while it's still hot. Not even all the way to his room. He can sneak a pill on the staircase, no problem.

The edges of the room grow sharper as the drugs wear off. Klaus had no trouble fighting while high. Combat training has been drilled into him since he could walk; it's muscle memory at this point. *Honestly*, he thinks, *it's harder to fight sober*. The stronger the drugs, the quieter the ghosts, the better he can focus. Another reason why his power is useless on a mission.

Already, there are voices whispering in his ears, tugging his attention away from his family. Klaus shakes his head in frustration.

Unlike the living, ghosts don't get tired. Ghosts don't need to stop for sleep, or food, or rest. And there are *so many* of them. Sometimes he thinks that his siblings, even Hargreeves, can't conceive of how many ghosts there are. There are so many millions more ghosts than there are people currently living on Earth.

"Well, how was your evening?" Hargreeves prompts. "A success or a failure?"

Luther's booming voice declares their evening a success.

"Really?" Hargreeves asks, stroking his beard.

"Dad, I know you're upset that we snuck out," Luther continues hurriedly. "But thank god we did. You would not believe what happened."

"Wouldn't I?" Hargreeves echoes, and Klaus notices Ben sitting up straighter.

"Holy shit," Ben says. He shakes his head and turns to face Allison. "You were right. It was too much to be a coincidence."

"What are you talking about?" Luther asks. "I'm trying to tell Dad about Ryan—"

"Dad doesn't need to be told about Ryan," Ben says flatly.

Hargreeves continues his interrogation as though Ben hadn't spoken. "And did you succeed in neutralizing the threat that Ryan represented?"

Luther looks confused, but Allison breaks in. "We did," she says, her voice calm and even. Whatever it is that Ben's figured out, Allison's has, too.

"Well done, Number Three."

"*Well done?*" Viktor echoes incredulously, catching on to what Ben and Viktor are talking about. "You sent us there to kill him?"

Hargreeves looks at him in surprise. Viktor isn't usually a part of the debrief. It's then that Klaus realizes that's exactly what this is—they may be spread across couches instead of perched around the dining room table, but this is definitely a mission review.

"I didn't send *you* anywhere, Number Seven." Hargreeves's voice is as calm as though he were discussing the weather. "In fact, I didn't expect you to go. But I suppose all children surprise their fathers from time to time."

"Surprise?" Ben repeats. "You orchestrated this entire night. Even Pogo telling us that the alarm would be off—that was for *your* benefit, not *ours*. There was nothing surprising about any of it."

"What are you guys talking about?" Luther and Diego speak almost in unison. Klaus was thinking the same question, though he didn't feel like making the effort to actually ask it. Besides, he's beginning to understand, too.

Ben turns to face Klaus, anger clouding his face. "Did you know? What did Dad promise you if you got us to the right party?"

Klaus blinks, trying to bring the room into focus. He's starting to feel sick, and not just because the drugs and alcohol are leaving his body.

"I didn't know," Klaus says softly. "I just wanted us all to have a night out together."

"We're on missions together all the time," Diego breaks in.

"That's different!" Klaus points out. "I wanted us to do something *fun* together."

Ben looks at him carefully, and Klaus knows Ben believes him.

Diego stands suddenly, his fingers twitching like they do when he wants to hold his knives. It reminds Klaus of a junkie jonesing for a fix, though he's never said so. It's the kind of comment that would make Diego throw a knife in his direction. "Will someone please explain to me what the hell you're talking about?" Diego finally asks.

"Dad planned the whole night," Ben explains. "He sent us there to find Ryan."

Hargreeves smacks his hand against the dining table. "I sent you there to complete the mission you botched this morning."

"We didn't botch this morning's mission!" Diego says. "We saved all the people in that town. Thanks to us, not a single person died in that earthquake."

"That may be so, but you didn't *complete* the mission."

"What was the mission, if not to save lives?" Luther sounds truly confused.

Before Hargreeves can answer, Viktor speaks, his voice still hoarse. "You wanted them to kill Ryan."

"I wanted the Umbrella Academy to neutralize the threat he posed."

"What did you think was going to happen?" Viktor growls. "Of *course* they killed him. You knew they would. How else could they *neutralize* him?"

Klaus doesn't think he's ever heard Viktor sound so angry. He's not used to hearing him sound like much of anything at all.

"We did what we had to do," Diego insists.

"And we didn't kill him," Luther adds. "We tried to get him out of there, but he wouldn't leave."

"I know," Viktor says. "But the point is that *Dad* wanted him eliminated." Viktor's voice sounds as though he's speaking to little children who can't understand that one plus one equals two.

Klaus wants to ignore the sound of his siblings' voices. Beside him, Ben is quiet. So is Allison on the couch opposite him, arms folded tightly against her chest. Ben's hands are gripping his knees. Klaus wants to look at Allison and Ben long enough to figure out what they're thinking. But it's too loud in here to concentrate.

The ghosts are back. *Of course they're back. They always come back.*

They only quiet when he's high. So what the hell is he doing spending any of his time sober? When have the ghosts ever done him any good?

It wasn't so bad during the séance, though. It was almost . . . *nice*. He asked questions, and they actually answered. The grandmother, the fraternity brother. They wanted so badly to be part of the conversation. He was almost able to manage them. They appeared because he asked them to, instead of just showing up uninvited. Without Hargreeves barking orders at him, Klaus could be distracted by the dead without being criticized for it. Hargreeves has never understood that he wants the impossible: He doesn't want Klaus using drugs to silence the voices of the dead, but he also doesn't believe that the voices of the dead should slow

Klaus down in the least. Tonight, Klaus got to choose when to listen, and when to turn them off.

"Enough!" Hargreeves announces, standing. He turns to Luther. "Number One, I expect a full report on my desk in the morning. Before training."

"Yes, sir," Luther says.

"When is he supposed to sleep?" Allison asks.

"If you were so worried about sleep, you wouldn't have snuck out in the middle of the night."

"You *wanted* us to sneak out," Allison says.

"It was still your choice." Hargreeves snaps before leaving the room.

Ben laughs humorlessly. "As though we have free will in any of this."

There's something in Ben's voice Klaus has never heard before—an anger, an edge, that's new.

If Klaus sneaks out now, maybe no one will notice. He slides off the leather couch like a snake and tiptoes toward the door. But before he can make it to the stairs, there's Pogo, balancing a mug of hot chocolate on a tray.

"Here you are, Master Klaus."

"Thanks, man," Klaus says. He sits on the bottom stair and clutches the mug close to his chest. He's so sick of the voices: Hargreeves, his siblings, the endless ghosts. He pulls the sleeves of his mesh shirt as far down as he can. In the morning, it'll be back into the uniform. By the time he gets back from training, the clothes he stole tonight will be nowhere to be found. He wonders what Mom does with all the outfits she finds stuffed beneath the bottom of his bed after his nights out, the ones he forgets to leave in the sewers.

Tonight wasn't a total bust, Klaus tells himself. Before the fight broke out, his siblings *were* having fun, he's certain of it. Next time they go to a party, they'll have some idea what to do, and that's more than he could've said last night. And sure, Hargreeves may have orchestrated the whole thing, but they did sneak out, they did make their way across town (Dad'll have to get Hermes in the morning), they did pick out their own clothes (questionable though some of his siblings' fashion choices may have been), and they did party. So maybe the night didn't turn out all that different from what Klaus had been hoping for.

Klaus digs into his sock and pulls out a pill. He drops it into his hot chocolate, where it floats for a second among the mini marshmallows before sinking beneath the surface. He drinks it all as quickly as he can. The tension in his shoulders begins to ease.

LUTHER

Y ou guys are looking at this all wrong," Luther insists. He recalls how it felt when that boy hugged him—the one who'd had snakes for hair like a gorgon. Hargreeves never lets them linger after a mission, reflecting on what they did right instead of what they did wrong. He certainly never let them actually spend time with any of the people they saved. It felt so good to actually connect with someone tonight.

"Tell me how we should be looking at it." Ben slouches on the couch, like he wishes he could sink right into the leather and disappear beneath the cushions.

"Two missions in one day. One completely solo—no Hargreeves in charge. It sucks that Ryan had to die, but think of all the people who *didn't* die because we stopped him."

Luther shakes his head. He's never seen the team look more devastated about *good* news. Ben looks incredulous,

Allison crestfallen, Viktor's face is streaked with tears, and Diego looks like he wants to rip something's head off. Klaus—well, Klaus snuck off, but what else is new?

"We saved lives tonight!" Luther can't believe he has to point this out. Again. "Don't you get how *good* this feels? Allison, come on—saving the world should feel good!"

Luther rolls his shoulders down his back. He's glad he ended up wearing his uniform sport coat all night. He's proud of the insignia embroidered on the chest. Of course, he ended up leaving it behind at the fraternity house after he used it to extinguish some flames. He wonders if the fire department will find it in the rubble.

"Yeah, it should," Allison agrees halfheartedly. "It's just . . ."

"Just what?" Luther is genuinely confused.

"Do you think it feels good because—I don't know, because it's what we've been trained to do?"

"I don't think you need training to feel good because you averted a disaster that could've sent the Earth spinning off its axis." Luther shudders at the thought: All those kids causing earthquake after earthquake, shifting the tectonic plates beneath their feet, releasing toxic dust into the air. He can see it in his mind's eye: Earth spinning out into the solar system, no gravity, no tides, nothing to keep it from swirling headlong into the sun.

"I know." Allison nods, chewing her lower lip. "But . . . maybe there's a reason we feel like we're the ones responsible for whether Earth is turning the way it's supposed to."

"Yeah, because we're good people," Luther supplies. Isn't it plain common sense to want the planet to spin the way it's supposed to?

"Maybe there's more to it. Don't you ever feel a little bit . . . I don't know."

"Brainwashed," Ben offers.

"Brainwashed?" Luther echoes. Now he's the incredulous one. "Because we want to *help*?" Luther can't imagine anything more important than rescuing innocent people.

"Because we feel like we *have* to help," Ben explains. "We wanted to go out and have fun tonight. Instead, we ended up fighting."

"So we were supposed to stand by and do nothing when Ryan posed an existential threat to the planet and everyone on it?"

"Of course not," Allison says. "But we started fighting even before we knew what kind of threat Ryan posed."

Ben continues, "And then, when we figured out what was going on with Ryan, we fought *more*. We escalated things. Because that's what we've been taught to do."

"Not me," Viktor says softly. "That's not what I was taught to do."

"I never wanted to kill Ryan," Luther interrupts. "I thought we could bring him home, and Dad could train him like the rest of us." That was his goal all along. His siblings were the ones resisting it. "And yeah, I'm bummed it didn't work out that way, really I am, but we still saved a lot of lives tonight."

Luther shakes his head, getting to his feet. How can his siblings just sit there? He's full of the sort of energy he feels every time they complete a mission. He wouldn't be able to sleep tonight even if Dad hadn't given him the task of writing up a full report. He bounces on his feet.

"If one person had to die so that literally everyone else on the planet could be safe, then I say mission accomplished."

"But that's the thing," Allison says, her voice almost as soft as Viktor's. "*Did* Ryan have to die for the world to be safe? What if tonight hadn't turned into a battle?"

"Yeah, and what if we hadn't gone out tonight? Ryan would've kept giving those kids powers, and they would've kept releasing fumes and causing earthquakes and—"

"So you're saying Dad did the right thing, tricking us into going out tonight?" Ben asks.

Luther pauses, thinking. "Yeah. I guess I am."

He hadn't been as excited as the rest of them about sneaking out. He did it for Allison; he did it because Diego would've made fun of him if he hadn't. But he'd take a mission over a party any time. He can't help it that he's happy this particular party turned out to be a mission.

Maybe the others don't understand because they're not Number One. It's not their job to take the lead. And even though managing his siblings felt like herding cats at times, Luther took charge tonight, just as he'd been trained to do. Heading a mission, saving the day—nothing feels more *right* than that. So what if Dad was sneaky about it? Don't the ends justify the means?

"Luther," Allison says finally, pulling him down to sit beside her. The dress she picked out so proudly is ripped and wrinkled and filthy with dust and grime. "You're right. If we hadn't been there tonight, things might have gone haywire in a million ways. But we *were* there, and they went haywire in a million different ways. That's what makes it so complicated."

"What makes what so complicated?"

"This," Allison says, holding her arms up, gesturing to their siblings, the room, the academy. "It would be easy if we knew for sure that we were helping, but we don't. All those robberies we stopped—maybe the police could've stopped them without us. Maybe the body counts would've been lower without us. Or maybe they would've been higher. We don't know. We *can't* know."

Luther shakes his head. "We're not normal, Allison. Like Dad said, we were born extraordinary."

"Yeah, but we weren't born the Umbrella Academy. If we were, then Dad wouldn't have had to buy the seven of us away from our birth moms."

"Six," Ben corrects thickly.

"Okay, then," Luther concedes. "Let's say it's because of Dad and the academy that we have this urge to save the day instead of using our powers for anything else. What's so bad about that?"

There's nothing Luther would rather use his strength for. Maybe he wasn't born a leader—maybe Hargreeves made him one. No, Hargreeves must've sensed Luther's leadership skills from the day he brought him home as a baby. Otherwise, why would Luther be Number One?

For the first time, Luther tries to imagine himself as an infant, brought to this enormous house. He tries to picture himself tiny and helpless: It's impossible. Still, he *knows* that he was once small and vulnerable. He wonders if Hargreeves ever held him, but that's even harder to imagine. He can picture Mom holding a baby, even Pogo, but not Dad.

"We're not normal," Luther continues. "We never had a chance to be normal. None of the October first babies did, even the ones who weren't adopted by Dad. Ryan proves that. At least Dad taught us to channel our powers into something useful, into *saving* the world instead of *destroying* it."

Tonight, Luther was a leader without Hargreeves pulling the strings. He led his siblings to a victory. And it felt *great*.

That's the truth, even if the others can't understand it.

DIEGO

The last thing Diego wants to do is agree with Luther, but Number One's got a point. They were never going to be normal. Not after growing up in this house. Not after being raised by an animatronic mother, a chimpanzee butler, and a father who was at once distant and overbearing.

Diego can't remember why they got so riled up a few hours ago, when Hargreeves all but challenged them to a night of common teen hijinks. Why did they take the bait? How did Hargreeves know they would?

Diego shifts in his seat, feeling his knives beneath his too-tight pants. When he found them at the thrift shop, they were perfectly black, but now they're smudged white with dust. Soon, Diego will leave them crumpled in a ball on the floor of his room, and tomorrow morning Mom will pick them up and throw them away when Diego isn't looking. By then, he'll be back in his uniform, with the custom-made compartments Mom sewed in so patiently.

But Diego loved fighting in these clothes tonight, clothes that *he* picked out himself. No sweater-vest, no blazer, no mask. All black, just like he'd envisioned. Nothing cutesy about it; nothing that matched with his siblings.

Diego stands and paces behind the couches. He should be exhausted after everything that happened tonight, but instead he's filled with that same nervous energy he felt when they arrived at the party earlier: his fingers twitching, his pulse racing, his jaw clenched.

He feels like he could take on a dozen Ryans. A dozen armies. Luther thinks he led them to victory tonight, but Diego knows the truth. From the start, *he's* the one who understood that there was only one way to end this. Ryan had to die. Cut off the head of the snake and all that. A *real* leader would know that. A *real* leader would do whatever it takes to keep his team safe, however unsavory. That's why Luther will never be a real leader. His cheerful Boy Scout mentality will always get in the way.

Diego runs a hand through his close-cropped hair, coughing as dust falls onto his face. It felt *good* to fight tonight. Not just Ryan and his horde, but before that. Shotgunning beers didn't settle his nerves, but throwing punches did. Diego didn't need Hargreeves's supervision to win a fight, and he certainly didn't need Luther calling the shots. Diego was right about Ryan all along. He's never felt like his contribution to a mission mattered more than it did tonight.

Dancing with the girl with the red hair and blue eyes and freckled cheeks felt good, too. Flirting with her—making jokes, smiling at her—felt good. Diego recalls the way his fingertips played against her hips, smelling the scent of her cherry lip balm when her face was close, the aroma of her vanilla shampoo when she spun away. It felt good when his body moved to the music. His body knew exactly what to do, same as in a fight, but he'd never been trained to dance.

He wonders what else his body can do that it hasn't been trained for. Wonders what else might feel so good. Maybe Allison is wrong: Maybe they're more than what they've been trained for.

Diego knows one thing for certain: It didn't feel good when Luther broke in and made the fight all about him, just like he always does. Luther couldn't see that Diego didn't need his help. Diego was pulling his punches, prolonging the fight, lulling his opponent into a false sense of security by creating the illusion that he could be beaten. But all along, Diego knew exactly how the fight was going to end. He'd been postponing the inevitable for the fun of it, something a Boy Scout like Luther could never understand.

Diego doesn't need the Umbrella Academy to win a fight. He doesn't need to be part of a team to save the day. Maybe he's meant to be a lone wolf. Diego looks at his siblings—scanning them, one and then the other. He even looks at Klaus splayed out at the bottom of the stairs. They laughed tonight, they worked together—but they also got in each other's way.

There's no such thing as Number Two when you're on your own.

ALLISON

Tonight's mission was handpicked by Hargreeves after all. It only felt different because they didn't know it at the time.

"I really liked those girls," Allison sighs. She barely spent twenty minutes chatting with them before accidentally goading them into a fight. Still, she's sad to think that she probably won't get another chance to be their friend.

"Liked them?" Luther echoes. "It looked like you were at each other's throats."

"No, we weren't," Allison says. The others were at each other's throats. And Luther doesn't know what Allison knows: They didn't seriously want to hurt each other— they'd stopped themselves from using their powers on each other. And later, when one of them was really in trouble, they dropped everything to get her help.

Luther shrugs. "It doesn't matter. You'll never see them again."

Allison hears something in Luther's voice she doesn't think she's ever heard before. It takes her a second to identify it.

Luther's *jealous*. Before tonight, Allison never showed the least interest in befriending anyone else. She never thought she *needed* anyone else. She knows that Luther loves her; she loves him, too. But one person's love isn't enough. Allison wants more.

It felt good when those girls were talking to her. Sure, she'd rumored their admiration—for her dress, her hair, her attention—but it felt good nonetheless. It reminded her of the days when she used to be on magazine covers and talk shows, when fans were waiting every time their car pulled up to the front door. But this was better somehow, because instead of screaming fans from afar, it was actual conversation up close. Allison learned about Jenny's, May's, and Letitia's inner lives: She didn't rumor them into having fears and doubts, only into revealing them. Letitia cheated on an algebra exam because she'd been scared that without cheating, she'd never get into college. Jenny struggles with an eating disorder because she's scared that if she can't control her body, she's not valuable. May steals clothes because she can't afford the latest styles, and she believes no one will like her without them.

Is that so different from what Allison did—rumoring them into talking to her, complimenting her, listening to her? They all did something they were ashamed of because they were scared of what might happen if they didn't, of sitting in the discomfort of all the ways they weren't enough.

Then—just like Allison—Jenny, Letitia, and May got angry. And they fought.

Allison isn't so different from those girls. But somehow, knowing that doesn't make her feel *less* special; in fact, it has the opposite effect. There's something so very special about not being alone. And when those girls—those cool but insecure girls—told her they liked her dress, her shoes, her hair. That felt even *better*.

Luther gets that kind of high from leading a mission, but Allison had never felt that kind of high before tonight—at once a part of something and the leader of it.

Where else can she find that heady combination: the acceptance of her peers alongside their admiration? The feeling that, at once, she isn't alone, but she's also the most special girl in the room? She isn't sure where to find it, but she's determined to figure it out.

One thing Allison knows for certain: Her high vanished the instant their night turned into a mission, even before she knew that it had been orchestrated by Hargreeves all along.

Which means she can't get that feeling if she stays here. With Hargreeves. With her siblings. With Luther.

She can't stay here forever. Not if she ever wants to feel that good again.

Still, she smiles. For now, it's enough to know that feeling is out there, waiting for her to find it again someday.

BEN

Ben isn't sure he's ever felt so angry before. He's covered in toxic dust that's making his skin itch, his new clothes are ripped up where his tentacles fought their way through the material, and he nearly died a little over an hour ago, then lifted the dead body of someone exactly his age from the rubble.

Hargreeves engineered the whole thing. He *wanted* all that to happen. He planted the idea of sneaking out. He must've known that Klaus would lead them to the college campus, where Ryan's party would be unavoidable. Hargreeves knew that no one else could've contained Ryan and his horde the way Ben and his siblings had.

For a moment, Ben feels as though Hargreeves has wormed his way inside of Ben's brain. Not only does Hargreeves control where he goes and what he does, but even Ben's *thoughts* aren't private. The idea makes Ben squirm in his seat.

What else could Hargreeves know?

Ben shakes his head even though he's not talking to anyone but himself. Hargreeves can't know Ben's secret thoughts. Recalling the disdain with which their father used the word *normal* at dinner tonight, Ben knows that Hargreeves never would've guessed that the Umbrella Academy would've promised not to use their powers tonight. He could never understand *why* any of them might want to be normal.

Allison questioned whether things might not have escalated without the Umbrella Academy's participation, but Ben knows for certain: the police, the firefighters, even the National Guard couldn't have done what they did tonight. Hargreeves was right about that.

But that doesn't mean what they did was *good*.

That doesn't mean what they did was *right*.

Here's something else Hargreeves doesn't know: Tonight, Ben decided he's never going to use his tentacles to kill another person. From now on, when he's given an order on a mission, he's not going to rush to please Dad and his timekeeping. Ben's going to allow himself to hesitate. He'll choose to save lives—even if it takes a little bit longer, even if it's a little bit riskier. And there's nothing anyone can do to stop him.

Tonight's mission was different, because Hargreeves wasn't there to call the shots. And that felt better. Looking around the room, he gets the sense that his siblings feel the same way.

"Dad acts like we were born to save the day," Ben says suddenly. "Like our powers are gifts. What if it's something else?"

"Like what?" Luther asks.

Ben shrugs, even though the word is on the tip of his tongue. Their powers aren't a gift, but a *curse*.

Ben says, "Think about it. No one else could've contained Ryan and his friends tonight."

"Damn straight!" Luther cheers raising a first in the air, but no one else looks so gleeful. Allison pulls Luther's arm back down into his lap and shakes her head. Diego rolls his eyes.

Ben continues, "But if we and the rest of the October first kids had never been born, there would've been nothing to contain at all."

"What's that supposed to mean?" Diego asks hotly.

Ben stands, recalling that the crowds standing outside the academy weren't always admirers. Sometimes there were protesters mixed in among the fans. There were people with signs declaring their existence an abomination, a sign of the end times, something unnatural. Something that needed to be imprisoned, contained—even destroyed.

Ben knows his tentacles aren't normal, but they're perfectly natural: He was born that way. Just as Luther was born strong, and Klaus was born talking to ghosts. Actually, Ben supposes that's not entirely accurate. Klaus couldn't have been born talking to ghosts. Even now, Klaus's command over the English language is dubious at best. Ben looks around, ready to make fun of his brother, but Klaus has already disappeared. What else is new? Anyhow, even before he could speak, Klaus could communicate with the dead.

"I don't know what it's supposed to mean," Ben answers honestly. "But do you ever think maybe the world would be better off without us?"

"No," Diego scoffs. "But maybe we'd be better off without—" Diego cuts himself off abruptly.

"Without what?" Luther prompts.

"Nothing," Diego mumbles.

"Without what?" Now Luther stands, planting his feet firmly on the floor like he's bracing for a blow.

Ben rolls his eyes. "Are you really going to start fighting *again*? The rivalry between the two of you is getting boring."

"*Boring?*" Diego sounds offended. He puts his hands on his hips, his fingers drumming against his waistband.

"Rivalry?" Luther sounds offended, too, though not for the same reason. Ben knows that Luther doesn't consider Diego so much a rival as a subordinate. Which Ben supposes isn't entirely Luther's fault, given the way Hargreeves raised them.

Ben wonders what it's like in other families. Sibling rivalry is common, isn't it? Maybe the competition between Luther and Diego is one of the few things about their family that's *normal* after all. The thought almost makes him laugh. What could be more commonplace than siblings bickering?

He wonders what gift he'd have selected, if he'd been just another one of Ryan's friends tonight. He wonders whether

Ryan might have had the power to give him normalcy—to take his tentacles away. Then again, Ryan's powers probably wouldn't have worked on Ben, if they didn't work on Viktor.

"It's been a long night," Ben says finally. "I'm going to bed."

"Me, too," Allison agrees.

"Me, three," Luther adds. "Well, not to bed, but to my room to work on the report for Dad." Ben marvels that Luther's voice still sounds cheerful. For a moment, he wonders if that's Luther's true superpower: the ability to see the best in everything.

"Dad's probably gonna wake us an hour early tomorrow just to teach us a lesson," Diego grumbles as he follows his siblings toward the stairs. "If I could control my own schedule—"

"If you could control your own schedule, you'd sleep till noon." Allison pokes Diego in the ribs, giggling.

Ben can't help it: He smiles. That's the thing about his siblings—they can be at each other's throats one minute and palling around the next. It's inevitable, with all their shared history and inside jokes.

Ben went hours at that party with his tentacles safely tucked away. He doesn't care if his power is perfectly natural; being without it felt right for a change. He doesn't care if the Umbrella Academy saved the day tonight. He's sick of feeling like a puppet on a string. He wants free will, like every other person on the planet.

"You coming, Viktor?" Ben asks.

"Sure," he says. "Though Dad won't make *me* get up early," he adds with a grin. For a moment, Diego actually looks jealous of Viktor.

Ben and his siblings head toward the stairs. Ben sees Klaus curled up on the bottom step and pulls him up to stand. Luther takes his other side and they stumble up the stairs with Klaus draped between them.

"Thanks, mon frères." Klaus slurs in badly accented French.

"I considered leaving you here," Ben says, hefting Klaus higher on his shoulder. If he used his tentacles, it would be a whole lot easier. But Ben likes the feel of his brother's weight; he likes how it feels to support him.

"You know, you pulled it off," Viktor says.

"What?" Ben asks.

"You wanted a normal night out, right?"

"I hardly think we had a normal night," Ben insists, but Viktor keeps talking.

"What could be more normal than sneaking out, only to get caught sneaking back in by your dad, and punished with extra chores in the morning?"

Ben opens his mouth to argue—Hargreeves didn't catch them, he knew they were gone; they're not being punished with extra chores, but with extra training—but instead, he finds himself laughing.

"You're right, Viktor," Luther says, grunting under Klaus's weight. "It was a perfectly normal night."

"Yeah, I mean, I gossiped with some cool girls," Allison adds.

"And I got into a fight with a drunk asshole," Diego adds.

"And I made friends playing pool," Ben supplies.

"And I got high," Klaus mumbles.

"And I hauled your ass up to bed," Luther adds, pulling Klaus from Ben entirely and swinging him over his shoulder.

"So what do you say," Klaus asks, his voice muffled against Luther's broad back. "Same time tomorrow?"

Ben and his siblings laugh harder as they trudge up the stairs.

Suddenly, their night out doesn't feel at all like a failure: not because they used the powers, not because Hargreeves orchestrated the whole thing. In fact, tonight feels like a victory.

The six of them started out together, then each found their way separately, and then each made their way back together again. And like Viktor said, there's nothing more normal than sneaking out and getting caught on the way back in.

It feels like a victory because they're laughing as they walk up the stairs together now, like a family.

VIKTOR

And I bonded with a loner in the dark," Viktor adds, but his siblings are laughing too loud to hear him.

If his siblings had known all along that the party was a mission, they probably wouldn't have let Viktor come with them. No, not probably—*definitely* not.

If he hadn't gone tonight, he'd never have met Ryan.

If he'd never met Ryan, he wouldn't have discovered that there was someone else in the world who feels—felt—as powerless as Viktor does.

Viktor shudders, thinking of the lengths Ryan was willing to go to in order to feel *powerful*. He knew he was endangering people, and he didn't care. For Ryan, anything was better than being left alone with his own weaknesses.

Hargreeves taught Viktor's siblings that the best way to deal with someone like Ryan was to dispose of him. Viktor thinks back to the people the Umbrella Academy has hurt on its missions over the years, the bodies they've left in their wake in the name of completing a mission, a job well done. Viktor wonders whether Hargreeves kept a body count alongside the rest of his numbers and figures.

Hargreeves may have sent Viktor and his siblings to find Ryan, but their father doesn't know everything. Hargreeves thinks he watches the members of the Umbrella Academy so carefully, but he's too focused on timekeeping and performance reviews to see the things Viktor sees. Or more to the point—Hargreeves doesn't *care* about the things Viktor looks out for.

Viktor sees that Luther never feels better than when he's successfully led a mission. When Hargreeves criticizes his performance, he reminds Viktor of a wounded dog, begging for another chance to prove he can do better.

Viktor sees that Diego is sick of being Number Two. He isn't willing to live like that forever.

Viktor sees that Allison longs to be a star, adored by fans, surrounded by friends. Viktor doesn't know—he's not sure even Allison knows—whether she might be willing to leave all of them behind to chase that.

Viktor sees that Klaus will do anything to silence the voices in his head, and Viktor worries Klaus could go to lengths that might destroy him in the process. Viktor also knows Ben worries about Klaus, too.

Viktor sees that Ben hates going on missions, hates using his powers. Tonight, Viktor thinks Ben hated it more than he ever has before.

Hargreeves doesn't know what Viktor does, because he

doesn't pay attention to these things. Hargreeves may watch the members of the Umbrella Academy, but he doesn't understand them like Viktor does. For the first time, Viktor can see that his empathy is a sort of superpower. It's given him the ability to see what no one else has yet: His siblings aren't going to stay here, in this house, together forever. Viktor isn't sure who will be the first to leave or how they'll do it, whether they'll stay away or come running back. But there's not a doubt in his mind: The Umbrella Academy isn't going to remain the same.

And that includes Viktor. There's a world out there full of people who don't care about the Umbrella Academy and their particular sort of superpowers. There's a world of people like him—people who want to find where they belong, to be loved for who they are and not for what they can do. People who will recognize that Viktor is special, even if it's in ways that are different from his siblings.

Viktor doesn't think he'll be the first to leave. Maybe not even the second. He knows that he's not the bravest among them.

But Viktor also knows that tonight, *right now*, no one— not even him—wants to leave. At the moment, they're too happy laughing together to think of leaving. Despite everything that happened, Viktor and his siblings actually had fun tonight. They worked together, with no Hargreeves there watching.

Viktor hopes they can feel this way again. Someday.

ACKNOWLEDGMENTS

Thank you to the lovely and talented people who were instrumental in this book's creation: Steve Blackman, Angie Busanet, Emily Daluga, Brann Garvey, Mollie Glick, Anne Heltzel, Pete Knapp, Diegs Lopez, Marie Oishi, Elliot Page, Kelsey Parrotte, Alex Rice, Michael Rogers, Andrew Smith, Stuti Telidevara, Susan Weber.

And once again, thank you JP Gravitt, for everything.

Dogs' lives are too short. Their only fault, really.

—Agnes Sligh Turnbull